T.

TE

GW00507476

LASCE, M

SOMEWHERE HERE I SLEPT

SOMEWHERE HERE I SLEPT

I SLEPT

(The Alexis F Dossier)

Marek O Lasce

Book Guild Publishing
Sussex, England

First published in Great Britain in 2009 by
The Book Guild Ltd
Pavilion View
19 New Road
Brighton, BN1 1UF

Typeset in Baskerville by
Ellipsis Books Limited, Glasgow

Printed in Great Britain by
CPI Antony Rowe

A catalogue record for this book is available from
The British Library.

ISBN 978 1 84624 326 4

for
Jacek Obtułowicz
(1949−1986)

Part One

One does not have to believe stories;
only that they can be told.

John Fowles
The Cloud

one

In which we are introduced to Alexis F; and whereafter the chance sighting of a young woman and her child will prove to have far reaching consequences. We also meet Wendy.

Alexis F has come to idle away his afternoons in an old coffee shop. There leisurely to browse through poems. Through essays, his books. Occasionally he glances at a newspaper. Once the staunch advocate of impulsive and eccentric behaviour, he has gradually learned that habit lets him meet people, gives them a chance to get used to him and so overcome their embarrassment.

It's a small shop, traditionally furnished. Walls of panelled oak, light fittings of brass, a white ceiling between original timber beams, panes of fish-eyed glass in the bay windows that flank the door. It's his retreat. His escape from bar stools, from today's ever present chrome and plastic, from imitation to the bygone sedateness of starched linen and set silverware.

In trim, white-laced aprons and black dresses, two waitresses tend the dozen or so tables. They smile when they serve Alexis. He has his own place, a nook beneath the hanging newel post of a dog-leg stair at the foot of which there's a Victorian hatstand, its bentwood arms discreetly pointing out that upstairs is private.

His cup is refilled often. Though by evening, when the local country gentlemen and the odd travelling salesman gather here for tea – hot toasted muffins or buttered scones – he is well on his way to the library. A few hours' study before it closes. There are poems to be translated.

For some reason he has stayed longer than usual, but makes no move to leave. The other tables have yet to be occupied and there's plenty of coffee in his cup. Outside stands a man, a silhouette strangely distorted by the curve of the window. Now other shapes join him. The man's arm holds the door open. She walks in. The child is with her. She squats before the child, helps him take off his coat and scarf. She is whispering to him and he grins, but says nothing. And she brushes aside the fair locks that have fallen across his forehead. Wind has coloured his cheeks (high cheekbones) and forced tears to his fawn-grey eyes, his mother's eyes. He also has her chin, but no trace of her proud, Mediterranean nose. He bears no resemblance to the man who is hanging up their coats.

Her eyes have picked out a table. The group move towards it. They are tired. They're passing through the town? Heading for home? She notices Alexis F, immediately to look away. Curious. She will look again, later. And the child struggles on to a chair while his mother watches in case he slips. She sits next to him. Her back to Alexis. How often has he seen that back? In subways. Staring at the soporific sound of fountains. At the bullfight. No, not there, the sight of blood troubled her. Perhaps skipping through meadows or shuffling in supermarket queues, just ahead. And ever walking away. Blue black hair resting gently about the shoulders of an expensive suit. Was it her clothes, her tastes that first attracted Alexis to her? Her away from him. He would go after her, then up to her, but turning, always amble off in other directions.

(Coy, she sat naked close by the body on his bed, not letting him love her because he has no contraceptives. She's afraid of the pill. Yesterday he broke a window and snowflakes flutter into the garret. Already this morning it has rained and hailed with short bouts of sunshine to cover the mistakes. Now it snows. Neither

4

of them speaks. They have slept badly. Sharp, her fingernails score minute circles into his chest, her gaze focused on the mouth of a poor Munch reproduction. *The Scream.* He shall never write of this.)

The child can't make up his mind what to eat. The crumpets are merely evil necessities before such a vast array of pastries and cakes. He chooses something that is mostly whipped cream, speckles of multicoloured flecks with a cherry on top. His mother comments. And the man's moustache curls up at the ends as he laughs. They are both laughing. They are happy. And so is the child.

(Water sprayed by buses. They dodged puddles and went into a café to get away from the drizzle. There was time before the film began. She didn't like sitting next to him because then he was bound to see her profile, her nose. In the cinema she would lean forward and, bowing her head, hide her face behind her hair. It will take him many months to convince her that her nose is beautiful.

He would have liked a chilled beer, but at once dismissed the thought knowing how much she detests his drinking, again and again amazed at the quantity he can consume without becoming drunk.

'It's a good job you don't have a car.'

'I'm a good driver.'

Though still unsure whether he wanted to eat or not, to her undisguised disgust, he ordered soft roe on toast and a poached egg. She was happy with tea. They talked about William Empson. She, preparing papers for his exam, down in the mouth and certain that she will fail. He, of the eccentric poet's long, wispy Chinese whiskers that bobbed up and down on his chest as he spoke; but this did nothing to lighten her mood. The Rolling Stones had recently released their album *Aftermath*, so, as if inspired, he leaped to his feet and did a passable impersonation of Mick Jagger singing 'Paint it Black'. This at least raised a fleeting smile and, for better or worse, was acknowledged by several other diners with the stilted applause of reserved approbation.)

The man is explaining something to her. His hands move as though to describe intricate pieces of machinery. Something small and precise. She teases his enthusiasm. Alexis hears her laugh and sees the man shrug his shoulders, spreading out his arms – a foreign gesture.

(He skipped into the air and clicked his heels together. Once, twice. For three weeks he has been away and she has spent long hours crying. There are deep brown hollows under her eyes. She has been afraid to tell him. Afraid that he might hate her.
    'I'm pregnant.'
    'Great!' Skipping, heels clicking.
    'D'you mean that?'
    'Yes.'
    'And you want it?'
    'Isn't that up to you?'
    'You won't marry me.'
    'No. But always say it's mine, I'll never deny it.'
    And they both laughed till the tears mingled on their lips.)

With her own napkin she wipes smears of cream from under the child's nose, from his chin. Carefully, she refolds the napkin.
    The bill is paid. They make ready to go. She has finished dressing the child who waits, looking around. He catches sight of Alexis F. His mother fastens her own coat tightly. She's drawing her hair from under her collar, and as she tosses her head to settle the soft strands on her shoulders, she too glances at Alexis. Quickly. Turning her face away, yet her eyes linger a while longer. The child stares on – a mixture of fascination and fear. The man takes the child by the hand and they leave. Through the distorting window-panes the woman tries to peep back into the shop. To where Alexis is sitting.

In a coffee shop full of chattering people. There's the tang of home-made marmalade.

Wendy, the more attractive of the two waitresses, comes to Alexis F's table.

'Some more coffee, sir?'

Alexis F shakes his head. He would smile, but it only makes the scars look more repulsive.

two

In which it becomes apparent that one's Alter Ego invariably has a mind of its own; and that Alexis F's, be it in the guise of pure Reason or fanciful Imagination, is no exception to the rule. More of Wendy.

This is highly improbable, if not altogether impossible. Not even I, with a surfeit of social timidity, which all too often I try to disguise as indifference, I could never have sustained such complacency. I would simply have rushed out of the tearooms, undoubtedly forgetting my hat and coat, let alone remembering to pay the bill. Outside I would have paused just long enough to catch sight of the family heading towards the river. The man nearest the kerb, their heads slightly bowed into the seasonal breeze, and the child between them trotting to keep up, his arm fully outstretched to hold his mother's hand. I would have followed at a respectable distance, only to be caught short when the woman, who on and off has been glancing at her reflection in the shop windows, abruptly stops to point something out on display in the newsagents, which besides papers, magazines and stationery, also sells gifts and souvenirs in the form of cheap imported bric-a-brac and locally crafted artefacts that supposedly typify the cottage industry of a small market town.

A pace ahead, the man turns in mid-stride and now, facing the woman, still takes a step or two backwards. He checks his wrist-watch. There's an exchange of words and a change of mood. Uninvolved and alone aware of my proximity, the child peers in my direction, absent-mindedly toing and froing the picture postcard rack, which he can just reach and which squeaks on its rusted pivot. The woman shrugs. And they continue on their way. Having twice retied my shoelaces, I would have straightened up and hurried on after them.

Just before the humpback bridge they cross the road and, making for the municipal car park alongside the water's edge, they turn into a lane to disappear from view.

Soon I too would have reached that corner, just in time to see the man seat himself behind the wheel of a green sports car – a sleek, draughty model of an era long since past, though meticulously maintained. And I would have willed myself to approach. As the man leans to his left and unlocks the nearside door. As the child scrambles into the tiny luggage space in the rear and wedges himself between two overnight bags. As the woman prepares to slip into the passenger seat. As, picking my moment, I would have overcome my shyness, calling out and waving, perhaps to catch the woman unawares, just for a second frozen with her right foot off the ground, her coat unbuttoned and her skirt riding up over her thighs, her back bent, a hand clutching at the soft-top roof for balance. Then erect, resisting the temptation to glance over her shoulder lest in fact I might be trying to attract somebody else's attention, she would have looked at me, her head cocked to one side, on her face an inquisitive frown.

Searching her eyes for a sign of recognition, I would have asked her not to go. Any clouding of her expression would not have deterred me. I would have told her to get her child and stay, if only until morning, but at all costs not to continue her journey. The questions forming in her mind – who are you, why are you saying these thing to me, what do you want? – remain a jumble and unspoken. From confusion to consternation, she is wanting to object, but doesn't quite know how, and, briefly catching sight of her equally wide-eyed and perturbed child, she looks to the man for help. Surely by now he should have been at her side, and would have been had he not entangled his shoe in the seat-belt.

No longer capable of controlling my emotions, begging, pleading, I would have reached towards her. Her, backing from me, refusing to believe in the reality of what is happening and all at once truly frightened. My hand finding her shoulder but, in our opposing movements, slipping to lay hold of her wrist. Her mouth open to a scream that can find no voice. Is she bending to her knees in gratitude, or struggling? Or is she cowering in some sort of gesture of supplication? Freed, his moustache curling at the ends above a fierce snarl, the man is leaping over the bonnet of his car. Anger has overridden fear. I am losing my grip. Suddenly released, the woman stumbles and falls, perhaps laddering her tights. The man goes to help her, to comfort her. Obviously I would have been knocked to the ground, bloodied and bruised. And only then, in my single-mindedness, would I have noticed that my behaviour had attracted a considerable crowd. Newcomers would have been treated to a variety of explanations and commentaries on the progress of events hitherto. An ice-cream vendor's van would have mysteriously appeared, tinkling out its Pied Piper's melodies, and children would have started pestering otherwise and better occupied parents. Taking advantage of the ready-made audience, two street entertainers, a juggler and an escapologist would have been found vying for prominence. Clowns would be seen selling balloons. And Wendy, still wearing her black dress and lace-trimmed apron, would have wandered through the throng, passing a hat, which looks suspiciously like the one I left hanging on a bentwood hatstand.

Once roused I am not one to be put off that easily, and so I would have launched into my own brand of play-acting with a cathartic outpouring of exclamations, half-uttered words and unfinished sentences ever beseeching the woman not to go. In the distance the siren sounds of the approaching emergency

10

services would have gathered force, while nearer to hand there would be heard the throb of native drums. A troupe of exotic dancers from some foreign island happening to be in the vicinity would have engaged upon a tribal dance of exorcism, for were I naked and hairy and pointing the prophetic finger of some demonic deity I could be no more absurdly demonstrative. To compound my outrage, tears would have blurred my vision, and for all my histrionics, I would have recognised but not accepted defeat as soon as the man and woman began walking away, arm in arm, discussing their preference for toffee apples over candyfloss. Relentless in my efforts and in the final frenzy of being totally ignored, at last I would have been appropriately restrained; settled into the back of an ambulance and pacified with the odourless contents of a hypodermic syringe. Telling this kindly paramedic that one day he would be called out on an emergency and arrive to discover that his child has been the fatal victim of an accident would have been to no avail. Already my jaw would be stiffening, my mind wandering.

At this juncture would a spontaneous fireworks display be considered too far-fetched? Perhaps not. Perhaps across the river on the grounds of the manor house it could be milord's son's birthday and his guests are celebrating around a bonfire, setting Catherine wheels spinning, shooting rockets skywards and sending Roman candles to light up the darkest recesses of the surrounding woods.

And as the ambulance moves off at a leisurely speed (our driver secure in the knowledge that sanctuary is to hand), the media – only the local media at that – would have reported these events as an incident. And of course not a mention of my participation, my involvement. But then who am I to make demands or to have expectations? Am I not the Voice of Reason? Am I not Emotion? Surely here I am those very feelings in Alexis that at this moment he would dearly like to shun.

While in truth, the only incident of note that takes place that breezy October evening is a snippet of conversation between

Winsome Wendy, waitress of this parish, and her colleague Plump Pam.

'You can't be serious!' exclaims Pam, utterly revolted but nevertheless intrigued.

'Never more so in my life.'

'But, but ... but ...' Pam is not exactly lost for words, it is just that all of a rush her thoughts stumble over each other. 'Imagine waking up with that lying on the pillow beside you!' she eventually blurts out.

'You've obviously never looked into his eyes,' is Wendy's calm and calculated reply.

'What if his whole body's like that?'

'Of course it's not.'

'How can you be so sure?'

'That's for me to know and you to–'

'Don't tell me you've already–'

With an exaggerated wink, Winking Wendy cuts across Pam's highly pitched incredulity, and then taunts her friend further by tapping the side of her nose with her forefinger.

'Well, my girl, I think you're letting yourself in for a lot of trouble.'

'Don't be silly.'

'You never know where these sort of games can lead.'

'Who said anything about a game?'

'It's unhealthy that's–'

'Unhealthy!'

'Yes and you should think about getting advice.'

'Advice!'

'It'll end in tears, you mark my words ...'

Whereas throughout, and all the while lost in reverie, Alexis F is seen sauntering westwards, heading for the bare ruins of a rambling mansion, which he has recently planned to adopt as his ancestral home.

three

Wherein we learn of the tragic consequences brought about by Alexis F's attempt to somehow atone for, and thereby hopefully eradicate, the failure of one love by substituting it with another.

(In the attic there was an L-shaped room. The door opened on to the squat, gloomier bay and against the steep slope of the roof. Raffia-caged Chianti bottles – dust-gathering monuments to tenants past – were swung from a white-washed beam. A red chintz-covered settee cut across the corner where the two spurs met and faced a small table on which stood a portable television. Coils and loops of improvised antenna had been hung above, pinned to the rafters, which supported a clumsy hip joint, awkwardly splayed to marry the deep pitch and the vertical wall. Sunlight sifted through a musty window set in the taller gable end. Hardboard was taped over a missing pane.

Summer.

They were watching television – a film. He sat on the settee, she was at his feet, nestled between his calves with her arms hooked over his knees. Her head rested gently against his thigh. From time to time he toyed with a strand of her soft dark hair, which had settled into fragile bunches about his legs. They tried to kiss upside down, but his goatee beard scratched her nose.

During the commercials she looked at the unwashed plates on the floor and thought, 'He never does the washing-up, he just waits for me to do it. What's the use of telling him? Last time he did it the cutlery came back sticky and there were bits of egg yolk glued to the coffee cups.'

She leaned forward and turned up the heater. He got up and turned down the volume. Summer.

'I'm going out to buy some cigarettes.'

Three months later he came back.)

'Are you thinking of her again?' The voice fluid, mellow. Her skin is bluish-black. She is called Nina O and sometimes Veigh'Vi and she paints.

'Yes.' Alexis barely stifles a yawn. 'In fact I'd just reached the point where I was about to go for some smokes. Wouldn't you like to know her name?'

'Drink and travel will make you forget.'

'And I intend to do plenty of both.'

'But for now you're content here.' The words, husky, white down about to fall.

'I've always had a preference for the countryside, after all, the kind of furnished accommodation I can afford in town leaves a lot to be desired.'

Nina O refuses to let Alexis see the canvas she is working on until it's finished when it will have to be submitted as part of her finals exhibition. Alexis sold his typewriter so that she could buy more paints. Then they made love. Her blackish-blue satin body between yellow and green sheets. His fumbling hands, pale and grub-like and fumbling. A collage. Then she cried. She does not understand how anyone has the right to judge her work. How can they say to her, 'You've passed,' or 'You've failed . . .'? Alexis tried to comfort her, but he doesn't understand either. If she passes she'll get a scholarship to study in Paris. She leaves in January.

One eye half closed, her head at a tilt, the artist steps back and surveys the canvas. She takes another step back and upsets a jamjar of brushes and oily green turps. For a long time she looks down at the mess, which soaks into the bare floorboards and then, on impulse, she drops the brush into the viscous pool.

Again she looks up at the canvas while wiping her tacky hands on her rump. She takes off her glasses. And then puts them back on. With cat-like mannerisms she turns and moves towards the window through a maze of pots, cans and beer bottles. There are green specks on her shoes.

An orchard backs on to the cottage, and beyond the orchard the Derbyshire moors. Millstone grit; keen winds; gorse. And there they have chased sheep.

'It'll be dark before long.'

'You should paint in Scotland.'

'Scotland?' And with a sharp intake of breath she shudders.

'At this time of year it gets light at half past three in the morning and stays that way till after ten at night.'

'Then why not the Arctic?'

'You'd never get any sleep.'

Abruptly she turns and, leaving her glasses on the sill, smiles at Alexis, the tip of her pink tongue like a tiny animal peeping out from between her full lips. And she laughs at Alexis sprawled out over the unmade bed. He asks:

'Do we need cigarettes?'

Without replying she walks across the studio, through the alleys cut into the ever varying contours of paint tubes, canvas and stretchers, over to the trousers, which hang from a nail driven into the naked beam. On her way to the bedside she scoops up a T-shirt and, handing Alexis the clothes, says:

'You'll have to find your own underwear.' Then, as he begins to dress, 'Will I see you again?'

'I'll be in France.'

Alexis F zips his fly.

'It's finished,' she whispers, and taking his hand, leads him to the painting.

(Three months later he came back. Their names had been taken

15

from the list by the doorbell, but Linda still lived downstairs. He hated her, her ideas, her self-righteous pretensions and the pompous, calculated promiscuity of her affair with the Italian teenager next door. He felt sorry for the lad, especially on cold nights when the poor boy had to leave the warmth of his lover's bed and in the wee small hours cross the fence back to a mother who neither spoke English nor approved. Alexis decided that it would be unwise to disturb Linda.

He climbed down the mouth of the coal chute and into the damp basement. At the foot of the stairs stood his old leather suitcase. Mould-gnarled straps and bent buckles held its bulging form. On top lay a clear polythene bag, and inside that there was a plastic belt, a toy gun and a photograph of them in evening wear taken at a formal dinner and dance. Two piles of sodden manuscripts were propped up against the flaking wall. Alexis took the two bags.

He felt hungry. He went upstairs and into the ground-floor kitchen. A dog was sleeping under the large table. It opened one eye, but took no further notice of Alexis. Perhaps it belonged to the people who now lived in the attic. There was some bacon and an egg in the pantry. He put them into his pocket. Linda walked in. She screamed and ran off down the hall back to her room, her nylon nightdress crackled as Alexis left. Quickly.)

The terminus is vast. Cold. Too cold and too vast. Eight parallel slabs of concrete, like the outspread fingers of a Cubist's hand, lie under the vaulted roof of steel and glass. Of these platforms only two are serviceable, giving access to four tracks; the remaining six are permanently closed, cut off by a temporary wire and matchwood fence. Clumps of moss advance along cracks in the unkempt stone, between which, among redundant rails, grow tall weeds and nettles. Above, dividing broken and bare panes, the heavy latticed arches rust. Yet from the line of the fence over the utilised platforms, they have been daubed in grey paint, hurriedly, leaving careless brush strokes on the mottled skylights, which already dampen a weak sun.

Alexis stands still, alone, about halfway along platform 2, looking down at the rails and beyond to the overgrown fence. A scraggy cat stalks and weaves through the upright posts, arching its back against the wire transoms, but he ignores it and looks towards the vanishing point from which the train will come – a lacerated panorama with no bend, no bridge as a concession to perspective.

(They have driven on to the moors. The road open, deserted. For them. Hills roll along the horizon and one tree holding on to the last of its leaves stands close by. It waits with them. They wait for dawn.

She would miss the train because of him; but no, she was there waiting a long way off along the platform. She waved. Her hair tied into a ponytail, which hung over one shoulder, over her expensive jacket. A beige suit. Did she ever feel embarrassed because he wore jeans and a yellow corduroy coat, stained? Because he refused to travel first class.

No, not she. She buys a corduroy miniskirt to match his jacket. He doesn't want her to wear it because it shows too much of her long black legs. He doesn't want other men to see her thighs. They'll want to see more. They will want to touch her, to feel her flesh and be convinced that it is flesh and not black stockings of the purest silk. She says that she would like to have her hair straightened. Alexis doesn't approve. The crinkly short hair, almost shaven, shows off the perfect proportions of her skull.

And he kicked the leaves and stomped in the gutter. She wouldn't hold his hand and said that he splashed her clothes and that they were expensive. He leaped over pillar boxes and split his jeans. And he laughed. She was in a bad mood and would not speak to him. Hiding her face behind her hair she crossed to the other side of the street and walked off alone. She was thinking, 'Will he never grow up?' He was thinking, 'How else can I give her my happiness?'

With her black, black eyes and lips pouting she chases sheep. She teaches him to love autumn; to be autumn, to be kind to

17

leaves. The green and the yellow, the black and the white. A collage. She drums calypso tattoos on his buttocks. The trees discreetly turn their backs and, spreading bared branches, guard their solitude.)

A foreign voice disturbs Alexis. '*Le train de Paris est arrivé à quai deux.*' People spill out of compartments, porters shout and whistle, carry bags, greetings pass in many tongues, carts and trolleys meander, dodge, move baggage.

She is there, talking to a porter. She has brought the Jamaican sun and she will teach Alexis to be spring. She sees Alexis and begins to walk in his direction, her coat flapping about her yellow miniskirt. Men's eyes are watching. Alexis stands still, not knowing whether to move towards her or not. His hand slips into his pocket, into the lining. Her pace quickens, she is almost running. There are green specks on her shoes. Her luggage overtakes her on an electric trolley. It nears Alexis then passes him. In amongst the bags and suitcases there's a portable typewriter embossed with his initials. She is very close. She doesn't hear the click of his switchblade opening. Nina is in his arms. Her hands clutched behind his neck, her mouth on his, on his cheeks his nose his eyes. She smells of familiar linseed oil; of spring. He whispers:

'I don't have the strength to think of you both.'

Her finger lifts to hush his lips and slides across his chin. Surprise waters her eyes. Understanding. She smiles, warmth and sunshine, the pink tip of her tongue between her full lips. Gently she lowers her forehead to his shoulder.

four

In which Nina O is eulogized; and thereafter the afore mentioned Alternative Self, under the aegis of Reason Personified, takes on the function of chronicler, critic and commentator.

My personal preference was always for Veigh'Vi. Somehow she gained in substance when addressed by that name, which, while offering passive lip-service to its European pronunciation, not only pointed up her self-sufficient demeanour but also her uncanny yet unobtrusive air of immediacy and presence. Then again maybe it did little more than aptly reflect her Ivory Coast origins, even though she had been born in the Caribbean, orphaned at a very early age, and thereafter brought up in South London by a variety of removed aunts amidst a host of even further removed cousins. Somewhere along the line she acquired a more than passable French, which she spoke with a singularly endearing accent. It might therefore be considered fitting that she should have died in a country which, over the years and during many prolonged visits, she grew to love dearly – Parisians notwithstanding.

In view of my susceptibility on occasion to get carried away, it might seem odd that I can approach Veigh'Vi's murder (it was undoubtedly a premeditated act) with no overt sense of outrage. Although I shall never come to terms with her death, and its memory as ever evokes a confusion of futilities and grief, my apparent detachment stems from the fact that I no longer know anyone on whom I can vent my fury and frustration.

To some extent and at one time or another, the desire, if not exactly the need to kill is visited on everybody. Violence comes to life all too soon.

So it was that one spring morning, very early, Alexis found himself in the garden with his mother. A dedicated horticulturist, she hoped to pass on some of her ardour, if not altogether instil in her son a measure of zeal comparable to her own obsession. He was then perhaps two years old, maybe a little older, and she bore him in her arms in such a way that he sort of half sat in the crook of her elbow with his chubby fingers about her neck. In his other hand he held an apple. As they wandered from shrub to shrub and flower to flower, mother enthusing about texture and shape and colour, something glistening caught his eye.

A spider had spun its web between a drainpipe and the stem of an exceptionally tall mallow, a single bloom, which grew in majestic isolation against the wall of the house. The web was speckled with dew and the morning sunlight embellished its subtle geometry, its fragility and its unabashed beauty. Filled with awe, Alexis insisted that his mother bring him closer. Just then, the spider ventured out on a sudden sortie and its unexpected appearance made Alexis jump with a kicking of legs and a reflex wave of his apple in some atavistic gesture of defiance. Angry, and urged on by his mother, he sought retribution for having been startled, and punched a hole in the web, sending the spider tumbling towards the ground. Briefly he was filled with a sense of remorse, but then, averting his face from his wanton destruction, he bit into his apple with relish.

The dismembering of flies, woodlice and other insects was to follow, as was the slicing up of earthworms – ostensibly to discover whether the residual segments could independently survive. But the realities of fallen fledglings, mousetraps and car-squashed hedgehogs were soon to put physical suffering into perspective. Vying reactions ensued. There were those who taunted the riverside stoats and water-rats. Those who stoned the wading birds and raided their nests for eggs. And there were those who would stand in defence of the animals and do battle for their safety. Allegiance to camps and attitudes would change from year to year. After all, we were only country boys indulging in country boy pursuits.

The advent and passage of puberty brought on not only a new-found familiarity with girls, but a growing expertise with rifle and twin-bore. Alexis became an excellent shot. Farmers were never averse to our spending a seasonal afternoon leisurely walking their lands and ridding them of vermin. Though in a sense we hunted out of a want for something better to do, it was never in deference to some barbaric blood-lust. Our kill was carefully measured and always destined for the pot. Even to this day I'm more than partial to a helping of home-cooked pigeon pie or rabbit stew.

For sport we turned to the noble art of poaching – that age-old, honourable offence – the ins and outs of which were handed down to us by Cider Sam, so called not for his predisposition towards imbibing that particular tipple, but because of his uncanny knack of being able at short notice to lay his hands on a side of everything and anything, be it beef, venison or lamb. Sam's knowledge of the river, its currents, eddies and pools was legendary, and a taste for salmon at breakfast once developed is hard to break. In or out of season, pheasant is always fair game. Time and circumstances have somewhat culled my appetite, but every now and again, when the moon is just so, I still get a strong hankering for a night's adventure in woodland and copse – the bailiff to outwit, a bird to ensnare then neatly dispatch.

And yet, despite such hard-learned and enviable skills, Alexis refused to buy weapons. Neither shotgun nor rod stood propped in his kitchen closet. These would be readily borrowed when required, and though he could skin a hare faster and more deftly than most, never was he seen to own so much as a penknife. The calculated procurement of a switchblade must have caused him much consternation if not outright distress. Had he chosen a swordstick, I might have been less surprised.

Perhaps Veigh'Vi need not have died as she did, though she did so instantly, painlessly, and with a rare grace and an even rarer understanding; almost as though she had brought about the very nature of her own demise and from the first had accepted Alexis knowingly, aware that he would be her lover and, as such, inevitably her executioner. In the jargon of officialdom, the event was eventually labelled as regrettable. Alexis would have added necessary. But nothing could be more absurd or further from the truth.

Ever predisposed to cut off his nose to spite his face, Alexis pondered often and at length what it would feel like to kill another human being, especially on a one-to-one basis. In speculation, there can be a state where no compunction is felt, no guilt, only the cold and impersonal indifference of the abstract act. But the killing of Veigh'Vi was no experiment, nor was it an attempt by trial and error to acquiesce to some psychopathic bent. It was wilful and, albeit aesthetically executed, macabre in its fervour.

Temporary insanity, a crime of passion, however it comes to be filed, few can expect to stab people to death on railway stations without suffering consequences. Alexis was arrested on the spot (later to effect a somewhat subtle escape). Some held that he offered resistance, but he was only trying to assist the paramedics carry their charge into the ambulance. He desperately wanted to ride with her to the hospital (where she was to be pronounced dead on arrival and immediately transferred to the morgue), but this he was denied.

I asked that she might be buried in the vicinity of Oscar Wilde, a writer whom she admired above many others. The authorities not only raised objections but took distinct umbrage at my interference. Oddly enough none of her paintings were ever signed, so I had the monumental mason carve the single word Veigh'Vi on her headstone. Her grave is adorned by a solitary sunflower. It might be growing anywhere; were it not for the woman (she or her doppelganger now speeding along country lanes on her last journey), and were it not for the child and were it not for the man with the curly moustache and were it not for the if game. But the if game is a dangerous one and destined to play into the hands of eternity.

In this long drawn-out evening, during a shift that for Wendy Waitress wears on and on, Alexis sits at home. Uncharacteristically (for he seldom drinks alone), he has poured himself a large brandy. Fingers working with the urgency of burrowing things, he completes his daily pipe-loading ritual, but before he puts a match to his tobacco, before he even takes a sip from his glass, he slips into a fitful doze.

five

Showing that Alexis is perceived to be the perpetrator of offences he did not commit; and wherein we are asked to consider certain aspects of Crime and Punishment and how they might have related to Alexis F's predicament.

'Wake up! Thirty-Seven! It's time, Thirty-Seven! *Wake up!*'

The words backfire. Instead of jolting Alexis out of his sleep they close about him in a cocoon of mounting resentment, but then as he grows more outwardly attuned to his surroundings, he tries to lock himself away from the persistent roar of the uniformed man who demands to be called *Mistah* Baker and is forever yelling, 'Wake up! Wake up!'

He encores with a rattling of his exaggerated key-ring against the cot's headboard bars:

'We've found you a new 'ome, Thirty-Seven, you *nonce*! Perv! Get up, *perv*!'

Resistance against this incessant turmoil and clatter is futile, so Alexis staggers to his feet. The violence that follows is demonstrative, almost figurative and merely token pain is inflicted. Mr Baker persists:

'You're going on a little trip, far, far away . . . you lucky sod! Who's a lucky sod?'

In this instance Alexis is not expected to answer.

'There's a cosy little job on the funny farm, all just for you.

Been asked for special you 'ave. You see we know all about you, don't we? *Don't we?*'

Alexis deems not to reply, but a well-appointed jab under the ribs has him say:

'Yes, *Mistah* Baker.'

'And we're gonna be a guinea pig, not an 'ampster, but a guinea pig. Ain't that right?'

'Yes, *Mistah* Baker.'

'And who said you could speak . . .'

Alexis stares into Mr Baker's face. Mr Baker stares into Alexis's face. He makes no attempt to conceal his revulsion and, with undisguised menace, engages staccato speak:

'And we ain't as daft as your Froggy friends, not 'alf as soft as any of them snail-eatin' foreign bastards . . . poofs and kiddie-fuckers the lot of 'em. D'you 'ear . . . nonce? Kiddie-fucker . . .'

Mr Baker sees nothing in Alexis F's eyes. To punctuate each of his next words he prods Alexis in the chest with a hairy forefinger.

'Think you're special don't you. Well if I 'ad my way I'd string you up by the foreskin an' go to work on your balls with a cheese grater . . .'

Then stepping back, swaggering towards the cell door, he pauses; and bent on creating an atmosphere that has flourish, like a confident signature at the foot of a death warrant, Mr Baker adds:

'I 'ear electric shock treatment really 'urts. Now get yourself ready!'

The transfer passes without event or incident. The transporter van is not designed for comfort and at times the seemingly interminable drive becomes bumpy. The wood-slatted seat scores his buttocks. Prisoners are not expected to have the luxury of windows so Alexis has no idea where or along which route he is being driven. They could be passing through villages, towns, or the ever varying landscape of open countryside. They could be in a different country altogether. Incarceration is much the same anywhere. It varies only with the degree of pleasure the custodians expect to derive from tormenting their charges, from inflicting misery, be it mental or physical.

'Sit down.'

'Thank you, sir.'

'D'you play chess?'

'Yes, sir.'

'You're fired.'

'I beg your pardon, sir?'

'Hired! You're hired, what did you think I said?'

'Fired.'

'Fired, don't be ridiculous. You can't be fired. Yet.'

'No, sir.'

'Fired indeed . . . did I really say fired? Well it only goes to – oh never mind, Hilary will show you to your quarters.'

'Shan't you be wanting my name, sir?'

'Name? Yes, I'll think of one.'

Then Hilary said:

'The Master will want you to serve coffee in the lounge, you've half an hour.'

Alexis asked: 'The Master?'

Hilary said: 'That's what we all call him, sometimes Prof.'

Alexis asked: 'We?'

Hilary said: 'The Household.'

Alexis asked: 'What's wrong with Guv . . . or the Guvnor if you like?'

Hilary said nothing.

A divan, a bedside lamp and a table. A chair, bars across the sash windows. A built-in wardrobe with a full-length mirror. This room right at the top of the mansion overlooks the driveway, the road that leads back to town. Alexis's new uniform has been laid out on the bed; dress trousers and a waistcoat of red and white pinstripes with silver buttons. The back is of black silk and he has difficulty adjusting its buckle. As he stands before the mirror he wonders what the Guv's last man was like. A fair size larger?

But when he heaves in his stomach and thrusts out his chest he presents the perfect picture of a gentleman's gentleman.

A hot summer afternoon. No clouds. Ideal weather for strolling through a park or sitting on a bench, maybe reading or just looking at people; at small children coming home from school with their mothers.

Distant spurts from a lawnmower percolate through the french windows, which open on to a terrace. Cooler air freshens the musty lounge, dusts the chandeliers. Alexis pours coffee from Regency silverware. The Prof lifts his hands to Alexis's shoulders and, craning, peers through his pince-nez at the scars perpendicular to his lips. The leather armchair creaks.

'Remarkable . . .' he mutters. Running a sensitive forefinger along the fleshy grooves. 'Remarkable, truly remarkable . . .'

Alexis is dismissed early. It's yet light, but the sun has set behind the swaying poplars, beyond the road that leads to town. He sits at his window unable to decide whether to read or go to bed. The Guv and Hilary are the only two people he's seen since arriving. Crickets are chirping.

With a marked predilection for baggy tweeds, bow-ties and Fair Isle pullovers, the Guvnor has the grizzly look and shapeless deportment of an absent-minded bear; a cuddly, playful beast that could turn exceptionally nasty at a moment's notice. Ruddy-cheeked and blue-veined with a stub of a nose on which are permanently perched the obligatory half-moon pince-nez, he has unwittingly served as the model inspiration for many a cartoon character (or vice versa) and could be anything from 40 to 105 years old. He has decided to call Alexis Thirty-Seven and today he specifically wants to show him something.

As if on a guided tour of the building, Alexis follows the Prof up the main staircase. He follows him through rooms, through halls with portraits in gilded frames. Occasionally the Prof indicates an opening or a corridor with a nod of the head and describes what lies beyond as the 'Post-Bauhaus Ballroom' or the 'Ming

Music Room', 'the Deco Dorms', even a 'Microchip Midi-kitchenette'. An alabaster bowl and an aspidistra, now a tapestry, and those Tudor stools remind Alexis that they've already twice passed this way. When at last they stop, they face a pair of double doors, which the Guv waits for Alexis to open.

They enter a library, a cathedral honeycomb of bays and alcoves. Tall bookcases, carved like Gothic pews in rank and file between lofty arched windows. Alexis is overwhelmed. So taken aback that already he is a few paces behind the Guvnor, his eyes flitting from left to right, straining to glimpse familiar titles, friendly names. Half-heartedly he moves to catch up, and on towards a spacious wing where silent men and women relax in easy-chairs reading, or at a table toying with therapeutic building blocks, a jigsaw puzzle. Clay and Plasticine. The Household.

All stand on the Guv's approach. A gaunt, shrivelled man wearing grey flannels shuffles forward. Poised, about to speak. But catching sight of Alexis in the background, he lowers his eyes and returns to his book, the page marked with his thumb.

'Sit down, sit down,' mumbles the Guv, hands by his side pawing at the air. The Household obeys, but eyes glare at Alexis, jealous eyes. Master and Servant move on, a new aisle, and the next, and more and ever more books. Eyes behind them leering.

Near, from an alcove sounds a sigh. Another. Maybe superseded by a groan or two. The Guvnor stops. He stares quizzically, kindly at the young woman wedged between the end of a bookcase and the wall. Her pleated skirt is concertinaed above her waist, and with slender fingers she clutches the walnut casing to herself, knees dug deep into the ogee moulding. She writhes. Shoulders squirming against brickwork. Her breath comes short and quick and gulped. Neither man stirs, but Alexis shams indifference, becoming fast absorbed by a loose stitch on the Guvnor's collar. All at once the woman senses their presence. She slips out and into full view. Ignoring the men completely, she adjusts her clothing. Then she selects a volume at random and, apparently unconcerned, strolls back to the main area.

Turning into a narrow aisle, Alexis and the Prof walk on, dwarfed by tier upon tier of books. A low door stands before them and, to its right, a chess board on a tripod. Some two-thirds of the game has been played – black at first glance showing the advantage. The Guv, noting Alexis F's interest, sweeps the pieces to the floor. A rash gesture? He says:

'Pick them up and put them back as they were.'

'I'm not sure that I can.'

'But you do play chess?' And without hesitation he replaces each piece (except one white pawn) exactly as it had stood before. He knows that Alexis is aware of his mistake and, pleased, he cries:

'Excellent, that's my move! You have yours on the way back.'

They go through the door. The room is arranged like a cinema. The Guv motions Alexis into a seat facing a makeshift screen while settling himself at a control panel of knobs and switches set into a desk top. Lights go out. On. Life-size schoolgirls flicker and jump across the whitewashed wall in a game of netball. Supple bodies that are cross-hatched by a mesh, a wire fence, as though the pictures had been taken from outside the playground. Alexis can feel the Prof's gaze, knows that he is studying him, his face. Perhaps he is making a film of Alexis watching a film.

Days meander into each other. Nothing continues to happen.

Chatelaine and housekeeper, Hilary has stopped locking Alexis F's door at night.

No patrolling guards, no underfed dogs, not even geese; and although a high stone wall marks the perimeter of the grounds, it is coped with neither broken glass nor barbed wire. A Romanesque arch and a wrought iron gate pierce the south boundary and give on to the reedy banks of a sluggish river. Outside there are no visible listening devices, no carefully secreted cameras.

Alexis feels no desire to run away from Lear Hall – as he has affectionately dubbed his current home. There are no belligerent warders ever threatening violence and he is provided with regular meals. He has adequate shelter and comfortable sleeping accommodation; warmth, and unrestricted access to more literature than he could ever hope to read. In as much as staff and inmates constitute one and the same, his duties are light and administrative rather than manual. Still the Household insists on keeping its distance. The vegetable gardens, a few head of cattle and the piggery fall within the realm of Alexis's responsibilities, though being at the Prof's erratic beck and call can be frustrating in the extreme.

There's also a spacious, vaulted wine cellar, furnished with modern home-brewing equipment and here, ex part-time alcohol abuser, Hilary, further excels as master vintner and alchemist *extraordinaire*. To compound this subterranean Gothic atmosphere, a small locked room, off to the left, has been furbished with scientific paraphernalia and resembles a Victorian laboratory. Hilary has developed a passion for toxicology; for gathering plants and herbs; for extracting, combining and distilling their juices to create poisons, undetectable potions, some of which kill instantaneously, while others will stimulate heart attacks, induce catalepsy or partial paralysis. There is no shortage of rats for experiments.

In the course of his duties Alexis learned that the Prof's birthday was not far off. He approached Hilary with the suggestion that it might be nice to arrange a surprise celebration. Hilary consulted the Household. Unbeknownst to Alexis, a committee was formed and meetings were convened with both agendas and motions. Schemes that included a barbecue, a bonfire, a garden fête, orchestras and fireworks were put forward and debated. Individuals were appointed to look into the feasibility and logistics of implementing the various proposals and the entire Household fell into a cohesive (albeit clandestine) enthusiasm until it was learned that Alexis had been the original instigator of the idea. All at once, allotted tasks became impossible to achieve and deemed entirely impractical. One by one, committee members resigned, pleading urgent prior commitments, and in the end the day simply passed unmarked and went unnoticed.

However, that evening, Alexis was returning from the pigsty when he was overtaken by an urge to take a stroll. It was an hour or more before dinner and so, skirting the west wing of the house, he wandered off towards the once well-trimmed, elm-lined walks, which, though now long overgrown and unkempt, nevertheless still led a haphazard and surreptitious path towards the river. Soon he found himself near the south gate, which, much to his surprise, stood wide open. Passing through, he immediately stopped in his tracks and abruptly took a side-step into the shadows. A cloud-washed moon vied with the grey fade of light and on the lush, marshy bank a figure moved with a measured, rhythmic tread. Using scrub and tree for cover, Alexis crept nearer. He quickly realised that the figure was performing some practised rite, some ritual dance that was forever gathering pace. It was the bookcase woman from the library. She was naked. Her almost breastless body was smeared with grime and her face, caked with mud, had been moulded into a grotesque, leprous mask. The whites of her eyes shone. Reeds and roots were woven into her hair. Like some demonic and frenetic Isadora Duncan, she gradually seemed to gather together her far-flung gyrations until they were concentrated into a single wild cruciform spin. Alexis began to fear that she might whirl herself into harm, but her odious head, streaming sprigs of slime, filliped with balletic precision to keep constant focus on a single point – the gate.

Stupefied, Alexis watched as a second figure appeared. This one was dressed in a white monk's habit, but despite the cowl, Alexis recognised him as the man who usually wore grey flannel suits. In contrast to the woman, he approached with a stilted though calculated grace as might a practitioner of t'ai chi; each studied movement being punctuated by the decisive utterance of an unrecognisable word, a sound like 'fawsse', the vowel stretched and drawn and snapped into a sibilant hiss. He had the semblance

31

of some medieval wizard casting spells or some mystic entranced in the throes of exorcising an evil spirit. His advancing presence more and more slowed the woman until she corkscrewed into a collapse and then, like a primate on all fours, offered her fouled buttocks. The inevitability of the sexual act, which was destined to follow, had Alexis searching out an opportunity for fleeing the scene. Picking his moment with care and believing himself unobserved, he silently made good his escape.

When not in the mood for reading, Alexis had taken to watching the Open University. He had become captivated by a course of lectures on Wellington and the so-called Catholic Question. Since domestic video recorders had yet to be made available to the public at large, he made a point of remembering and underlining the published time of transmission. It being late and the way the Household generally shunned him, objections to his choice of viewing were never aired, so that night he was astonished to find most of the chairs in the television lounge occupied. He expected the inmates to sheepishly file out one by one on his entry, but instead, they rose and faced him in unison. As if by some prearranged signal, half donned hideous masks of deformity, each with an exaggerated, penis-like nose daubed a gaudy brown. The other half clipped on caricatures of cardboard cut-out spectacles. Alexis turned to leave, but was arrested by the sudden onset of activity behind his back. Turning once more he saw that the masked had paired with the bespectacled and stood frozen in lewd poses. He made as if to leave and again the inmates stirred into a hasty motion behind his back. The couples changed partners; new positions were adopted, equally obscene, breath-held and rigid. Mischievous children playing adult variations on the age-old game of 'Statues'. Alexis never did bother to learn whether the Iron Duke eventually resolved his less than cordial differences with Huskisson.

The taped conversations with the Prof seem to get longer and longer, but if not meaningless, remain as enigmatic as ever. Their games of chess become more intense. Nothing continues to happen with monotonous regularity until one morning Alexis barges into the Prof's office without knocking. The older man sits at his desk. There is a substantial pile of typed paper in front of him and he peers over his glasses at the intruder, a frown of consternation quizzing his brow. Alexis says:

'Guv, I'd like to marry Hilary.'

'Marry! Marry! Are you serious? No, it's out of the question. Impossible! D'you hear, impossible . . . How does Hilary feel about it anyway, I suppose you've asked him?'

'Yes.'

'And he agrees?'

'Yes.'

'But that's ridiculous. It's illegal! I mean I'm not even sure whether I approve of the operation in the first place. What's more I'm not sure that Hilary's transsexual manifestations are genuine, or that he would even make a suitable candidate.'

'But we'd like to get married, operation or no operation.'

'That's just daft . . . if you don't mind my saying so, and definitely against the law. Don't think I don't know what you're up to. I can see through your little game and I don't much like it. No, sir, I don't like it at all! Besides I don't think my constitution could stand all the excitement, ha! What kind of deviant are you anyway? You're supposed to have a fancy for school kids . . .'

'According to whom?'

'It's all here in your file.' He rests his hand on the stack of paper. 'All in black and white.'

'According to whom?'

'Well there's no other satisfactory explanation . . . nothing else fits the eemmm . . . Listen . . . I know you two have been shacking up together, but marry? Well I ask you? No the authorities simply wouldn't . . . and there's my research . . .

'Thirty Seven, underneath it all you're a decent fellow and I need you here . . . In the long run, if you like, with your co-operation, I'll be able to do you some good . . . to really help you. But marriage . . .'

(Hilary stopped locking Alexis F's door, instead, night after night he would come in and they'd talk for hours, learning to understand and trust one another; to swap intimacies. Hilary has an ornate snake tattoo on his thigh and he too had been transferred to the institute with a recommendation for a prominent staff position. Alexis discovered that he had not only to expect but accept the label of upstart or usurper and to be forever at enmity with the Household. After all, the head post had been granted to him immediately on his arrival, a newcomer, confined on a charge by many deemed barely worthy of the name misdemeanour.)

'Well . . . yes . . . Marriage . . . I suppose theoretically it's possible. No doubt you hope that technically it would constitute sufficient grounds for your release . . . and his. Fat chance! Then again . . . let me think about it. Maybe I could claim some measure of progress in terms of your treatment. A tangential success . . . It's all very highly irregular. Mmmm? I'll let you know.'

He waves Alexis out of the room. By the door stands a chess set. Alexis sends the pieces scattering to the floor. The Guvnor's move, and whatever he does Alexis will take his queen.

News of the Professor's unexpected and untimely stroke, which left him paralysed and comatose, was reported in the national press. Worldwide, the various social sciences were then undergoing an extended phase of unprecedented revisionism and any radical academic or self-styled behaviourist who could raise adequate funding was encouraged to propound and develop new theories, specifically by experiment and observation – and often the more outlandish the better. Nevertheless, much to the chagrin of many liberal scholars, it was decided that there was no one competent or sufficiently well informed to carry on with the Guv's somewhat idiosyncratic programme, so Lear Hall was closed. All his essays, notes and findings were later published and are now arguably acclaimed as the standard pioneering reference in what still remains a highly controversial field.

Hilary sent Alexis a copy of the book in which he circled every mention of Fourteen, underlining the passages where it appears in connection with Thirty-Seven. The work is prefaced – detailed case histories of each subject. Thirty-Seven's is difficult and upsetting to read.

For a while, in long frivolous letters, Hilary wrote fanciful anecdotes about his job as a research chemist for a pharmaceutical and cosmetics firm. He hints at an affair with one of his lab technicians. Alexis on the other hand secured a post at a privately owned school for blind children in a small town in Derbyshire. Occasionally he has thought of paying Hilary a visit, a surprise visit. But this would undeniably mean retracing steps that Alexis is disinclined to take, there being no point in going back unless it is in fact to go forward.

six

In which, among other matters, Wendy is briefly allowed to take centre stage; and whereupon it is to be noted that any resemblance between her and Peter Pan's Wendy Darling is purely intentional.

Something is gravely amiss. This excursion into homosexuality (fashionable as it then may have been) smacks of the contrived and the absurd. To my knowledge Alexis has never mentioned nor displayed any sexual preference for his own gender, though he did on one occasion talk of a pubescent experience, a rather playful if not altogether experimental incident, which took place on a cycling holiday with some obscure relation, some distant cousin or other. Moreover, he has been known to be both open and quite boastful about his promiscuity, a well-remembered procession of women having always catered to the satisfaction of any of his lusts, which may have demanded an uncomplicated outlet. Where love is concerned, Alexis has already demonstrated his reluctance, if not inability to cope with that emotion and, as Veigh'Vi might have testified, he invariably fell into its outward physical expression with much innovative ritual and acrobatic enthusiasm. Beyond this, his general attitude toward the sexes remains unambiguous. He considers neither to be superior and will treat each with an equal measure of complacency. As to Hilary, I have grave doubts as to whether Alexis consummated his conveniently professed predilection – yet what man has never wondered what it must feel like to be penetrated? Nevertheless, I suspect that their entire escapade is fabricated, along with the Prof, his somewhat unconventional establishment and its cast of fanciful deviants. Even so it would be typical of Alexis to find himself in the hands of some free-range therapist as batty as himself.

Though in most civilised societies provisions are often made for the study of the criminally insane or the socially perverse, their places and manner of detention are subject to levels of orthodox procedure and certain modes of control, no matter how lax the mood of the times. If Alexis is to be believed, then his eccentric professor appears to have been given a free rein and allowed to function without external licence or in accordance with any known code of restraint. Also there is no available documentation regarding Alexis's transfer from the French authorities into the hands of the British. A case such as his would find no precedent for extradition and no records of any such process exist. His adventures, though suspect, are not necessarily fictitious. Reading between the lines, Alexis is undoubtedly telling a truth albeit one of his own making. Thus, as is my imaginative wont, I would offer a different, perhaps more attractive scenario.

Somewhere he was institutionalised and there granted enough independence to make not only his presence keenly felt, but to turn his ironical sense of self-preservation to dominant advantage. Given time and place, an initial escape into the anonymity of the French Foreign Legion is not as implausible as it first might seem. *La Legion* was not always as fastidious about the background of its recruits as it now claims to be. Even today it frowns on homicide not because of the criminality or the immorality of the act, but because a murderer is considered potentially unreliable. Alexis would have found running away to the Legion most appealing. It has after all had its fair share of artists and poets. Alexis could well have been captivated by its shrouds of chivalric myth and its lingering memory of Victorian Romanticism where crimes of passion might not only go mindfully unnoticed but even find clandestine favour. He would have welcomed the harsh military discipline, subjugating himself to its legendary brutality with a quasi-masochistic resignation. He would have drawn strength from the banality of a mechanical routine and relished the exacting constraints of satisfying arbitrary trivia. The sheer physical exertion demanded from basic training would have left him gratefully relieved of all thought and feeling. It might well have been a way, even subconsciously, of inflicting a punishment on himself far more severe than any he would have encountered in a civilised jail. It is also highly likely that he would have made an effort to attract the surreptitious attention of his commandant or some superior officer, while further engineering a more intimate bond with a comrade-in-arms. In it all there would have been a design.

Dien Bien Pheu was not all that distant a memory. Vietnam was still on the global agenda and the Legion, famed for its ever ready supply of mercenaries, remained actively involved in central Africa. It would have been excruciatingly hot there. A regular patrol would have approached that particular copse in the wilderness with textbook caution. Not everything can be anticipated. Skirmishes and ambushes happen and the wounded are sometimes left for dead. A battlefield makes not only for corpses. It provides opportunities for accidents to occur (intentionally or otherwise), for maiming and disfigurement, for pain and anguish (perhaps to be remedied), for personalities to change and identities to be misplaced. Granted, none of this takes into account the somewhat lame allusions made to paedophilia. Surely if a man cannot take delight in sitting and watching boys and girls at play, if he cannot bask in the careless yelps and giggles of unfettered innocence without arousing suspicions of a criminal nature, then something is definitely amiss. On the other hand could it be that two or more incidents are being deliberately confused here in order to obscure the available facts? And could not those events described as taking place at Lear Hall have occurred prior to Veigh'Vi's death? After all, suppositions present themselves to be tested and a variety of explanations can always be put forward. Then again, the depth of Alexis's musings this evening are not strictly speaking my immediate concern. Let him sip his brandy and smoke his pipe. Let him live his life at the back of his mind and in his darkened room invent whatever reminiscences he will; leaving me single-handedly to entertain a certain anxiety for Warm-hearted Wendy.

She will have noticed that Alexis had left her a larger tip than usual and will have jumped to the conclusion that this was an inpromptu expression of his fancy for her. The assumption will have struck her as unwarranted and she will have felt shamed by her own sense of vanity. It will have been superseded almost at once by thoughts of her boyfriend; the boyfriend about whom nobody knows, not even Precocious Pam, tempted as Wendy might be to tell all. To tell of their secret wedding scheduled to take place in less than a month; of their secret plans to leave this backwater town for ever, to secretly run away this very weekend. But, going about her business of clearing tables, laying fresh napery and setting places, she will have remained mum, neither happy nor sad, yet as always displaying an unlearned grace and a deftness, which typifies her casual demeanour.

She makes no effort to look attractive, but succeeds, even when her henna-streaked hair is in need of a wash, raggedly parted, tucked back and bound with an elastic band into a Manx cat's tail. Loosened from their quiff, careless strands trail over her forehead. Tiny studs pierce her ears. Her healthy complexion is highlighted by the remnants of a summer tan. With fingernails cared for and unvarnished, her hands are strong and worked, yet remain shapely. A single silver ring adorns the right. She has a solid yet curvaceous figure, which carries not an ounce of fat, but denies her a marked waist. Her shoulders attest to a childhood of river swimming. Freed from the constraint of undergarments, her breasts will neither spread and fall outwards nor will they droop and point down, but keep firm in their athletic mould. Her ankles are slender. Her feet are small. It's a practical body born of what once might have been termed good peasant stock and will bear her years with consideration and confidence.

Everything being just so and readied for opening in the morning – the till checked, the float balanced – Pam and the manageress of the coffee shop will have brewed a pot of tea, put their feet up and smoked a cigarette, but by then Wendy will have been on her way, a well-filled box of unsold cakes, pastries and patties in her string bag. She will have skirted the car park and crossed the bridge. Inadvertently she will have glanced in the direction of the old manor house, which certainly ought to be somebody's ancestral home, but she will not have seen it for the woodland scrub and the thick cluster of horse chestnuts, which obscures the view.

Wendy's mother gave birth to all her five children in the cottage towards which her only daughter will have been heading. A stone's throw from the water's edge and on the crest of a gently sloping bank, it once stood almost mysteriously alone, but the town has grown to span both sides of the river and the property developers have robbed it of its seclusion. Between low hedgerows, a winding, gravelled cul-de-sac leads from the barren lanes and drawing-board lawns of a modern private estate to a loose-hinged, wooden gate in an unkempt privet. In the fast fading light, Wendy walks these oft-trod paths with a casual surety of foot but with a focused air, as if looking at these all too familiar surroundings for the very last time. She is both channelling and toying with her memory.

Six years ago on a blustery evening not unlike this one, Wendy's father called his children together into the parlour. This had never happened before. With mounting anticipation they bunched into a semicircle about his chair. Smiling a somewhat sad but warm smile, he looked at each in turn, and then, as if addressing a point far, far away, he said:

'Your mother's gone. She won't be coming back.'

The short, stunned silence gave way to an uneasy fidgeting. The twins, who at seven were the youngest, began to whisper, 'Gone away, gone away . . .' over and over until they fell into playing their very own special mirror-mime game. Their baby-like expressions creased into sorrow, they enacted a range of simultaneous hugs, kisses and caresses, seemingly to find some consolation in their reflected gestures. While Wendy and Toots exchanged furtive glances, neither being able to keep eye contact with one another nor yet being able to arrest their gaze elsewhere, Curly whimpered:

'I knew it . . . it's all my fault . . . I knew it and I'm sorry, it's all my fault.' He moved into a corner and, facing the wall, continued to blame himself, bemoaning his lot and sagging under the weight of all the cares of his nine-year-old world.

'Where's she gone?' asked Toots.

'I don't know,' answered his father.

'Why—' and realising the question would solicit the same inadequate answer, Toots cut himself short. In a suppression of tears he fled upstairs, only to be heard pacing from room to room.

As the eldest, Worldly Wendy told herself that she had to understand. She sought to find a measure of comprehension in her father's tired and careworn features but saw only an impenetrable void. At almost 15 she was a woman, and falling back on the singular stamina of her sex, summoned her strength to come to terms with the feeling of both knowing and not knowing at the same time. Though she wanted to climb on to her father's lap and curl into a ball under his chin, she gently rested her hand on his shoulders and briefly brushed his brow with her lips. And at that moment she knew that from now on and in most things she would have to replace her mother. She scurried off to the kitchen to see what might be cobbled together by way of a meal.

No one was hungry that night and without being told to do so everybody went to bed early. Unable to sleep, after restless hours of tossing and turning, Wendy tiptoed downstairs for a drink of water. Much to her surprise her father sat slumped at the kitchen table, his back to the door, his head cradled in the fold of his arms. He was staring hard at a full bottle of whisky and an empty tumbler, which stood directly before him. Without a word Wendy retraced her footsteps, her thirst unslaked. In the morning she discovered the bottle still unopened and the tumbler still unused.

As days became months, try as she might, she could not think of her parents being other than happy. The thought heightened the melancholy numbness that enveloped her. She remembered her father as always laughing, reckless and bubbling with a surfeit of time to spare for his children. He had taught her to swim, to ride a bicycle and a love of Gilbert and Sullivan. He had unearthed conkers with his boys, taken them fishing and to football matches. For their own good, he had banned catapults, knives and airguns. With mother, Wendy had tended the herb garden, had gathered wild currants and blackberries, had jarred pickles, preserves and jams. Mother allowed mixing bowls to be licked and it was she who had told them stories of witches and fairies and all kinds of elfin folk that lived in the forest. She also knew of magical lands that lay abundant in wealth and riches there just for the taking. There was Blackpool and boarding houses; snowmen and sledding. Wendy's recollections were thus a procession of Christmases and birthdays. She refused to recognise her father's insensible idleness, his selective involvement in family affairs and his lack of either drive or ambition, let alone the mundane rounds of childbearing to which he had subjected his wife. These realisations were to come gradually and much, much later.

Meanwhile she patiently waited for her father to provide an explanation for her mother's departure, but never once thought to confront him. If he were to confide in her then he would do it in his own inimitable manner, but till then she would remain sensitive to his reluctance to speak, yet affronted by his prolonged inability to trust her. Overnight he had altogether lost his cheerful disposition and now seemed never to be at home, or when there, he would simply mope in an oppressive silence, which might rarely be punctuated by a forced and painful smile. They saw each other less and less. He ate alone at odd hours and, as the mood took him, rewarming whatever food his daughter might have prepared for that day. Though perhaps on the brink of despair, not once did he succumb to neglect and, without fail, every weekend the housekeeping tin on the mantel above the Rayburn would be generously replenished.

At school, the little that was said by her teachers and girlfriends was for the most part muttered in embarrassed innuendo. Toots, however, faired less well. His classmates revelled in the overt cruelty of pubescent boyhood. Eyes were blackened, noses were bloodied and teeth were lost. New words found their way into his vocabulary. Curly continued to blame himself, not only for his mother's absence but for any misfortune and mishap that occurred, whether the fault was his or not. The twins found their own equilibrium by choosing to be too young to acknowledge any significant change in their ever more self-contained lives.

Though having an appreciable aptitude for history, music and maths (especially algebra), Wendy's schooling soon showed a turn for the worse. In her surrogate role, the care of the boys took precedence over study, and any scholastic aspirations to which she may have been encouraged or which she herself may have entertained, rapidly fell by the wayside.

On her sixteenth birthday, having no academic qualifications, she found herself fortunate enough to be given a job at the local precision mouldings factory. Before long, her above average abilities lead her to positions of limited responsibility and the eventual choice of volunteering for unsociable shifts, which allowed her to work part-time at the coffee shop. This she will have been doing for nigh on four years.

Out of habit and necessity, she will have lifted the lopsided gate to ease its opening along the arc ever more deeply scored into the mud and cinder path, but, encumbered by her string bag, she will have struggled to close it, perhaps to leave it wedged ajar with an ineffectual parting kick. Nearing the unweeded and overgrown vegetable plot, forever sprouting spinach, she will have been assailed by the routine sounds of her home and paused as if to commit them to memory. A sudden burst of rudimentary chords from Toots's guitar. Nibs (the former bully who had so mercilessly tormented Toots about his mother) has persuaded him to join a rock 'n' roll band, which has already shown more than mere promise and stirred up much local interest. Curly setting and resetting the table with a clutter of platters, knives and forks, determined that everything should be perfect and to his complete satisfaction. It never is. He will have been looking after the cooking of the jugged hare, which Wendy prepared several nights before and, no matter how delicious the result, will profusely apologise for all the shortcomings only *he* can taste. For a while he experimented with playground drugs, but is now determined to atone and embark on a life of monastic deprivation, perhaps in the long-term to enter the priesthood. The other two will be out and about, safely hearing and seeing things that only they can see and hear. They have decided on a stage career and are perfecting their act as professional twins. Wendy entertains no fears for her brothers' futures, though she will undoubtedly miss them. Feelings about her father's whereabouts will have been long ago submerged under layers of indifference.

After supper the twins will have invented a new routine for doing the washing-up. Toots and Nibs will have gone chasing girls. Curly will have been visiting the rector (who has an exceptionally pretty wife) or at choir practice. Then Wendy will have dressed herself in jeans and sweater, put on her rubber overshoes, her sheepskin jacket and tied a scarf about her hair, but not before very carefully checking her make-up. In the dark, retracing familiar steps, she will have gone off across the fields, along little-used bridle-paths and over stiles. In no time at all she will have reached the old manor house. Drawn by the light, remembering her mother's fable about the moth, she will have crept up to the french windows and stood in such a way as to peep in between the undrawn curtains with little risk of herself being in sight. There she will have seen Alexis wake with a start; then heavily lift himself out of his chair, lumber over to the log fire and prod at it vigorously with a poker. The flaring embers will have set grotesque shadows dancing along the walls and she will have wondered what it is that has suddenly made him smile.

seven

Wherein our attention is drawn to the futility of hate and the destruction of one's enemies (albeit symbolically), even if the enemy happens to be oneself. Alexis F's first ever encounter with Nina O.

There had been a fire at the hotel. Helpers were still being recruited for the task of clearing debris, of repairing and redecorating. The proprietor, a short, swarthy and robust man who revelled in the name Don Juan, didn't much care for Alexis F's appearance, but since Alexis claimed to have studied architecture and had addressed Don Juan in his native Majorcan rather than in Spanish, Don Juan decided to hire him.

The work was arduous. And tedious. There were burned timbers to be removed and replaced. Much of the structure had to be made sound again. Then there were walls to be replastered; others merely stripped, but all to be repainted. Blankets and bedlinen had to be laundered. Carpets were scrubbed by hand, washed free of hose water and dried by large fan heaters, cacophonous blowers shaped like torpedoes, which needed constant tending and a frequent refilling with oil.

In due course, the builders' ladders are loaded on to donkey carts and sent dawdling along the melting tarmac roads winding back to town. The job is over, and Alexis finds himself wanting to stay on. The owner 'ums' and 'ahs' for a moment. But Alexis knows that Don Juan has seen the extent of his capability, and that he doesn't shy from hard work. Don Juan also knows that Alexis speaks German – a language he is most eager to learn.

'A handyman would come in useful,' he's saying. 'Especially now that the holiday rush is almost on us.'

Pause.

'If I were to keep you on ... *if* mind ... I'd insist on two provisions. Every evening you must give me a German lesson, well once in a while, and you must at all times be out of the way ... of the guests that is.'

Don Juan assigns Alexis a set of duties.

He often works 15, 16 hours a day. Maintenance. Daily, the bar stock has to be checked and replenished. Deliveries have to be received and stored. Sinks have to be unclogged; door handles fixed; curtain rails remounted. He polishes mirrors, straightens pictures and attends to the supply of logs used for burning under the hotplates on which Señora Benitta attends to all the cooking. Huge tortillas and endless paella. She is Don Juan's wife, marginally taller than her husband and uncharacteristically has blue eyes. She also lisps naturally, which in turn plays havoc with much of her pronunciation. Alexis is paid a pittance, even by Spanish standards, plus bed and board; but then Alexis has no expenses to speak of and Don Juan repeatedly reminds him:

'Everything's okay. I've fixed it with the local police,' and he winks with a wrinkling of nose and cheeks.

From about three in the afternoon till eight in the evening Alexis F's time is more or less his own. After only seven lessons Don Juan has abandoned German, or simply believes that he has sufficiently mastered enough words to please by far the majority of his clientele. So, unless catching up on sleep, Alexis spends hours walking. Away from the scatter of breeze-block hotels, which make up this new and fast growing sea front resort. Away from the ancient, fortified mother town of Capdepera. North, across bays, three popular beaches. And on to a narrow dirt track that snakes through the forested foothills of two mountains. Heat and mosquitoes follow him under the trees.

Occasionally leaves rustle, twigs snap. And mocking, the shadows consort.

On the ridge top, in the hollow of the saddle, the overgrown path divides. Seaward, there's a plateau; to the west, the higher peak – Pui Águila. Each of its slopes offers a different ascent. The sheer and the gentle. To tackle with mood. Should Alexis choose an awkward route, he'll reach the summit shortly before dusk and in uncanny silence; the sounds of day dead and those of night – the crickets and bullfrogs – still dormant. In isolation. But no; the poems return. On odd scraps of curled, sometimes charred paper. And more and more often written in Spanish.

Alexis opts for a leisurely climb. Before him the Mediterranean stretches wide. Clear, blueing, darker, black. To Sicily, Malta and Crete. To Libya. Familiar circles. Ripples spreading from the small volcanic isle, which wart-like squats some quarter of a mile from the beach. The stronger swimmers, ants climbing over its potted surface. Holiday makers, sunbathers and their resort. Tiny bleached cubes of bad sanitation, strange food and strange customs. But a fortnight of blistering sunshine and a landlord who mumbles in their own tongue. The subsiding cry of someone falling. And Alexis sees him. As if in slow motion, a body is plunging from the edge of the plateau and down towards the sea, towards the spume of surf and the loose boulders where the lapping and swirling foams swirl and lap. Limbs that flail, relentlessly plummeting, all at once to jolt to a sudden halt and to swing inwards, as if the feet were tied by an invisible rope or cord. Dangling legs and arms, fingers and toes scraping for holds in the cragged face. Cling. Then upright, slowly the man begins to scale the rocks.

Many people have gathered on the plateau. Unaware of the climber, they watch a solitary figure barely 50 yards away, poised rigid and dangerously close to the cliff's edge. Alexis waits for the person to execute a dive, but instead, quite unexpectedly, somebody breaks free from the crowd and runs directly at the motionless form. They collide. Like a skittle, one topples, letting out a mournful howl that reverberates.

47

Crowds are jeering. Faces. Distorted and angered at public assemblies. Toothless. Solemn in processions. At fiestas crowds are aimless, lost or drunk. Meandering tourists in pantomime. A single roar in the corrida. To wave and eddy at carnivals. But the entertainment on the plateau is esoteric, shrouded in rites for those familiar with mysteries, which Alexis doesn't understand.

Even with no path he gets to the plain quickly, there to be assailed by the pungent smell of horses and asses and the hot odours of a throng, which appears to be segregated into two groups. Some, though all are peasants and fishermen, queue in a ragged, haphazard file facing the half-doors at the rear of an old gypsy trailer. Symbolic plants, complex loops and curls decorate its barrel-vaulted roof below which one long wall is folded open and held level by heavy chains of orange and green links to project like a broad tailboard. At the corners, fluted, timber poles capped with large brass spheres support a scarlet canopy. And all around this stage there is a mob, milling and noisy, but penned in by a makeshift fence of rough-hewn posts and twine.

A tall, gaunt man with a pencil-line moustache and close-cropped sideburns stands on the platform He is dressed in a gypsy's costume. His three-quarter length trousers reveal the floral design scored into the calves of his leather boots. His vest jacket is intricately and colourfully embroidered. A velvet sash spans his waist. As he lifts his hand, a signal for order, his flared sleeve slithers back to his biceps. Sweat trickles across his brow, disappears under the rims of his dark glasses. He is shouting a number. A woman steps from the wings. A fisherman is pushing through the audience, waving, clutching a small, worn rectangular card. He is weaving through the leering faces and from amongst fellow villagers and friends some of whom pat him on the back and mutter congratulations.

Others jibe.

The gypsy examines the fisherman's ticket and they exchange a few words. Laughing. Together to inspect the woman who somehow looks ageless, her eyes weary and downcast, yet proud, partly hidden by strands of blonde hair.

Still nodding his appreciation, the fisherman leads the woman to the precipice. There he positions her with her back towards the sea, towards the drop and to his own satisfaction. To yelps of encouragement and whistles of disapproval, he returns to the stage. Grinning. Turning, running at the woman. To hit her. And he hits her, his shoulder squarely between her breasts and with such a force that he almost follows her over the edge.

The rabble stays mum. The scream is a haunting wail, ululating and undulating, diminishing. Then gone. To a thunderous cheer.

Alexis glances at the old man who queues last in line on this side of the barrier. Unperturbed, he waits. He is carrying a portrait, the size of a postcard in a gilded frame. Alexis asks:

'What's going on?'

From deep within folds of parched skin, languid eyes peer at Alexis in amazement. The old man's brow furrows, as if to gauge the question – is it a joke? He looks down at his small painting of an elderly matron. Back at Alexis. Then in a voice soft but full of vigour, he says:

'We smite our enemies.'

'Sorry . . . ?'

'Hurry! Bring a picture of those you hate, of him who is your enemy. Take it to the Maestro. Tomorrow you too will push them into the sea, hurry!'

And as an afterthought:

'But you must pay.'

A mischievous grimace. He is wagging his finger, beckoning for Alexis to draw his ear closer to his lips. Alexis obliges him and the old man whispers:

'They're only actors, tumblers. They never fall, not all the way to the water. Watch. They shackle their feet to ropes, secretly. They climb back later. I know. I am old, but these others . . .'

He nods in the direction of the babbling crowd.

*   *   *

49

Don Juan is a philanderer ever visiting Palma ostensibly on business, but more often than not doing the rounds of brothels and bars. True to his Latin perceptions, he also considers all foreign women fair game and his hotel seems to cater to a preponderance of 18- to 20-year-old females, single and of Nordic extraction. Nevertheless, despite his claims, he has far to go before he can aspire to the successes of Miguel, the head waiter, and Lorenzo, the cocktail barman. These two have a slate in their room on which they record their conquests and by week three of the season were both well into double figures. Perhaps because Alexis poses no threat to the tenets of machismo, Don Juan has gradually evolved a certain liking for him, if not altogether a special, albeit one-sided relationship. It is as though Alexis has become a pet or a favoured curiosity, so much so that recently his master took him on a day-trip to the capital and there, by way of a treat, escorted him to a whorehouse. Oddly enough, no amount of bribery or cajoling on the part of the madame could induce any of the girls to oblige Alexis with their favours. Yet none of this constitutes real grounds for hatred, not even the obvious heartbreaks Don Juan causes his wife. Alexis has long since developed an easy rapport with Señora Benitta. She at least can laugh at herself and make fun of her own speech impediment.

The local photographer lived on the outskirts. He stood Alexis against a whitewashed wall. He adjusted Alexis F's collar and asked him to look straight ahead. All of sudden Alexis felt very apprehensive. The photographer bent under the hood of his camera and made some adjustments. When he emerged, he smiled and said:

'Sorry, we must be patient.'

The sun glinted off the photographer's gold tooth. They waited. The sun sank a little lower. The photographer bent under the hood of his camera. He emerged and smiled. They waited. The sun sank a little lower. Alexis still felt very nervous as the photographer took his photograph.

The prints will be ready later, by nightfall. And the gypsies on the hill are bound to be performing again tomorrow.

Alexis has given notice. He is leaving. At the weekend, the day after, soon. Don Juan wants to know why.

'Because it's time,' Alexis tells him.

'What time?' he's asking. 'Why not stay? Stay to the end of the season and I'll pay for your flight to the mainland. To anywhere in Europe. It's inconvenient for you to go now.'

'But I must.'

'Why? You'll have no more wages till you tell me why, not even what I owe you already.'

In anticipation of obstinacy, Alexis has formulated a reason Don Juan might just understand.

'I've entrusted my wife to the care of a lunatic,' he says. 'A mad irresponsible oaf. A poet who drives old battered sports cars, badly and too fast. I must get her away.'

'A wife?'

'Yes.' Explanations about commitments in cohabitation would only prove fruitless.

'Well why didn't you say?' Don Juan's tone harbours scepticism. 'Send for her.' As much a challenge as a suggestion.

'Impossible.'

'Impossible?' In jocular disbelief.

'There's the child.' Alexis is thinking on his feet.

'You have a son?' When it comes to children, Don Juan's inbred precedents leave him no option but to be concerned.

'The boy's in grave danger.'

'What kind of man are you to abandon his own son?' And there is no mistaking that the revulsion and repugnance has become genuine.

Nevertheless, on Alexis's last evening bottles of champagne are freely uncorked. In the kitchen, Señora Benitta dances. Her mother plays the guitar. Nobody volunteers to sing, but the rest of the staff who are not on duty along with one or two guests clap out rhythms and beat time. Miguel persuades Imgard to join him for a midnight swim. As if firmly conditioned by habit, Alexis tends the flames under the hotplates. He burns scrap paper, sheet after sheet neatly covered in writing. At one point he almost starts a fire and, extinguisher in hand, Don Juan laughs.

At dawn Alexis will pack his bags and cross the twin peaks to the new holiday camp in Cala Mesquida. There he'll bum a ride.

In Ortego's bar a driver is breakfasting on melon and sipping cognac. It's his job to ferry ever more rowdy batches of English campers to and from Palma.

This early morning journey bears the hallmarks of depression. After a long night of fulsome revelries, the holiday-makers sit quietly subdued. Under-slept and over-drunk, they nurse sore heads, sore stomachs and freshly tender patches of peeling skin. Even the self-appointed jester that such a group invariably produces can do little more than bemoan his delicate lot. Sympathy is short. There is only the Duty Free shop, the hopefully undelayed flight and the predictable drizzle of home to look forward to.

Alexis sits at the front near the driver. They too have little to say to each other. An uncomfortable anxiety has curtailed Alexis F's practised repertoire of polite small talk. He feels certain that he is being not only watched, but malevolently scrutinised. The hairs on his neck rise and he dares not look over his shoulder. When the bus eventually stops to let him down before the airport turn-off, he feels a genuine sense of relief and for some moments watches the vehicle drive away, but no one gives him a backward glance.

Some time after the bus left, probably just long enough for its existence to have been all but forgotten, a body was washed up on the beach.

The policemen assigned to the task soon gave up keeping back the inquisitive tourists who one by one came to join the ring of onlookers. To ask, then nod, meaning to stay, but walk off and then away from a circle that somehow always remains unchanged.

Then the ambulance crew arrived. Sweat stains had tanned the armpits of their white tunics.

'Bitching heat!'

The policemen agreed.

In spite of its battered and mangled limbs, the corpse was turned over as a prelude to being lifted on to a stretcher. The circle spread. Someone gasped. The face before them was severely corroded and hung gnawed in gangrenous lumps. Later, a much closer examination revealed the disfiguring to be nothing more than a mixture of greasepaint and latex make-up.

Weaving through the clutter of cast-iron tables at a cheap quayside café, the waiter brings Alexis a beer. She is visible from a distance. Both the waiter and Alexis stare. The very way she walks – with the fluid grace of a gazelle or an antelope in flight – would make her stand out in a crowd; but there is no crowd, only one or two dockers and stevedores enjoying an unscheduled break. They seem momentarily too stunned to jeer or for raucous comment. Without hesitation or once averting her eyes she makes directly for Alexis.

'May I join you?' she asks. The waiter hovers.

'Be my guest,' Alexis replies.

'I'd sooner pay my own way.'

The waiter hovers.

'As you wish.'

She loops the straps of her rucksack over the back of a chair, which scrapes the stone cobbles as she sits. She orders a kir and crosses her legs. The patina, the smoothness of her colouring is the depth and stillness of safe waters.

'I saw you on the bus,' she says in a matter-of-fact tone. 'You don't know what a joy it was to see you weren't one of them.'

'A tourist you mean?'

'That's one way of putting it.'

'So how did you get on the bus?'

'I mingled with the mob. They were all too comatosed to notice.'

'I find that hard to believe.'

'You didn't see me.'

'Not exactly.'

And so very soon they are engaged in an animated conversation as might normally be enjoyed only by people who have known each other for a long time. They are both catching the late crossing to the mainland and on the ship their intimacy, bolstered by copious tots of brandy, will lead them to sharing Alexis F's cabin, but not his bunk.

'I would dearly like to make love with you,' she has said, 'but this is not a good time.'

'I understand.'

'Do you . . . ? Yes I think you do . . .'

And their chatter and their storytelling go on well into the night.

When they wake, they are assailed by an odd sensation. There is a strange, tacky odour in the air. On leaving the cabin they are confronted with an all but spent confusion, the smell of disinfectant and vomit. Decks and gangways are awash and littered with puke bowls. They learn that they have slept through the worst thunderstorm on record and that parts of Barcelona are flooded. It will be a while before they dock.

Once on dry land they approach their farewells without sadness.

'I have a cottage on the moors, less than an hour's drive from the Arts School. You'll come and stay with me there,' she says.

'Of course.' Alexis jots down her address.

'I have to spend a few days here in town. There are some people I have promised to visit.'

'And Gaudi.'

'Yes . . . and Gaudi. I'd invite you to join me, but I can't. It would be rather awkward.'

'There's no hurry and much to see. Sooner or later we'll meet up in England.'

'Yes, you look like a man who still has far to go . . .'

eight

Illustrative of how even fragmented memories of childhood will often bear the seeds of a today ever to be viewed as the portent of things to come.

'Travel indeed! One need travel no further than to the church . . . and back!' That's what his mother had said. 'If God had meant us to . . .' This comes as a neat and generalised reply in the vein of all her profound platitudes to some duly forgotten question put at an age when Alexis knew for certain that there were different lands and different people beyond the white peaks that ringed the village. He recalls her words without fail whenever he is strapped into a bucket-seat and quashing anxiety while waiting for the aircraft to taxi along the runway.

After Alexis F's birth (no doubt an uncompromisingly complicated delivery, the agonies of which perhaps germinated an extreme religious zeal) his father was barred from his wife's side. Her obsession with the evils inherent in all men – Original Sin in the Serpent personified – led to a belief that chastity alone could safeguard her sainthood. Two divans therefore, separated by the entire width of the room, replaced the nuptial four-poster. To retaliate, father drank. He slept on a straw-filled pallet laid in a cupboard under the stairs and to curtail his frustrations made cardboard cut-out effigies of nineteenth-century soldiers, which he then painstakingly painted in minute detail. Alexis is an only child.

The family cottage, built of timber and stone, was typical of any in a highland village. A close-neighboured chalet within easy reach of the church. The lower floor, raised and levelled on a plinth, was a simple kitchen in which the windows faced the main street and where pots and pans hung over an open grate burning beneath a crude iron grill. A large kettle stood perpetually on the boil, and seemingly ever to hand, an enamelled hip-bath added to the clutter. It was a cramped area with steep stairs to the three attic rooms above, one hardly more than a closet. In the yard, there was the privy hut and other lean-tos, a toolshed, a barn. Alexis has a goat, but he desperately wants a wolf cub.

Mother limps. She tells Alexis about hobgoblins and griffins and crawly things with legs; lots of legs. He doesn't quite believe her, though secretly he is afraid of being turned into a frog – prince or no prince. She also tells tales about cloven-hooved trolls who live in clocks, steal time and carry off naughty children. At home there's a tall clock by the pantry. With this clock comes the memory of an old, stooped man who every once in a while appears from nowhere bringing yarn and ribbons, needles and pins. Sometimes he has a suitcase full of baubles, trinkets and charms. He sharpens knives and scissors and speaks of other things. The things called wise. Their clock is even older than the man because it has just one hand. But the peddler can see the time in its wry, yellowed dial. He shows Alexis. Yet though he often tells Alexis of these things called wise, he never talks of the clock's eye. The eye that has to be prodded and twisted. An eye that Alexis has seen shining in the dark.

Sundays begin noisily. Mother yells at father who, heedless, snores on. Her normally upright and slender height seems to collapse on itself. Her shoulders hunched, she is cursing. Her hair, usually bound flat to cover her ears, is dishevelled. Furious, her eyes sparkle and each crease of her clothing is animated. The chaotic rush, a weekly attempt to arrive at Mass on time. Alexis is pulled up the hill, ever faster, in an act that tends to disguise

lameness. Lurched, glancing over his shoulder for glimpses of
father following, dawdling. He's suffering from last night's
unabsorbed alcohol. Nearing, greeting a friend. They share swigs
from a bottle in a brown paper bag.

And always they are late. And always take advantage of the
'everybody-stand' confusion to march to the front pews while the
gospel is read. Father, his tie straight, the hay no longer under
his collar, inches in at the back and stays there with the rest of
the men. Throughout the sermon Alexis longs for the day when
he's grown up and can stop there too. Freed from kneeling.

Mother is dead. Today she is buried. The priest, his breath
sweetened by holy wine, speaks to Alexis of things neither
understands. Father is drinking.

There are lots of places where Alexis can be alone. In the
forest on the eastern slopes high above the sawmill, or in the
disused mine, but he chooses to sit in the corner of the toolshed.
In the barn he hears the goat chewing. He fiddles with wood
shavings. He swings the vice handle to and fro. The toolbox is
locked. He finds a rusty nail. He is carving lines into the palm
of his left hand. The grooves pale. Slowly blood oozes. It is harder
to cut his left hand.

Father has appeared in the doorway. Alexis is up, both fists
clenched inside his pockets.

'There you are . . .' his father mumbles. 'What're you . . . why
are you here all by yourself?'

Blood seeps through Alexis F's trouser pockets and trickles
round his thighs. He makes no answer.

Father stoops to hug him, but at a distance, as if at arm's
length. The feel of his whiskers prickles. The smell of alcohol
catches the throat. A broad palm on Alexis's shoulder and father
is leading his son to the house.

There is a woman in their kitchen. Alexis has seen her before,
once when he peeped into the bothy. She had been talking with
father who is now saying:

'Son, this is Lucy, she's –'

'Don't, not now,' says Lucy to father, and, 'Isn't that right, young man?' to Alexis. 'Not yet seven and a braver fellow than most I'll wager . . .' She is smiling.

Alexis is grateful to Lucy (though she is slightly wrong about his age) for father lets him go and he runs off towards the pond where he washes his hands, bandages them in rags.

Lucy has come to live with them. To cook. To clean. That evening she sees the scabs on Alexis's hands.

'What happened? Show me.'

She inspects the scabs. Alexis says nothing. Lucy seems satisfied. Not to probe, never to take any notice of him. But he can't help staring. She has such large breasts and buttons her blouse so as to leave them half exposed. Alexis is sure they are going to leap out at any second and he mustn't miss them. They will.

One day a lady named Auntie Beth came to visit. She packed Alexis F's clothes and some toys into a trunk. Alexis said goodbye to his goat because he didn't have a wolf cub and because he was going away with this lady who owned a house in England. He was going on a journey across the mountains.

'Would you care for a drink, madam?' the air hostess asks the passenger across the aisle from Alexis. They are airborne. Every now and again a choppy Atlantic breaks through the bumpy bank of thick cloud.

Heavy, a fearful odour of scent assails Alexis F's nostrils. The hostess is smiling, her painted lips pout. And steadily, and steadily, so very steadily, a foreskinned phallus slides from her mouth. It grows longer, firmer and longer, like a sacrificial bilbo shedding its sheath. The all too familiar vision taunts him, will haunt him till he no longer feels free to look any woman in the face.

He snaps shut his eyes.

In a far-off cemetery his parents lie next to each other sharing a peaceful irony.

nine

In which the exegesis continues unabated, red-herrings and unwarranted diversions notwithstanding; and wherein it begins to transpire that Wendy's role is perhaps not entirely all that it might seem to be.

Oh yes, that'll be right. I specifically refrained from comment earlier because I am fully aware of Alexis's propensity for if not exactly hoisting himself on his own petard then for inextricably enmeshing himself in his own embellishment of the truth. This digression to the Balearic Islands (plucked at random in an epitome of his utter disregard for sequence) is no more than a feint. Anybody would think that Alexis had invented bungee jumping, though in all fairness at that time the activity was very much confined to the Indonesian islanders and their ethnic displays of native masculinity. Nonetheless, there is something to be said for conjuring up visions of carnival. Why not run away to the circus? It would have been easy enough for a young, strong and healthy chap to find work with a travelling fair; especially someone who could handle a heavy goods vehicle no matter what its state of disrepair. The waltzer, the dodgems, the wall of death; it is by and large a rootless society of latter-day adventurers who thrive on sex, drugs and Wurlitzer rock 'n' roll. On a merry-go-round, hungover and never quite sober yet never drunk to incapability, Alexis would have felt at home amongst these anarchic itinerants fucking their way from town to town through an endless procession of faceless teenagers destined for tears. Sharing a caravan with the stale stench of feet, junk food and everyday's clotted semen; with which weekend's girl much passed from bunk to bunk, from Liverpool, Bradford or was it Leeds, who still lies curled and rejected under sweaty laundry in a stupor in Newcastle or is it Carlisle and whose name has long since been lost to the sweet decay of insouciance. Of course eventually Alexis would have been sacked. He would have become bored and done something spontaneously dangerous just for the thrill and funfair of it. Perhaps he set the drive of the gig wheel in reverse, in motion and laden. Perhaps I too 'have now stupidly veered into a red herring and laid myself wide open to accusations of postulating unwarranted diversions, though I cannot avoid further noting the way Alexis seems to be making an issue out of kitchens – wood-burning stoves, kettles of boiling water and their kin. Am I expected to infer that it was something of this nature that caused the mutilations? Or is it, as I suspect, just another cunning aside.

When it actually comes to the crux of the matter, no sooner do I credit Woebegone Wendy with an unfortunate past, than Alexis deems it necessary to create one of his own. Admittedly, I didn't really notice or even begin to know him until late in high school and it's possible that he has foreign origins which in turn might account for his facility to learn languages without effort. He speaks five fluently and has a working knowledge of two more. The woman I have always assumed to be his mother might well have been an aunt, though she never struck me as a foreigner and certainly never spoke with an accent.

Whoever she was, the constant image she evokes is that of a slight person with coarse unruly hair splaying outwards from beneath a chequered cheesecutter. Perennially dressed in a grey, elbow-holed cardigan and tweed skirts, she is ever to be seen shod in heavy-duty wellington boots, their tops folded over. There is a pair of secateurs in her hand and somewhere in the picture a falcon or a goose or an owl. Though in the country animals are seldom

60

reduced to the status of pets, she seemed to be always in their company. At night, hedgehogs congregated on her back porch where she would leave them saucers of milk. Should they perchance find themselves neglected of an evening, they would make a rasping rumpus and a din of such magnitude as is totally unbecoming of a creature so prickly and small. Badgers had burrowed a sett at the bottom of her garden. Once, much to the bewilderment of many a farmer, she saved three fledgling crows, which had fallen from their nest, and managed to rear them by discovering that they would open their beaks to be hand-fed only if she first flew either worms or thin strips of meat towards them. Already a veritable Saint Francis, her green-fingered renown reached legendary proportions after she inserted a dead twig into the ground to serve as a prop for a tottering sunflower and subsequently the twig itself took root and budded. On another occasion, she acquired a coffee bean from a coffee importer prior to it being roasted and in a northern climate cultivated a healthy coffee plant. Alexis could not help but undermine her satisfaction by, supposedly in jest, pointing out that her achievement left her liable to be prosecuted for cultivating cocaine. The story of the spider is second-hand and from a source I don't immediately recall.

It is therefore hard to accurately assess the influence she might have exerted on Alexis and his future exploits. Of the outward opinion that by a certain age children should be actively encouraged to fly the coup, she would thereafter take on the role of confidante, confessor and sometime advisor. Privy to other, less virtuous aspects of her character, Alexis may well be harbouring a deep-seated desire to discredit her public persona and so renounce her altogether.

Be that as it may, it is entirely his business as it is becoming Windswept Wendy's business to reveal herself, but having summoned up the courage to tap at the window she stays her hand. Alexis has lighted a kerosene storm-lamp and is making directly towards her. He thrusts open the window and marches off to one of the outhouses. It would be foolhardy to suppose that he is unaware of his uninvited guest, but Wendy nonetheless takes advantage of his absence and slips into the room. Alexis returns with his arms laden, the lamp precariously balanced on top of several logs. He places a couple of these on the fire, the rest he stacks alongside the grate. Lifting his lantern high, he leaves the room. Wendy follows at a safe distance.

In tandem and apace, they climb a narrow circular stair. Wary Wendy maintains her distance. Two storeys above and still comfortably separated, they enter a gallery. It spans the full length of the mansion and, like the clerestoried nave of a church, is glazed all along one side. Perhaps to keep visitors from getting too close and poking their fingers into unwanted places, a timber handrail some three inches wide and at hip height runs a few feet from the opposite wall, which, judging from its pattern of faded rectangles, was once hung with paintings. Alexis clambers on to this balustrade and with arms akimbo, but bent at the elbow like a priest reciting from the holy missal at Mass, he embarks on a tightrope stroll. The lantern swings from his hand and at the halfway mark illuminates an enlarged black and white photograph pinned into one of the empty rectangles. Posed at possibly a dinner party or some formal function, a young couple self-consciously grin at the camera. They are flanked by two other prints, but these are too small to make out clearly.

Wendy stands mesmerised at the entrance to the gallery. On reaching the end of the rail, Alexis about turns and starts back. More confident of his step now he moves faster. The light undulates. He completes this second trip and sets off on another. Though he cannot help but have seen Wonderstruck Wendy, he has so far done nothing to acknowledge her presence. All at once she is aware of a distant murmur and, as Alexis turns yet again relentlessly pursuing his balancing act, she realises that his lips are moving and that he is mumbling. The nearer he draws to her the louder and more distinct his words become. His voice reaches a perfectly pitched modulation. He is projecting with the practised precision of a performer. And he is playing to the gods.

ten

Demonstrating the Child to be the Father of the Man; and wherein First Love invariably needs must be confined to the annals of Lost Love.

It's a puppet show. Handed down from generation to generation, the marionettes are comfortably well worn. Their bruised cheeks, chipped noses and fissured fingers have been much patched and often painted, so that the various layers of varnish and gloss give their colouring an ethereal sheen. In a different context they would be glass-cased in a private museum or perhaps shelved in an overpriced antique shop. Yet despite their age, their joints remain supple, and their jerky movements across the stage are not to be attributed to some stylistic technique, but rather to a young operator's shaky inexperience, or else to an old showman's tremors, the mandatory demands of many late night yesterdays and too much traditionally gratuitous alcohol. It all adds to the magic, and Alexis is enthralled.

Five or possibly six years old, this is the first time he has ever left the protective ring of the mountains. There was the bumpy dawn ride to the station in Gustav's battered taxi. There was the enormous steam engine hissing and belching jets and streams of vapour and smoke. There was the cosy compartment with its wooden slatted seats that left an imprint on his thighs and his backside. The fine soot that flew through the window that Alexis had insisted stay fully open, and father's bemused consent. Then there was the grit that lodged in Alexis's eye, followed by mother's I-told-you-so concern and her earnest fussing with the corner of a lick-spittle moistened hankie. And in a blink, there was the city. The cathedral arches of the glass-roofed terminus and ranks of locomotives straining at the leash. The ceaseless noises of bustling people and the unfamiliar smells of strangers, waving and shouting. Alexis has never seen so many polished shoes and so many knees, such a press of crotches and bottoms, everywhere, spilling on to street and thoroughfare. Already his neck aches from looking up at buildings built by giants, but above all he realises that he must take care where he treads, for there are things called trams with screeching wheels and clanging bells, and it wouldn't do to get his foot caught in the rails.

The story the marionettes tell is probably not much older then they themselves. With their glass bead eyes they have seen the ancient walls and the city ramparts; with their wooden hands they have touched the guarded towers and the castellated gates. Their cloth ears have heard the good citizens speak the names of the fearless knights and the sainted earl who all fought the beast, and in honour and courage laid down their lives, but to no avail. The dragon lived, and by decree supped on a maiden a day.

Still they came, bearing past glories or seeking future fame, both young and old from near and far, and with sacred weapons and valour, with promises and faith, each eagerly took to the fray. Each was slain. The creature would not be killed. Terror turned the townsfolk on each other. Fathers no longer knew how to protect their daughters from the wiles and the clutches of their neighbours who sought to appease the dragon with the sacrificial blood of others. Not even nuns were safe.

Then, unexpectedly, as if by chance (and in fulfilment of a prophecy, some were later to say), an unknown shepherd boy arrived on the scene. Having spent the summer months on the very high mountain pastures and plateaux, which many suspected did not really exist, he had heard nothing of the beast or the plight of the city's virgins. Even on being graphically told about the tragic situation, he did not appear unduly concerned, but merely decided to rest his flock on the gentle slopes outside the city walls. In the way of all shepherds, he had a marked philosophical bent; after all, what else is there to do when tending sheep but ponder the mysteries of the universe or occasionally toot on a flute. His musings led him to the conclusion that if the dragon could be persuaded to eat something more succulent than the flesh of female innocence, peace and harmony might be restored to the countryside. Therefore, according to a secret, special recipe, he prepared two of his best fatted sheep (which at their worst would have been tastier than any others in the land), and that evening – in truth not so much to help the people, but more by way of experiment – he presented them to the dragon as an hors d'oeuvre before the stupefied gaze of a petrified 16-year-old novice bound hand and foot at the stake, the skulls and whitened bones of her predecessors scattered about her feet.

Not being one to look a gift horse in the mouth, and also attracted by an appetising aroma, the dragon sampled the first of the sheep. It was so much to his liking that he tossed his head backwards and, with a flap of his majestic wings, let loose a plume of flames several hundred feet into the air. Not knowing what to make of this unprecedented pyrotechnic display, the spectators on the city walls fled from the ramparts to hide under their beds. The dragon set about devouring the second sheep and disposed of it with as much, if not far more relish than the first, his gastronomic contentment doubling the height to which the flames soared from his drooling jaws. When he then turned his attention to the pretty novice who, wide-eyed, cowered trembling and traumatised by fear, the creature found to his great amazement that he was totally sated and couldn't possibly force another morsel of food past his lips. 'From now on,' he announced in an appropriate dragon-like roar, 'you will provide me only with sheep served by this man.'

The townspeople who had heard the proclamation from under their beds spontaneously poured out their thanks and blessed the shepherd boy. However, all too readily they came to realise that before long there would be no sheep left for either the dragon or themselves and their old animosities towards one another re-emerged as ferociously as before. Fortunately, the shepherd boy had plans, which naturally he kept to himself.

A week later he made his usual offering, the dragon being by then well and truly addicted to the sheep – so much so that he wolfed them down with hardly a chew, just for the satisfying afterglow that would immediately emanate from deep inside his cavernous belly. Beast and boy had already established a certain rapport. They even managed to exchange the odd pleasantry about the weather, though in fact the night was fast drawing in and becoming decidedly chilly. No sooner had the dragon swallowed the second sheep when his customary rumble of appreciation was cut short, to be transformed into a gasp of sparks and the fizzle and pop of cartoon stars. Disappointed and perplexed, the dragon looked at the shepherd boy and the hurt that showed in the creature's glazed eye sprang not from the excruciating cramps that now raged in his stomach, but from the agony of betrayal. Desperately trying to catch his breath, the dragon about faced and, giving his tail a mighty swish that inadvertently blew up a wind of sufficient strength to splinter trees and to lift and scatter innumerable slates and tiles, he stomped off towards the broad river on which the town stood. Lowering his massive jowls into the fast flowing waters, he drank and drank. And drank and drank. And drank some more. But the burning pains persisted and so he drank and drank. The river level began to fall drastically and still his thirst was unquenched. So the dragon drank and drank. And drank. Until all at once, like a broken laugh, he burst into a thousand pieces – but no fairies were born of that horrendous sound.

The sigh of relief that fills the auditorium is accompanied by the false start stutter of applause from one or two parents who stand in familial clusters at the back of the hall, while their children sit on the parquet floor in cross-legged files and open-mouthed entrancement. Alexis has never dreamed that the world could be filled with so many boys and girls of his own age. They clap and cheer when the shepherd boy is proclaimed king of the city and the pretty would-be nun his bride, having of course confused her vocation with an impoverished father's persuasive and forgivably practical concern for her best interest. Even so, Alexis cannot help but blink away an as yet unaccountable sadness, an almost tear. Then the lights come on.

And then there are cakes and jellies and jugs of gassy lemonade and games and burst balloons and shouts and squeals and cries and howls and a squash and a jumble of delights and distress. It is a time when for once mother and father seem to indulge in each other's company, talking effortlessly, even smiling and joking. But there are disappointments. Alexis is told that two of the girls, Jola and Mela, with whom he has happily been playing blind man's buff, are the daughters of his mother's best friend, and very nearly, though not really really, his cousins. Alexis is told that Mela is his girlfriend and then when they are both grown up, she will be his wife. So what does he think of that? Dumbfounded, the shock of the suggestion fills him with dread and trepidation. In silent embarrassment he stares at the fresh scuff marks on the toes of his shoes. Surely, if he is to be married instead of having a wolf cub, why can't it be to Jola? She is younger and ever so much nicer and doesn't have that odd smell.

Alexis retreats to the safety of the all-boys' adventures. But these too are fraught with unexpected and inexplicable dangers. A good head taller than the rest, a lad called Mirek, with a great deal to say and a self-serving flair for telling others exactly what to do, suddenly and viciously punches Alexis on the upper arm. Alexis stands in stunned confusion. Nobody has ever hit him before and he doesn't know what he is supposed to do. The pain spreads to his shoulder, but he is no stranger to the rough and tumble of mountain living, so shrugs it off. Then on some spontaneous gut impulse, he launches himself at Mirek, bringing him to the ground, pummelling with his tightly clenched fists, blackening his eye and splitting his lip. Alexis has blood on his hands. Adults are intervening. There are shouts and squeals and cries and howls and a squash and a jumble of anger and indignation. But eventually apologies are made and apologies are accepted. Calls for recriminations subside and with some reluctance blame is not apportioned. An arm's length peace is restored.

And then after much shaking and kissing of hands, farewell hugs and kisses on the cheek (but pointedly not Mela – don't be so shy) it is time to go; at last to escape, ever in a rush, back on the tram, back on the train in a compartment with the window mother-checked and firmly closed, with heavy eyelids that refuse to stay open to father's caring banter, 'You really gave that bully Mirek what for, eh . . . Ha, he'll not forget you in a hurry . . . eeh?' or 'Wouldn't you've liked to have been that brave shepherd boy and stuffed the sheep with poisoned sulphur and brimstone and destroyed the wicked dragon?' Alexis is too tired to say, 'No,' because it would require a detailed explanation that might be misunderstood, and, cradled against father's broad chest in the crook of his comforting arm, it is so much easier and so much more satisfying to be simply overcome by sleep.

And overnight Alexis is twelve years old. Already he masturbates. His introduction to the facts of life took place under a lamppost, but the irony is still lost on him. Barry explained that his existence began as a glob of spunk on the end of his father's knob, which was shoved into his mother's fanny. Alexis thinks saying things like that is rather ludicrous and distasteful, yet he cannot bring himself to call Barry a liar; nor does he seek confirmation elsewhere, especially not from his surrogate parents. Then it dawns on him. For years he has watched animals mating, bulls and cows, geese, rabbits, ewes and rams, but he has never made the connection and extrapolated it to include human beings. After a swift, practical demonstration courtesy of Barry behind the coal bunker, followed by a few tentative experiments, which at first produced little more than a queasy sensation in the pit of his stomach and a strange jerk at the base of his spine, Alexis takes to the idea of sex like a duckling to water. In next to no time he is an ardent if not devout onanist.

The women in his fantasies are real, lascivious and submissive matrices of improbable flesh. Their material counterparts hold no tangible interest other than to stimulate variations on a theme, a configuration of anatomical permutations in wholly improbable situations that involve suspender belts and stockings. The very notion itself of meeting a female and having to chat-her-up (what is there actually to talk about?) with the sole aim of seduction (where's it actually to be done?) would require considered effort and rationally be a waste of time in the light of so much else that demands attention. There is Astronomy. And History, and Music. At an age when consequences are best avoided, Alexis has vital decisions to make – should he be schooled in the arts or the sciences, which will propitiate fate? He must see answers, and though with prank upon prank he aggravates his teachers to exasperation, suffers their accusations of being out on a limb and stoically submits to recurrent rounds of corporal punishment, he is ever eager to know. The need is insatiable and lies outwith the nightly turbulence of counterpane and bedspread.

Shortly before his thirteenth birthday, Alexis receives two letters, the first ever. They are both from abroad, from home. In one, the parish priest writes that father has 'found peace', along with a page or more of what seem to be prayers, condolences and cheering advice. The other comes from Lucy, a hurried note painstakingly drafted on stiff, crinkle-edged paper in an azure envelope bearing too few stamps and a musty odour. According to her, father has 'passed on'. Alexis feels under an obligation to cry, but the more he tries, the more his thoughts are dominated by Lucy's bosom. Its demonstrative proportions spur many messy consolations to screen a new terror, which has befuddled his mind. Each night he surges in on himself, pushes himself from himself and scans his shell as though it were a character on cellulose, misplaced and in some other-living film, while the ethereal him floats unreachable. In these confused confrontations there is a mysticism and desperation, which he knows he is not yet equipped to handle, so he flees to the safety of his feral imagination; or better still to the familiar comforts of everydayness where each sporadic memory of father falls short, overtaken by an idle and uninvited curiosity. What did father do? He had never struck Alexis as a man on a quest for peace, or on a search for anything else for that matter. How did he earn his living? Questions never gaining enough momentum to be voiced or answered, but systematically dissolving into visions of father's hairy knuckles and the massive span of his fingers forever fondling equally abundant breasts.

Feeling a mixed measure of pride and consternation, Aunt Beth watches Alexis collect his prize for Religious Knowledge at the school's annual speech day, and at the moment he shakes hands with the guest dignitary of some local, albeit dubious note, she sniffs and decides to send the boy away to a summer camp – for his own good. With his unaired grief (not that Aunt Beth approves of displays of extravagant emotion either in public or in private) and with his self-contained puberty marked only by the proliferation of crusty stains on sheets, blankets and pillowcases, Alexis will undoubtedly benefit from a change of scene.

The summer camp is run by an organisation not unlike the Boy Scouts, but with distinctly marked military overtones. The tying of knots and lyricless singsongs hardly feature in the programme at all. For six weeks the 30, maybe 40 participants (more or less of a maximum age of about 15 and from all parts of the country) are subjected to the rigours of marginally scaled down army manoeuvres. They bivouac under canvas on the edge of a forest and near a convenient stream – convenient for daily, ice-cold ablutions, but distant enough to make an arm-crippling chore out of fetching water for the field kitchen. Cooking is done in groups of five and by rote in all weathers on an open fire and for the entire ravenous complement. They sleep on straw-palleted beds each has built for himself from dead lumber gathered in the wood. Reveille is at 0600 hours, and a routine of exercises – including parade drill and full-kit hikes over all terrain; mock attacks and position defences; rifle and small-arms practice (not to mention being dumped alone in the middle of nowhere in order to find the quickest way back to base) – usually leaves all concerned fit to drop. By lights-out, often with a nostalgic sigh, only one or two addicted devotees allow fleeting, minimalist thoughts of sex into the equation. There is also sentry duty.

In the small hours, armed with a password and a Lee Enfield .303, Alexis circuits in and around the tents. He checks the quartermaster's store, the duck-boarded dining marquee, then ambles off towards the stream. Over an hour of his solo watch still remains. The live round in the chamber of his rifle makes him feel somewhat uneasy, even though he has been instructed to fire into the air in case of emergency. After all, bullets fired vertically have to come down somewhere – intruder or no intruder. At the water's edge he props the rifle against the trunk of a tree, lifts the leg of his shorts and takes a pee, jetting a high arc of urine into the darkness. Reassuringly it tinkles into the unseen current below. Alexis smiles. He sits on a dry clump of grass and gazes up at the cloudless sky, at Ursa Major (always first to catch the eye), at Orion and at what just might be the Coma Berenices, as ever to marvel at and revel in his own puny insignificance. He shines his torch heavenwards and laughs out loud at the feebleness of its beam, then turns it on to the pages of the paperback he has taken out of his ammo-pouch. The book, inscribed and signed by the headmaster on the flyleaf, is about fore and aft sailing ships and Alexis's reward for rehashing bible stories. Schooner, ketch and sloop. Alexis is to spend many fruitless hours trying to memorise these riggings in a bid to recognise them at a glance, as some of those to be envied can identify the silhouettes of obsolete fighter planes. Rustling noises from the woods disturb his concentration. It's either nocturnal animals going about their legitimate business or some of the bigger, towny lads stealing back from a jaunt to the girls' camp a couple of hills and several as-the-crow-flies miles away. Alexis goes back to studying sails, confident that his turn will come.

And it does. Out of the blue he is singled out as an achiever who not only shows distinct promise of leadership, but is to be regarded as a model recruit amongst his peers. Along with two of his elder colleagues he is awarded an accolade in the form of a discreet lapel pin at a midnight, moonlit initiation ceremony held in the depths of the forest where he swears a mysterious oath in what vaguely sounds like Latin and on the tattered remains of an ancient battle standard. He is now a bone fide Novice of the Organisation. Much to his delight it all smacks of medieval orders and knightly chivalry. But better still it means that he has been chosen to be a member of the coveted, deserving few who have earned three days rest and recreation as guests of the young ladies in the next valley but one. And *they* are billeted near an abandoned airfield in Nissen huts with running water, hot showers and toilets. Rumour also has it that they sleep on sprung beds with proper linen and mattresses. And there, marching along a disused runway, Alexis will first lay eyes on Angéline – Jelly to her intimates.

Though only twelve years old, Angéline has come from France all by herself to visit her cousin Matty whose mother, a Mrs Watkins, is a close friend of Aunt Beth's from long long ago, yet one whom Alexis has never met. Mrs Watkins is responsible for the Nissen hut girls' activities and welfare and it was she, incidentally, who had advised Aunt Beth to send Alexis to his particular camp where it would make a man of him. Alexis is learning all this directly from the horse's mouth. He rather likes Mrs Watkins and the way she trips over her words, then whistles and winks before rushing on, but ever since being formally introduced, he simply can't help casting prolonged, furtive glances at Angéline.

She has a rounded, Slavic face, pale green eyes and downy

blonde hair, which she wears tightly drawn into a plait hanging down to the small of her back. Her upper lip is very full, but doesn't quite meet the lower and so leaves her front teeth partially and permanently exposed, giving the impression that she is always about to smile. When she does smile, her pert nostrils flare a little, while sunbursts like constricted Roman candles go off in the pit of Alexis's stomach. She also has breasts, real breasts cupped in a redundant bra, which shows lace-trimmed through the flimsy material of her white blouse. A slender waist above boyish hips, a slender ankle over a sculpted Achilles tendon and an overall, would-be snug fit against Alexis's chest compound the irrepressible lure he already feels.

At supper they find themselves seated next to each other, but words refuse to come easily. Hardly more than dead-end grins and nods have been exchanged, until Angéline spills some salt, only to neglect to toss a pinch over her left shoulder. Alexis finds both her clumsiness and her lack of superstition endearing. Clearing his throat in an irreversible bid to dispel any lurking vestige of shyness, he launches into a sincere diatribe about witchcraft. Angéline listens carefully, asks pertinent questions and makes sensible remarks. Her English is excellent, her accent coquettishly charming. Alexis decides that chatting girls up is actually a piece of cake, just as Angéline offers to serve him dessert from a selection of pastries, which, inexplicably, he refuses; then self-consciously changes his mind and chooses a rum baba. And all too soon the meal is over. The girls clear the tables, set about washing-up and tidying the kitchen. Alexis and his companions are ushered off to their quarters. There is to be a bonfire that evening and homespun entertainment to be considered. A form of charades sounds promising.

That night, hot-showered and tucked up in fresh linen on a sprung mattress, Alexis finds it difficult to sleep. The day's events tumble about in his mind, over and over, ever for his memory to focus in on the moment when, seated cross-legged in the fire-glow, he had linked arms with Jelly in one of those side to side

73

swaying chorus songs. Surely his elbow had first brushed and then nuzzled against her breast. And she hadn't minded. As tomorrow she will not mind him stealthily taking her by the hand or slipping his arm about her waist whenever they find themselves alone, now that they have become inseparable. Alexis tells her about the kind of house he would like to live in, the kind of car he would like to drive, the number of sons he wants to spawn, much to his utter amazement, for he has never thought about any of these things before. Sentences seem to purr out of him freely, uninhibited and unedited. Jelly responds in like manner. She too likes Astronomy. And History, and especially Music. She plays the piano and the flute, but longs to learn the cello. It is as if they are flying courtesy of some kind of automatic pilot, both gloriously happy and surprised to discover how much their tastes, their interests and their ambitions seem to be the same. It's all a revelation. And it's all too soon time for parting, for Alexis to return to the 'Front'. They kiss once, very briefly, with just a twinge of embarrassment. Mrs Watkins proposes to visit Auntie Beth when camp is finally over, so nothing can prevent Alexis and Angéline from seeing one another again.

They meet at the top of the steps outside the abbey church. But it's all unplanned. It's all wrong. It's Sunday and the service is over. Nevertheless, the Organisation has scheduled a special afternoon session, which does not accommodate the unexpected arrival of Angéline and which Alexis, in conscience, dare not ignore; after all, he swore a secret oath at midnight and in the moonlight. Jelly whispers that she understands and, without another word, hands Alexis a small package, which he deftly slips into his uniform shirt. He watches Angéline as, without a backward glance, she skips down the steps and gets into Mrs Watkins' car. He watches the car drive off.

For almost a month Angéline has dominated his thoughts, fuelled his dreams and fantasies, but not those that have him reaching for his genitals – these are still confined to the capricious domains of seamed, fishnet hose and spiked heels. Jelly embodies something altogether different, ethereal yet tangible, sensual yet sexually unassailable. For almost a month he has been so looking forward to being with her again, but all of a sudden she is gone. Gingerly, he fingers the small package, draws it out from his shirt and peels back a corner of the wrapping. It's a tie. His knee-shorts pockets are already full so he tucks the tie back under his belt, secure against his bare flesh. The old, battered Morris van at the foot of the steps sounds its feeble horn. His comrades are urgently beckoning for him to join them. They are setting off for a royal park where a herd of deer still roam wild. Perhaps Alexis will get back in time to see Angéline once more before she goes for good. But it's not to be.

Pleasantly tired from what turned out to be an adventurous day, Alexis lets himself into the darkened house. It must be really late. Not even Aunt Beth is waiting up. Nor does Alexis care for a glass of milk or even a biscuit and he goes straight to his room. Now is the time to try on his tie. But it's not there. Twisting and turning, he feels all around his waistband. But it's not there. He strips, fumbles through his clothes, shaking them, folding and unfolding them, checking and rechecking, emptying his pockets. But the tie is not there. He looks at himself in the mirror as if to make certain that he is naked, that the tie isn't still secreted somewhere about his person. He leaves his room, switches on the hall light and begins to slowly retrace his steps, peering intently at the floor. But the tie is not there. He goes outside, scanning from left to right, all the way to the road. But the tie is not there. He stands in the road peering after the Morris van that dropped him off and is long gone. It begins to drizzle. And then Aunt Beth is beside him in her cardigan and wellies.

'What on earth's going on?' she half whispers and half shouts, shaking Alexis out of his stupor and pushing him back towards the front door. 'Have you gone mad, you'll catch your death out here!'

'I've lost something.'

'You can look for it tomorrow. Now off to bed!'

But tomorrow brings no comfort. Wretched after a restless night, Alexis simply cannot understand how he could have lost a gift from Jelly, how he could have been so carelessly crass. He rings all the people that were with him on the exercise. Not one remembers seeing a small, soft package with its corner torn off. Mr Howard reluctantly agrees that his Morris van needs a thorough clean out, but though he searches it from top to bottom the tie is not there. Alexis is therefore left with no option other than to return to the royal park. It will mean catching buses, maybe a train. He certainly doesn't have enough for the fare and nobody is prepared to advance him a loan. Despite his anguish and a gnawing sense of helplessness, he will have to wait until the weekend for his pocket money, meanwhile earning a little extra by doing odd chores and running errands for neighbours, for the village post office, the grocer's shop. Even so, the weekend brings no comfort. With remarkable accuracy, over and over again he covers every inch of ground that he trod, ran or crawled through the previous Sunday. Everything appears to be exactly as it was, though on this occasion he does manage to come across a deer, head-on, but they merely startle each other and back away into safe postures of indifference. The tie is nowhere to be found.

In the dead of night, a defeated Alexis sits at the kitchen table. His frustration has finally turned to tears, to uncontrollable sobs. Aunt Beth enters in a blaze of lights.

'Good Lord, Alexis!' she cries. 'It was only a *bloody* tie!'

Alexis can't believe his ears. Stunned, he gawks at Aunt Beth, feeling a rush of jumbled emotions, hatred, confusion, despair. But then it's probably only human to completely miss the point, to be so insensitive, so brutal, so stupid, so very, very evil.

'I'd like to go to France,' he says softly. And sniffs.

eleven

Wherein Reason begins to show signs of fallibility, but buttressed
by an innate arrogance ensures the ongoing viability of his narrative.
Wendy at last rightly makes her presence felt.

So much for childhood. Toy soldiers and puppy love. I trust that's
the last of it. The innuendos are far too obvious and this persistent,
direct and indirect belittling of his mother (or Auntie Beth as
Alexis would have her be), plainly depresses me. Yet, without
wishing to dig up that old has-been Freud, perhaps this is actually
where it all begins, but then again, is having a recognisable
beginning really that important? In the long run it only begs the
issue of chronology, all that cause and effect nonsense. Nevertheless,
I must admit that I do find the idea of a clandestine, militant
brotherhood rather appealing. This quest for shared anonymity
is of itself intriguing and fits very neatly with earlier suppositions.
But it's not good enough.

Personally I favoured the plain and ordinary Sea Scouts, not
that we lived anywhere near the sea; and this too is significant
because sooner or later, if only ever so briefly, Alexis must make
time to confront the inevitable and the inescapable, no matter
how much it presently suits him to play the fox. Wily Wendy is
my bait and she will lure him out. Softly, softly.

I have to confess, however, I had expected Alexis to be much
nearer the mark by now. But then it's a bit like the retrograde

motion of planets, totally confounding until understanding simply dawns; or at the risk of mixing metaphor and simile, it's the bobbing and the weaving, that sparring with a daunting eventuality that ultimately must be faced down.

I had hoped that sending Wendy to him might have stimulated him to move more rapidly and in the one direction. But then again he still has to openly interact with her, to acknowledge her presence. At least he has finally stopped all that ridiculous declaiming and all that pacing along the beam. Instead, he is sitting on the railing; arms at his sides, his hands, palms-down, tucked beneath his thighs, his head bowed. Having given up counting the to and fro of his circuits after Lord knows how many completed lengths, Well-mannered Wendy approached slowly, silently, to stand a few paces before him. She is resisting the temptation to put her arm about his shoulder and console him. Rightly so. At this juncture any unsolicited display of affection might throw him into entirely the wrong kind of introspection. So they remain for some time opposite one another. Unmoved.

There is no rush.

It can't be much after nine o'clock and given the maze of narrow country lanes, their overall state of disrepair and the erratic appearance of chugging farm traffic, it's a good six hours' drive to the new motorway – even in a well-serviced sports car with an expert at the wheel. With senses keyed up, it falls to me to stay alert, to control my apprehensions and with difficulty accommodate those ever more potent surges of adrenalin; while in comforted insouciance, Alexis would have the world believe that his mind remains firmly fixed on other things. Higher things. The gamble of parenthood and the gambols of parental emotions; thwarted family feelings couched in pretensions to some neo-messianic exclusivity; enlightenment in a dubious seaside resort and a rationalised justification for denying basic human nature – who's kidding whom? Try conceit and selfishness compounded by eremitic aspirations in an immature and troubled psyche. Or better still, tosh and piffle!

With only the slightest lift of the head, he looks at Wendy and dispels the urge to smile, but she can see the controlled laughter in his eyes. A mischievous merriment that fails to fully disguise the pain, yet further feeds her persistent desire to mother him, to bring him tactile solace and the body-warmth of touch. She is about to succumb to her instincts and makes as if to move towards him when all at once he slips off his perch and takes her in his arms.

'Listen . . . and let the music take you,' he whispers in her ear as together they start to sway gently. And once again, 'Just listen . . .' as gradually he leads her into a dance. At first she can hear only the shuffle of their steps, untried and clumsy to begin with, but soon becoming synchronised into a rhythmic tread above the intermittent bend and creak of shrunken floorboards. Then, as never before, Wendy finds herself waltzing. The delicate forward pressure of his torso and the slightest squeeze of his left hand guides her backwards through trust and into the glide of blind faith; while his right hand, light on her waist, draws her towards him, yet ever a step removed. He can take her anywhere he wants to. New moonlight lends a carefree substance to the hollow gallery. Willowy Wendy is flying.

'Did you know I would come here tonight?'

Alexis gives no sign of having heard, so a little louder Wendy asks once more, 'Did you know I would–' but she is cut short by a curt, 'No.'

It is up to Alexis to dictate the tempo. Little by little their dance gathers pace. Wendy follows with an unexpected ease; then all at once, with daringly improvised heel-and-toe actions, she rids herself of her rubber overshoes, one by one. Yet a certain reserve prevails and she cannot, dares not abandon herself to the flawless, hypnotic pitch of their rise and fall. Finally her patience fails her.

'But you suspected?' she asks, as, almost before she has realised, Alexis has deftly executed a neat box turn and switched from English to Viennese.

'Suspected?'

'That I would come.'

'I considered it possible. After all, you did promise to do the spring cleaning for a week every year.'

'And now that it's happened?'

'It's happened.'

Alexis has brought the waltz to an abrupt halt. Still they stand holding each other. Wendy is looking him squarely in the face as she continues:

'Do you mean you feel nothing?'

'On the contrary.'

'What d'you feel?'

'It's time you got what you came for.'

'Oh and what's that?'

'First let me show you round the house, it seems that there's dirt and dust just everywhere.'

'Silverfish in the floor and red herrings under the stair?'

'We'll talk as we walk.'

'Better still, why don't you tell me a story?'

'Let's see. Shall we . . .' And Alexis offers his arm, but stretched before him horizontally as if gently resting on a cushion of air at near shoulder level, the elbow comfortably bent. Wendy smiles her confusion. Alexis indicates that she should rest the palm of her hand on the back of his. She complies. Gracefully poised, he sets off on the stately march of a polonaise. Peering at his feet, for an awkward moment or two, Wendy trips along beside him, but very soon picks up the step. Alexis has retrieved the hurricane lamp. It swings between them. And majestically they and a dignified host of their shadows promenade.

twelve

In which memories give credence to the notion that running from a problem only turns it into a similar problem, and that the traumas surrounding one's own circumstances are frequently mirrored and magnified by the plight of others.

Just as the longest journey proverbially begins with a single step, so taking three forwards and one back will at last bring the dancers to their destination – to a carefully choreographed bow, centre stage. Just as Alexis F has been nowhere, so he is going nowhere. Not a single car has passed him in either direction for almost two hours. The sun has long since tipped the zenith. And just as Alexis decides to find some unlikely shade for a much needed and belated siesta, so a blurred dot appears on the horizon where the heat-softening road shimmers into its own vanishing point. Intuitively, he knows that the oncoming vehicle is a Citroen van with army-brown, corrugated sides. Moments later, like the wheezing of some ailing sewing machine, the sound of its 2CVs will confirm his assumption. A yellow and blue sticker on its windscreen denotes that it's from the Ministry of Agriculture, a governmental department whose employees are forbidden to pick up hitchhikers. Nevertheless, Alexis raises his thumb, and much to his optimistic amazement, the van draws to a nodding halt.

Three uneventful days have elapsed since his arrival on the mainland. Well south of Murcia, Alexis is travelling towards

Almeria; crossing the desert, a crushed plane of volcanic rust encircled by violet mountains. Immense and misplaced, a ragged moon crater of crumbled reds. And 70 kilometres of endlessly monotonous, endless tarmac. Ever at eye-level, ceaselessly straight. For nigh on an hour he and the official have sat speechless in a mechanical silence. Terminally bored. Their thoughts are at a blank, subdued and oppressed by the unaltered whine of the engine and afternoon temperatures that even mundane conversation cannot override.

Then, without warning, the van veers off at right angles. At once, but as if in slow motion, Alexis glances at his driver to check that he has not fallen asleep or gone road-blind, only to realise that they have intentionally turned on to a crude track, its pitted and cracked surface barely posted by a verge of patched, coarse vegetation. So Alexis says nothing. Neither does the driver. The van bounces on, over barren, shallow mutations of burned colour, driving dust towards the peaks, towards a light-reflecting haze in unfinished outline – the tiny far-off buildings of a farm complex where the houses and barns are white and of mud and all but windowless. The tallest is in part three storeys high and overlooks a well or a spring, for here the healthier shrubs sprout to just above the ankle. A gnarled, solitary tree shoulders survival in the sanctuary of an inner courtyard, its one, sparse-leafed branch visible from over the flat tops of the lowest roofs.

Men stand waiting for the van. Swarthy young men already aged. Rigid. In nondescript work clothes and primitive sandals, they've stood their watch for a long time. Beyond them, propped up against a low wall, squats an old man, grown even older before the engine shudders to rest.

The official says, 'I shan't be more than ten minutes or so . . . fifteen at the most.' Though in shirtsleeves, he adjusts his official tie and stiffly climbs out from behind the wheel. With the opening of his door the arid air penetrates still further.

The men greet him with tired enthusiasm. Accompanied by two of their number, he walks off and away from the farmhouses to disappear from view where the ground dips into a significant hollow. The others also disperse to go about their business.

Stationary, it is now no cooler, no different than being outside. Alexis lifts one leg and then the other to ungum the sweat-tacky flesh of his thighs from the thin cotton of his trousers. The old man does not move. Nor does the wall. A fly stalks across his face. Slowly. Towards his eye.

Alexis F takes a crush-proof cigarette pack from his breast pocket. The cellophane wrapping crackles, damp to the touch. He can find no matches. He gets out of the van. Scratches at his ribs. Leaning from the waist, he slides his arm through the raised window flap to fish out his sombrero from the back seat. He begins to amble towards the farmyard. A woman in black stares at him. Even at a distance it is obvious that at first she is simply curious, but soon becomes fearful and urgently vanishes behind a hefty Moorish door. In the narrow shade, a child sits playing his four years into the powdered earth about him. Everywhere. With a sister who is perhaps nine. Both are olive skinned, have round, ebony eyes and fringes of long, matted locks. Both are anaemic. Both are dressed in torn, soiled robes, the boy's so short that it barely covers his midriff. He has no trousers, no underwear. Neither have shoes.

'Got any matches?' Alexis calls, holding up and rolling a cigarette to and fro between his thumb and forefinger. Droplets of sweat cloy under his hatband.

The girl scoops up the child who, startled by her sudden action, yelps into a prolonged whimper, his legs kicking. Hampered by her confounded burden, she flees, awkwardly scurrying off through the same hefty door.

For all of a minute the air seems to stir a mild excuse for a breeze. Alexis peels his hat from his head. Frees his hair. Sighing. Aimlessly, he turns to see the official with his companions crouched in the hollow. They are intently inspecting, prodding at their fruitless land. The dismalness of the soil is mirrored in the features of their faces, yet evokes heat-swamped notions of toil and ambitions of survival. Elsewhere.

83

The girl has reappeared. She stands four, maybe five feet away, on tiptoe; a book of matches in her fully outstretched hand. The child is calmly perched on her hip. Smiling. Alexis takes one step towards her, she takes one back. Alexis extends his arm. The girl drops the matches into his palm, carefully lest they should touch. Keenly aware of being observed, Alexis strikes a match, lights the cigarette between cupped fingers and inhales the tar-rich smoke, but shows little pleasure. When he looks up to return the matches, the girl is gone.

Then, in a mood shift of growing expectancy, there rises a murmur of low voices. As if on some prearranged, clandestine signal, people begin to saunter out of the buildings, in twos and threes, from behind the hefty door, from unseen nooks and crannies. There's the old man who, with the aid of a bent stick, has clambered to his feet, and the woman in black in the midst of others also in black. There's the girl and her brother-on-hip and a host of other scruffy children, teenagers and youths sprouting sparse moustaches. A much extended family all speaking at once, muttering, each having something to say as, ignoring Alexis, they congregate close to the van. Flanked by the farmers, the official has left the hollow and is making his way towards them. His presence brings them to order and he addresses them briefly and as a group. His words have no meaning for Alexis, but are accepted without query by an audience of expressionless faces, parched and anxious, and lacking the energy for anger. Again, as if on cue, the atmosphere changes, becomes less tense, while the gathering splinters into smaller pockets of conversation. There are smiles, half-hearted gestures and a prevalent sense of resignation. An occasional laugh is to be heard.

In unconscious parody of some antiquated portrait of poverty, the girl, the child and perhaps an older brother stand in front of their parents who seem to be exchanging conventional pleasantries with the official. Grinning, he rummages in his pockets and eventually produces a paper-wrapped sugar cube. There's a light coffee-spill smear on the side where it lay in the saucer. He offers it to the child who snatches, then tears it open suspiciously; sniffs, then licks, then greedily sucks at the white lump, an unbounded glee and joy in his eyes, as glazed and glowing as the first signs of the early evening that is slowly beginning to envelop him alongside those other eyes that are jealous, envious, yet calm. He is the youngest. His is the need.

Alexis F and the official get back into the van. They leave. Perhaps the family is waving. Perhaps the girl is at last smiling. Perhaps a fly is getting ever closer to an old man's eye.

Once on the highway the official gives Alexis an enquiring look, followed by a curt, hapless shrug.

After a considerable while, as if thinking out loud, Alexis says, 'Would it not be better for that child to never have tasted sugar . . . ?'

His driver says nothing.

thirteen

Wherein on the road to Myth and Fable stories are told within stories.

'That's not much of a story.'

'There's still a lot of the house to see.'

Wendy and Alexis have abandoned the pompous prance of the polonaise and are now ambling arm in arm like lovers of old standing, comfortable and secure in each other's touch; warmed by the close light of the lantern, which Alexis holds steadily aloft. All is as it should be, yet I cannot help but fear that Wilful Wendy is perhaps acting a little too fast too soon. I have of course left her to her own devices and am very much relying on her instincts. She is the best judge of the situation at present, but it wouldn't do to startle the hare until the hounds are straining at the leash. Too much can be made of feminine intuition and Wendy is, if in many ways unexpectedly mature, still rather young when it comes to certain areas of sensitivity. There may be nuances and subtleties beyond her grasp, though equally there is a great deal to be said for the innocence of immediate response. Ever mindful of what is safe or expedient, I naturally briefed her on a more or less need-to-know basis. The speeding sports car and its occupants, which incidentally is making excellent time, is none of her concern. I trust her implicitly, but this is dangerous ground she is treading. Some games are played for keeps and I worry.

Apace they have walked in and out of rooms, along corridors, through halls and up and down stairs. All are empty, anonymous and complacently gathering dust in the moonlight. Sometimes he and she will linger, not really looking at anything, though every so often Alexis will take advantage of the pause to fondly stroke the walls. Floorboards creak. There seems to be no end to the mansion and, for all Wendy knows, they are going round in circles. But then they would surely come across their own footprints. Wendy leans her head on Alexis's shoulder, drawing herself close into his arm, as if the better to hang on to his every word.

And that's just as it should be. But there are times when words, no matter how keenly heard, are not what they seem. Listening is not synonymous with understanding, nor reading with comprehension. Ever the Voice of Reason, I have all along tried to mediate, to keep things in perspective; yet even I must bow to the dictates of circumstance, to the wiles of events beyond my control. Any man of medical standing will avow that nervous breakdowns happen to the best of us, and given that Alexis is hardly the most stable of people, is it any wonder that in flitting about the globe, that in hiding behind or beneath the skirts of women in an attempt to flee the pains that have doggedly pursued him, he will eventually succumb to the inevitable collapse?

Nonetheless, a lack of sanity does not necessarily indicate a lack of logic. The mental and emotional processes of dealing with trauma are many and varied. So let those parts of the mind about which I know nothing and over which I have no command lead where they will. Sometimes tortuous and dangerous paths have to be trodden with a blindfold. That requires perhaps a leap of faith, a trust in the skills and the knowledge of an unseen guide, and the firm belief that everything will be made clear in the end, that pending disaster and disorder will be averted, and for the experience all concerned will emerge somewhat the wiser.

fourteen

Wherein, during a sojourn in America, Alexis falls prey to a nervous breakdown, which is liberally populated by a cast of characters who otherwise might be found playing bit parts in a nightmare.

The house is full. Full of mortgaged memories, full of imported misgivings and yet it is far too large ever to be completely filled. Uncharted nooks and crannies remain perpetually in the cold. Echoes in counterpoint, the rasps of saw-teeth biting into the wooden skis of an old-fashioned rocking chair kindle no emotion. On the other hand, sawing generates body heat. The kitchen surfaces are of vinyl, the stool is of aluminium and the Davenport is upholstered in leather. These do not burn. In the grate the embers sulk.

It's winter. Pocono snows lie two feet deep and deeper still in mounting drifts.

Alexis walks past her door. Does he not remember that the walls downstairs are of panelled pine, faded where the pictures used to hang, as he flops to his mattress and sleeps without thinking to wake her?

They would meet on the stairs.

'Good morning.'

'Good night.'

And again later:

'Good night.'

'Good morning.'

They can no longer agree and speak no more. In passing, eyes downcast, they learn to rely on the recognition of each other's scents and natural odours.

There was a time when they talked a great deal. All day, night? One sat on the Davenport and the other, gently nodding in the chair, unzipped chilled cans of weak beer. They drank. Enthusiastically. Alexis would improvise on the guitar and she would sing. They would play chess. Dawn, stale and mate.

The banisters, the steps, these are also of timber. Had she not burned the axe handle, she would fell them for the fire and leave Alexis stranded, cut off from her world and in innocent isolation. Stifling the sounds of her outside, under the pillow where he wheezes, the crisp air seems to creak, much amplified in his ear. Beside him lies an open book and his fingers still clutch at the wire frames of a pair of yellow-tinted glasses. Part of his foot shows from beneath the heap of blankets. Once fleshy pink and mother-kissed, mother-tickled and mother-covered with socks, it would have been mother-tucked away and mother-wrapped under the quilt – mother never suspecting that it had been left exposed on purpose and never thinking to check if Alexis is awake.

He showed her how to play the blues. She managed two, perhaps three basic chords, but though she concentrated hard, the fingering patterns proved difficult to master. She leaned forward to see what she was doing wrong and her hair got caught and tangled in the strings. They laughed.

Suspended, still in the breakfast room, the last of his cigarette smoke, like a warped halo spinning amoebic over the table, over the piles of coloured paper and round the typewriter, undecided which to sanctify. Could he not have banged on the door?

They pry and suspect, but never a mention, never a hint; only secret methods devised to found mistrust and silent objections. The thumbprint on top of his manuscript cannot easily be removed. She'll ignore that page. No trap visible on the next, but automatically she sweeps her hand along its surface. The dots of two 'i's and a colon come loose. She peels them from her palm and puts them on a small piece of transparent plastic. To replace them later. Is this colon necessary? A comment she resists writing alongside the text. That's how it begins. Involved, she is annotating a draft, scribbling suggestions and improvements in the margins. Then it's, 'Good night.'

'Good morning.'

He's seeing the unfamiliar, compact script, so unlike his own bold strokes and loops. The exegeses pencilled in columns on the orange sheets outrage him. Determined, he's striding towards the bottom stair, only to stop short and turn. He paces the floor. He turns. He paces the floor. Hour after hour. He'll play guitar. That night, fast sudden riffs, high notes bending, flee. They are bent on breaking without end, a rhythmic tread. And the front door is being unlatched. That other woman has come, bringing food, tobacco and a carton of cigarettes. It's acted out for all to hear, him sending her away, her sobs, her sad footfalls crunching the snow. The car uneager to fire. Then headlights picking out tall pines along the gravel avenue, which leads to the highway. To the merging sounds of traffic, a truck painfully shifts gear before the incline.

Hurriedly, sloppily dressed and hoping that Alexis has at least kept the cigarettes, 'Good morning.'

No reply. Now they will never finalise arrangements about the time of day.

No wonder the girl was confused. That other woman who might arrive as Alexis stops work to climb up to his room where they've whispered and giggled and cried. At times she has crept into the house (while he was preparing coffee), crossed the lounge, going at once to his pallet, and waited for him who'll wait on her. No wonder she's a bed-hopper, crawling into any cot to reconstruct the form of thighs, the scent of her feminine moans; in climax, to discover a new story typed on olive paper and which begins – It's happened again, I'm in bed with a stranger. No margins. But had he given them names they may have opted for other adventures.

And the day after he'll do nothing. And after the day after he'll do nothing. More and ever more he is unable to fall asleep. Ill-taut. This is the night that he saws up the rocking chair. He knows that she will turn up out of the blue, the front door pushed against emptiness, her voice quivering, her words indistinct, violent. His calculated and calm, 'Why have you come? I don't want you here. What d'you assume to redeem? I'm impotent. I warned you. So now go.'

Din raucous shrieks. Things being thrown. A door slammed, car engines churn. To get up little rested and find a broken window, the guitar amp smashed and neatly heaped food over the floor – rice in the kitchen, pork hocks in the living room, the earthenware jug of *crème de café* in the snow. Outside. There are no skid marks, no signs of melted rubber, not even an oil stain. The fire is unlit.

But he did wake her up, just to point at a young fawn as it forages by the house. A first winter and there's nothing to eat. Kneeling behind icicle cages, they watch from the same window. There is nothing to say. The yearling edges ever closer across the clearing, slipping and sliding on spindly legs. It slumps up to its chest in the deeper drifts. They long to feed it but know that if they were to move, if they were to open the door, it would bolt. The fawn sees them, peers at them. Motionless, a hungry pity in its glazed eyes. Then it lurches back into the forest, gingerly in the direction of the highway where a truck will kill it.

They can do nothing. Words still fail them. Alexis has bought a set of new knives and practises. Holding them by the blade or by the handle, he throws them into the rectangles on the walls. New toys, dolls, puzzles and a tricycle. A wheel squeaks muffled as, chuckling, he pedals through the vacant rooms. But the tricycle does not move. It is there on the porch, where it was left, traces of snow clinging to its saddle.

Tired in anticipation, he is expecting a letter. He destroys all

91

others in their envelopes, all those without an overseas postmark. Soon some fool will send a Christmas card. There is nothing to be done. The fire will remain unlit. Alexis waits for the arrival of a photograph of a child.

And somewhere in the background, an ill-tuned, cheap transistor radio is playing. And the voice of Mick Jagger launching into the chorus of '19th Nervous Breakdown' can be heard issuing from its tiny, tinny speaker.

Their parties are noisy, getting noisier. Sitting in groups, they'll remain in groups and chatter loudly, trying to impress their own reflections, their memories. Ornette Coleman plays 'The Riddle' and, having heard the riddle, Alexis avoids their dull expressions, their drunken questions, inevitable lead-ins to autobiographical answers. For a moment she was alone, wearing a simple, low-cut dress of purple crêpe. Breasts breathing, small animals asleep. Alexis wants to touch them. He approaches her.
    'Hello I'm—'
    'I know, I've been told.'
    Alexis raises his hand. She winces and jerks back, but her flesh brushes his palm. And she, spilling some of her punch on to the carpet, staring at the stain, the fabric's discolouring. And he, one arm held horizontally, foreseeing the reproachful tone. Yet she says nothing, only glances up, her curled lashes whipping, her fierce moss-agate eyes watering and staring. She asks:
    'Why did you do that?'
    Alexis's arm aches. He lets it drop, slapping his thigh. A retort. Then almost as if to mock himself, he whispers, 'What would you have said if I'd just asked?'
    'I don't know.'
    'May I put my hand on your breast?'
    'Yes.' No hesitation.
    He moulds his fingers to cup her shape. Delicately. She sighs. Small animals patter. He shuts his eyes to stay her penetrating

gaze. Her breath evens. He presses harder and her hand clasps his. She is easing it away.

They will meet in hotel rooms, often in uncomfortable beds. They will meet at more parties, book launches, previews and on stairs. They will say:

'Good night.'

'Good morning.'

The house is too large ever to be filled. So men in white overalls and peaked caps tow it away. Others in blue dungarees and rubber boots dig deep holes in the clearing where animals came to forage. One says:

'We're building apartments.'

Another: 'It's going to be a motel.'

Perhaps they expect to unearth a body.

More men visit Alexis in the city. Uniformed or suited with their ties loosened or undone, the quiet ones expect him to talk, their apprehensions feebly masked. Still others bring the outside in on their shoes. They have no manners. They ask many, many questions. Demand answers and explanations. It is probably they who suggest that Alexis should leave or is it just their envoys, observers with the insatiable need to see reasons but never the issue for itself? Their shadowed omnipresence prompts him to take flight. Again.

Rain nears the sad city. It too comes back, with allies, teasing the phallic threats of umbrellas and scorning the pitiful headshakes of tall buildings. Apartments too large ever to be filled. There Alexis sets the radio dial at maximum volume.

On the table cutlery rattles. Empty milk cartons; a stained sugar bowl; the sugar stained; bobs of ash like rabbit droppings; a fork squirming free of the plate to which it is glued. The coffee cup, its handle broken, burns his fingers and he clasps it all the more tightly. The chair creaks. He is sitting on something. Possibly one of her stockings. He lights a cigarette, knowing it to be his last and foolishly thinks to save some for later.

'Krystina,' they said. She corrects them. Wears white, a plain robe with broad crocheted sleeves showing summer tan and a pale band round her wrist for a watch or the loop of a dog-leash. She arrives late. Last.

And the same unidentified odour prevalent throughout the flat. Most noticeable, then bearable. Cat shit? Rotting vegetables? A mouldy dishcloth? She bought an aerosol spray to anaesthetise it, to put it down. But she has hidden the can or it is lost amongst the weeks, the months of garbage; bags which spill from under the table in rank and file to trace a path towards the door and line six flights of stairs, many shedding their plastic skins on their way out into the street where an oily patch by the parking meter reminds Alexis that her Dodge is real. Anyway, he prefers the scent of joss-sticks. Perhaps he'll go to the drug store on the corner and buy a pack of Winston.

'Krystina,' they said. She corrects them. Arriving late with other people and dressed in white, her long hair gathered into a bun. Someone holds out a drink. Alexis would offer her his chair but it creaks. And he's tired, in part distressed, in part disorientated. The immigration officer had been an officious bastard with nothing better to do than threaten to deny Alexis entry into the country. Maybe his wife had refused him his conjugal rights or overcooked his breakfast that morning, or maybe he is prejudiced against anything out of the ordinary, but letters and invitations to return were proffered as testimonials and eventually found acceptable.

Buses are delayed. Because of the snows, they run hours behind schedule. Alexis waits. At last to end another journey, to greet, to embrace half-heartedly, mindful least they embarrass one another as much as the onlookers. Coy, they are unsure, knowing there is much to say, but find it difficult to begin. It is over a year since they sat and talked this way in another dingy room, in another town, another land. They make tea, they eat Greek bread just as before. No time is past. Only a coffee cup has cooled and Alexis no longer hears the radio, but feels the jingle of the cutlery.

94

He stands, the chair scraping the worn lino and a stocking slithering from its seat. He locks himself in the bathroom, a reflex action, but he can't piss. He forces himself. Nothing. He drops his trousers and sits on the pan. The cigarette burns his fingertips. The cistern does not work, but there's nothing to flush away. In the kitchen he whisks up her stocking, hangs it over the chair-back, thinks of tuning in the radio (it's registering static) to Nashville and walks across the hall. The stocking slides to the floor. A cigarette butt floats in the pan.

'Krystina,' they said. She corrects them, smiles at the mistake and, looking away, refuses the drink that is being offered. Alexis is introduced to the people who have accompanied her.

'You remember Helen and Keith, and this is Ozzy and Jake and Nigel.'

Alexis says, 'Hello,' once.

'And this is Mona and the Painter Imogen.'

Alexis says, 'Hello, hello,' as from the earpiece of a long-distance conversation about to be interrupted by some operator who is 3,000 miles away. Here is a man who has travelled more than 3,000 miles to be 36 hours late and blame the weather, but to come back. Here is a man who has come back to a party and all that he left behind, exactly the same fresh leers now tagged Helen and the Painter Imogen, Jake, Keith and Lily (the Tigress), Mona and Nigel and Ozzy; a waterfall waiting to be amused, to chuckle at the clowns.

'Krystina,' they said. She corrects them, does not take his hand so that hers can adjust a wisp of hair that has strayed from the bun. Untroubled about the chair, refusing a drink, she moves provocatively in her white gown, drifting away to mingle, to shuffle labels in other rooms – leaving this one empty.

Where the bed is unmade and the walls are covered in raw hessian, Alexis falls heavily on to the sheets, over a stench of dead semen squirted from aerosol bottles. He is shaking his hand in the air to numb the sting. Then turning his head he sees the window. He is puzzled. The window is undamaged, nowhere even cracked and it shields the night. Alexis gets up and walks towards it. A drug store on the corner is flashing neon signs.

Above the drug store lives a man who owns a poodle. Every so often he carries his pet out into the street and positions it on the sidewalk. The dog sniffs, sniffles, never once to soil its floppy ears. Then, as though under orders, the dog shits in the gutter, much to the gratification of its owner who immediately draws a sheet of flower-printed toilet paper from his pocket and wipes the animal's arse. Much to the poodle's gratification. Alexis hasn't the courage to say good evening to this man, yet somehow manages to smile at him.

He pays for a carton of Winston and a bottle of Sominex. Passing an oily smear in the road, he is eyed by a suspicious police cadet hopefully not so bored nor as yet immune from memories of his schoolboy self stealing penny chews from the Five and Dime; not forgotten the Ave Marias and the swish of black trailing cassock. Content to hum, to drown the argument of his footsteps with rain that is raining at intervals of a block and a half.

Cars drone. Windscreen wipers pump. Alexis nuzzles his head between her breasts, a pendulum in dull motion to kiss alternate nipples. Again. Again. Noisily. She's giggling. Behind the wheel of every car that goes by and in search of anywhere that sells beer.

'It'll help,' she says and lifts his head, tugging playfully at his ears, asking to be kissed. But one ale house after the next is closed. The rain is relentless, warm and good. Left a block. Left a block. It's on nights like this that he kills.

She drives on. Waves. To toot her horn. At Alexis? At trucks slowing on the incline. Jabbing savagely at an inert brake pedal. She'll tell him that he's unique and he'll tell her that she's unique.

'Isn't it time for bed? For a parting of thighs?'

'Yes, yes!' cries Mona so forcefully that Alexis has to move the receiver away from his ear.

'But why didn't you ring earlier? We'd have gone to dinner at

Jake's. Lily fixed the most, oh never mind, hurry come quickly!'

Mona's apartment is painted silver. Perched beside a settee, a white bird lives in a black art nouveau cage. Plants grow out of the window frames. There Alexis pummels his fists into Mona's welcome body; bends, moulds, but can never shape the flesh to his satisfaction. To look like her. To feel like her.

Mornings she stands by his weakened form and mockingly holds wine in one hand, coffee in the other:

'Which d'you prefer?' she teases, knowing full well that he'll take the wine and stay on for dinner at Nigel's or Imogen's. Perhaps he'll snatch to distort Ozzy's flesh tonight and later play mouth harp, alone in some Bowery bar to the enthusiastic indifference of hardened drinkers; to bum a dime from a panhandler – the cost of dialling an answering service:

'The next bar we come to . . . will be open . . . The next bar we come to . . . will be open . . . The next bar we come to . . .'

And he steps from the telephone booth and he glances over his shoulder. And the rookie hasn't moved. And a girl is being pulled along the street by a huge mastiff, the leash cutting into her wrist. And she vanishes around a corner. And left a block. And left a block. Rooms that feed off people, spilling over on to rusted fire escapes.

The beer did help, but he almost slipped on an oil slick in the road. Could it be that she was already at the flat? Sniffing pots, tasting the curry days before it's properly ready to be eaten. Let's have it now! No, not till the logs for the fire have thawed.

'Burn the rocking chair,' is the suggestion.

First Helen apologises for the lack of heat. The fuel supply will be replenished within the hour. After that Keith apologises because they've run out of beer. 'But Nina has volunteered to go and buy some,' he adds, a full tumbler of whisky in his hand.

'Send the other comedian too!' roars Jake, at which Helen's and Keith's home resonates with a cascade of jeering. Labels swapped, they trade muses in this house of complex design, which fascinates Alexis, and in which one day he will climb the stairs.

There are no paintings on the walls, only stained-glass windows. Here water mixed with oil reflects the flashings of a drug store's neon sign. Out front kneels a police cadet, droplets of rain dripping from the peak of his cap; his palm is poised on the butt of his gun. He is peering into the gloom and up six flights of garbage-strewn steps right into the reek of cat shit, the crackling of a radio and through a hive of cells.

In a studio, the woman who is being painted these past three weeks remains unmoved. Her puce face might smile, just once, if only in unstarted scribblings scattered over the floor. She knows that Alexis is here, in the toilet emptying sleeping pills into the pan, his cigarette smouldering aimlessly in the ashtray. It's four in the morning and he will replace the stocking as soon as he has finished in the bathroom.

He switches off the light. Cockroaches scurry out of the walls and make for the kitchen. The glimmer of an occasional headlamp purls across the ceiling. But it's never hers. Sitting at the foot of the bed, correcting verses on the inside of discarded cigarette packs, she has watched him plough the dirty sheets and covered his bared foot. Is that her there laughing in the street or just some whore haggling over her price with practised mouth mimicking the wailing of a harmonica or the flush of a faulty cistern? She's down the road somewhere taking her dog for a stroll while Alexis lies in bed becalmed. But he's not calm, needing desperately to see her yet afraid to look up when anything moves, whenever the cutlery rattles. He knows that he will not see her today so rejects the idea, fearing that if he doesn't see her today he will never have seen her, that she is unreal, that he only imagines the slamming of car doors, the spinning of tyres on ice.

Dawn. Now he dares not fall asleep lest he miss any hour that she is awake.

'Come to dinner at Painter Imogen's . . . and to bed with me. Then you'll sleep. I'll give you wine.'

'Wine! Wine!' echoes an art nouveau parrot.

And the sun's on the hills and Alexis is on the hills with it. No more is he in a bedroom of net fabric walls with a stocking for a scarf, but in an outside cold in the outside good because she is there somewhere. Where boards, which prohibit trespassing, are bypassed, boundaries are violated. She also chases along foot slopes, kicking aside the garbage, short of breath, together being the spot beneath the sun.

But on the mountain they are building a highway to tow houses into the city. The tractors rumble, plum smokes spout and green leaves are being crushed, always leaving so little to leave. A dread of yellow cabs, which if observed closely will contort their dented bodies to lunge through the narrowest gaps between buses and curbs, between each other. A woman almost strangled on a staircase. And a subway ride, Astor Place to Times Square, or was it Grand Central? The compartment of bored rush hour faces. Different. Indifferent. Ears that hear screams, eyes that locate their source, only to turn in on themselves. Those nearest step back, push back and squash those unaware and furthest from what's happening, has happened. Alexis has had this sudden fancy to dance like a whirling dervish, to waltz these endless miles of endless tunnel to the whistling in his fears, because coming back there is always so little to leave. A Last Will and Testament, which makes provision for the purchase of two coffins (one so pathetically smaller than the other) and perhaps the dying squeals of a truck breaking hard before the incline.

fifteen

In which The Voice of Reason, true to narrative form, tries to rationalize and justify everything but that which might actually require rationalization and justification.

It would come as no surprise for Waggish Wendy to give a sigh, then ask, 'What kind of nonsense is that?'

Of course she would get no immediate reply. There's pain in the old dog yet.

'Is it a parable? A fable?' She frees her arm and steps aside. 'What is it you're actually trying to tell me, what are you trying to say? You see I simply don't understand.'

Their length and breadth tour of the manor has brought them to a halt before a set of continental-style double doors, the right leaf standing slightly ajar. Alexis glances at Wendy, does a double take, then, lifting the lantern even higher, looks her up and down as if seeing her for the first time, as if she has changed into someone else or merely become the shadow of her unrecognisable self. The appraisal seems to hang in the balance, a moment caught between the conductor's last wave of the baton and a surge of appreciative applause, which on this occasion goes unheard.

It is any wonder? For the most part I would tend to agree with Wendy. So much can and should be frequently dismissed as nonsense, yet in the long run who am I to interfere with how the truth needs to be told. I certainly would have marked up Alexis's stay in the States as a success, but then I am prejudiced. It was after all at my instigation and expense that he made the trip in the first place.

His pedagogic role in that backwater mining village in the north of England had been a blatant sham. Someone of Alexis F's capabilities eventually has to exercise them to the full, no matter how much they chase after the secure banality of a dead-end existence and fool themselves into believing that they have happily succeeded in achieving it. The waste could not go on. Alexis would never lay claim to an academic bent in the traditional sense, but his linguistic talents are exceptional and his translations, particularly of contemporary Slavonic poetry, remain second to none. At that time in America there was a healthy (or equally an unhealthy) and considerable interest in all things East European – other than immigrants that is. I had become associated with a small colony of writers who, for no explicable reason, had found a haven on the banks of the Delaware in the one-crossroad town of Milford. This was by no means a dropout commune; in fact the Milford Group expressed unreserved antipathy towards the Hippie Movement, seeing it as idolised, dope-fugged stagnation, as indeed it proved to be in practice. No, these were a handful of both young and old, published and unpublished intellectuals who, being scattered in the same vicinity, could if need be take advantage of daily contact for ready stimulation. Their stock-in-trade was debate and discussion – often heated and bad tempered – followed by bouts of concentrated work in isolation. Here Alexis should have felt at home.

He should have appreciated my efforts in securing that house for him on the outskirts of town, for introducing him to the company and providing him with Alice. She was not exactly one of my leftovers, but a free, uncomplicated soul in her early twenties and most amenable when it came to providing so-called creative people with unobtrusive companionship and practical comforts. In return she demanded nothing more than a kind gesture, a kind word; perhaps a mention by name. Experience had made her impervious to the mandatory frustrations and tantrums of artists, so much so that I find any demonstrative outburst attributed to her highly suspect. At best she might once in a while weep in the privacy of her own self-dented self-esteem. There's little doubt, however, that many people felt themselves mysteriously drawn to Alexis, and women in particular would presume to assert unchallengeable and exclusive rights to his person. It was not just his European accent. Almost overnight he became a major talking point and the supposedly off-chance arrival of Faye from California in the middle of winter should have spelled out clear warnings.

Alexis should have realised that involving himself with Faye and having her almost at once move in with him would lead to disaster. He should have foreseen that as an unexceptional, though competent and genuinely amusing poet, Faye would soon become jealous; not of Alice, but of Alexis's unused talents. He should have known that the quality of his work, though ostensibly second-hand was far superior to anything Faye would ever produce. Popular though her verses may have been, she had attached herself to a man who did nothing but unwittingly show up her inadequacies. For her a one-to-one emotional understanding or commitment was never the issue, neither was sex. Alexis should have grasped that all the jibing, the goading and the cajoling to get him to write his own material, as well as the mischievous taunting of him with presents of children's toys in response to his persistent complacency, was designed to exacerbate the situation beyond endurance. Perhaps he did.

I on the other hand should have anticipated the severity of the snowfalls in the area and made adequate provision for fuel deliveries. I should have organised even a temporary road to be cleared to allow the heavy gas trucks to get through regardless of the incline, and that goes for the collection of the garbage too. I also should have guessed that when it came to Alice and Faye, Alexis was doing no more than planning and rehearsing

102

some sort of revenge for a final farewell demonstration of male aggression towards women. All women.

Faye was obviously responsible for his move to New York and she should have been aware of the consequences. Perhaps she intended somehow to exploit her dismissal of him for her own gratification, but then again she could not have predicted the appearance of Krystina, nor could she have controlled the effect that Krystina would have on Alexis. This was an era when certain people fell freely and unashamedly in lust. It had little to do with the derogatory notions of promiscuity or permissiveness. The giving and taking of sexual pleasure became a worthwhile expression of regard and respect, which accommodated an exchange of partners without undermining the core of any stronger ties. Orgies as such were not uncommon and, if anything, tended to reinforce individual relationships. Faye's half-sister, Lily (or Tiger Lily to be more accurate) had become the self-appointed overseer of this particular East Village sect. She was the prime motivator in organising lunches, parties and get-togethers; making sure everyone had their fair share of each other, as it were. Though coquettish, cold and amorous by turns, she also managed to fulfil the function of a sort of personal agony aunt and in this guise saw a worrying waning of enthusiasm grip her friends. Likewise, having put herself last in the queue, her entire attitude was to change after her corporal indulgences with Alexis. Her self-confidence went into decline. She became withdrawn and indolent, all but entirely fading into the background. Yet, it was the introduction of Krystina into this group that somehow revitalised all the women and once more bonded everybody together at the expense of Alexis, especially since Krystina had this near obsession about using the diminutive Nina of her given name, which, as might be expected in the circumstances, was pointedly disregarded.

The way I see it now, Alexis took advantage of Faye's aggression initially to play on the sympathies of her half-sister's avant-garde set. Then, going against the grain of their supposedly unconventional conventions, he would have engineered an

103

acceptance of his own purported values only to pour scorn on to his converts by probably brutalising them both physically as well as mentally, thus throwing them into a state of misery and confusion. In short a triple bluff, which in the end simply backfired. As the newcomer and prime focus of Alexis's attention, Krystina would have presented herself as a common enemy and fostered united opposition. Moreover, she was immune to games. Self-contained, careless as to whether she was accepted or not and with an alluring band of scar tissue round her wrist, she would have been insufferable as far as Alexis was concerned. Yet not possessing her would have been even worse. To have his advances ignored, an agony. Her origins were Venezuelan and though she was nothing like her adopted Ivory Coast namesake the temperamental resemblance by association must have hit its mark. Krystina would never permit herself to be maltreated, so again Alexis would have had to have maltreated himself instead. In Krystina he should have met his match. As it happens it was she who telephoned to announce his latest disappearance, so brief and so sad a call. I should have known that he would go as ever without a word, only tonight to find his tongue.

'The master bedroom's through here,' he says, pushing the left-hand side of the door. It does not budge. For a second Alexis forgets himself and grins foolishly.

Not one to be fobbed off, Wendy says, 'You know if anything you're getting worse. And I thought you were supposed to be good at this sort of thing.'

'What sort of thing?'

'Making up stories.'

'Whatever gave you that idea?'

'Well I've watched you in the coffee shop. You're always scribbling.' Wendy prods the right-hand side of the door with her forefinger. It swings open on a creaking hinge. Alexis ushers her into the room. She takes but two steps when he says, 'Excuse me, but I better go first and see to the generator.' For a moment Well-grounded Wendy gets the distinct impression that she has walked into a maze. Alexis and his lantern veer off on what appears to be a zigzag path between chest-high obstacles. The light vanishes, leaving her in darkness. She does not dare move for fear of colliding with something unseen. Before her eyes can get accustomed to the gloom, from the depths of somewhere, she hears a faint choke followed by a stutter. Lights fade up in the room and just as rapidly fade out again. The stutter becomes an even, muted rumble. Lights fade up again, dip once, twice, and then maintain a steady glow.

Wendy discovers that she is up to her armpits in books. She is indeed in a maze built of volume upon volume. Stacks of hide-bound tomes, hardbacks and paperbacks of all shapes and sizes surround her in seemingly haphazard rank and file. The room is large and at the centre of the labyrinth, on a marginally raised podium, stands a brass bedstead above which hangs a formidable crystal chandelier. Being able to see over the piles of books, yet succumbing to the odd blunder, Wendy readily makes her way to the plinth. She tests the mattress with her hands. It feels comfortably firm. She takes off her scarf, her sheepskin jacket and her sensible walking shoes, then stretches herself out on the counterpane.

There's no sign of Alexis, but Wendy is sure that he is close by, that he can hear her quite clearly. Nevertheless, she does raise her voice a little:

'It's my turn. I'll show you how it's supposed to be done.

'Once upon a time . . .'

sixteen

Descriptive of Alexis F's search for barriers behind which he hopes to hide from the caprices of emotional and mental pain, only to discover that cures are not affected by a simple masking of symptoms.

Somewhere on the Mediterranean coast there stands an old fortified town. As a matter of expediency and in keeping with what has gone before, let's site it in Spain and call it Algeciras. A young woman, little more than a girl some might say, but already the mother of three, works as a skivvy-cum-chambermaid in one of the port's waterfront boarding houses, which caters mostly to itinerant mariners while also offering more permanent, though rotating accommodation to several prostitutes. The young woman – Mercedes is as good a name as any – works a daily 16-hour shift. Her olive complexion, chiselled nose and ebony hair strongly suggest a noble, Arabic ancestry. Originally she came from the countryside near the Portuguese border, but a childhood spent in caring for an ailing mother and tending to the machismo demands of younger siblings drove her to run away and marry in secret. Town life proved to be a short-lived improvement. After the birth of her first child, she once more became a captive of her penurious lot and, of necessity, an underpaid drudge. Her husband is an offshore fisherman who drinks.

From the basement window of the scullery, Mercedes sees the arrival of a young man on the quayside. He is tall and has hair streaked with gold. It is early morning. The young man sits down on the rough cobblestones. He dangles his feet over the edge of the dock and leans his back against his kitbag. He gazes across the bay. The hours pass unmarked.

Whenever her work takes her into the scullery where at least it is cool, Mercedes sees that the young man has not moved. He watches water idle, oily and murky and black. He watches the anglers, a long way off, casting lines from the harbour wall. He watches them go off for lunch. From time to time he stares at a motionless gantry. And whenever anybody comes near, walks by too closely, the young man automatically reaches for his waistband as if to check on something he has secreted there. This seems to happen often.

It is well after midday and he must obviously be hungry, for he gets up and strolls towards a *bodega*. He casts no shadow. Now out of sight, he perhaps orders a glass of cold beer and a *bocadillo* with sardines, peppers, tomatoes and some olives. Perhaps he helps an American sailor (who speaks no Spanish) choose between two prostitutes and acts as an interpreter pimp at barter for a fair price. Undecided, he seriously weighs up the reject.

'Wouldn't you like to play family too?' prompts the whore with a wriggle of her sheer-skirted rump on the bar stool.

('Will you stay with me?' she asked, though hinting at a sense of obligation rather than want. Her lips formed an uncertain smile.

'No,' replied Alexis.

'But must you go?' she sobbed, a dry exploratory sob.

'Yes.'

'But I'm going to have your baby,' she mumbled, 'I'm going to have your baby,' over and over again.

'Save your tears. It can't, it won't make me stay.' Alexis couldn't be more adamant.)

'Come on, let's play family . . . just for a little while,' suggests the whore once more, grinning encouragement and fluttering her false eyelashes. She crosses her legs, inching up her petticoats to display even more stockinged thigh.

The young man goes back to his place on the dock. Time passes unmarked.

Then all at once it starts, not a sudden downpour, but a heavy, menacing rain. The cobbles are loud with its barrage. The young man returns to the *bodega* and perhaps there learns that because of a seaman's dispute all scheduled ferry sailings to Ceuta have been cancelled until further notice. He buys two one-litre flasks of *anise dulce*, a bottle of orangeade, a large crusty loaf and almost a kilo of cheese. He enters the boarding house and registers with the concierge who is none too pleased about having her siesta prearrangements disturbed. Mercedes sees the young man climb the stairs, taking the steps two at a time to a twin room tucked under the eaves. He locks himself in. And it rains.

The only afternoon sounds in the building are those of water drumming, of water dripping, deadened at irregular intervals by the maid's tired footsteps. Wearily she clomps up and down the stairs, which link the balustraded landings, and wearily she shuffles along the lengths of these tiered balconies that, on three sides, overlook the worn flags of the entrance hall. The skylight leaks. Droplet after droplet falls the height of seven storeys into a chipped, enamelled basin. There's another outside the young man's door. Every so often he hears the maid change this bowl for an empty one.

The two ships on the right are depicted with their prows, their anchors facing the artist. They appear to be moored together. The third is visibly so, its hawser slack and drooping from its stern. The vessel in the centre is showing least canvas, but has the tallest mast. It lists to the left. A rating is sitting on its short cross-boom and is involved in the operation of hoisting or lowering a drunkenly angled lifeboat back into a vertical position. Many other sailors are grouped at the railings. The sea is choppy, as after the storm of a difficult voyage.

The young man turns from the unframed print on the wall

108

and looks out of the window. For a while he gazes over the roofs, the wet slates and terracotta tiles lost to the incessant rain. Then he pulls the curtains shut. Daylight still filters through the flimsy material.

Using a biro, he draws a chequered pattern on a sheet of paper torn from the centre of an exercise book. This he lays out on a chair between the two beds and, rummaging in his bag, begins to set up chess pieces on the improvised board. Stretched out on his back, he peers at the ceiling and wonders at which point the rain will penetrate, will finally work its way through. He stares at the game. It is unbegun; a black pawn missing. Repeatedly he swallows sickly-sweet mouthfuls of the orange-diluted anise from a plastic tooth mug. Now and again he nibbles at the cheese, chews the bread. Whenever he gets an erection, he paces the floor, then swaps beds.

Drowsily he uncaps the second bottle of anise and mixes yet another shot.

The hours pass unmarked.

A slamming of doors! A shout! The young man has been dozing. It's dark. Still disorientated, he climbs off his bed to put on the light. He gropes for the switch by the door. Nothing. He tries another by the hand basin and immediately snaps shut his eyes from the stabbing glare of the unshaded bulb. He eases them open and drinks from the tumbler to swill clean the scum and sleep tastes out of his mouth. Somewhere in the building, not far off, he can hear a scuffle. There are moans. There's a scampering and the nearing tread of someone running, a pounding over the stairs and a clatter. The young man unlocks his door. On the landing the maid has dropped her bowl. The one already there, still half empty, catches a drip.

Mercedes lets out an unchecked sigh and a whimper. She heaves herself at the young man with such a thrust that to keep his balance he is forced to stumble back into his room. Her hands clamped about the young man's waist, Mercedes presses her cheek hard against his chest. Her frail body quivers. She sobs.

The young man folds his arms about her shoulders, gently hugging her tighter with her every shudder. For a moment she stops, shudders once more and is stilled. She loosens her grip and places the tips of her fingers against his ribs, softly, to ease him away. She peeps up at his face, then bursts into tears, swaying as he holds her.

She is calmed. The young man leads her to the bed and sits her on it. He closes the door, reaches for the key in the lock, but then thinks better of turning it. Then he fills the second tooth mug with anise. Mercedes' head is bowed; her palms cover her eyes, swollen and bloodshot. The young man taps her on the thigh, lightly. She twitches and looks up. Dishevelled, her hair streaks her furrowed brow. She takes the mug, at once refusing it, handing it back and shaking her head and mouthing, 'No, no no.'

His hand cupped round hers, the young man urges the mug towards her lips.

'Go on, it'll help.'

She drains the measure in one gulp and places the tumbler on the chair; her hand still trembles. A damp ring forms on the paper chessboard. The young man picks up the tumbler and refills it. Mercedes objects, but then slowly sips at the syrupy alcohol. Every so often a shiver flees her back. She gazes down at the threadbare patches of carpet at her feet; at an old cigarette burn. She too looks old, worn and burnt out. Her hands are coarse, her nails both ragged and cracked or chewed to the quick. Too many creases border her liquid-brown eyes, stunning even in their distress. Her nose, the delicate arc of an unstrung bow.

They sit opposite one another and drink in silence. The young man is puzzled, curious, but refrains from asking questions.

Without warning, Mercedes jumps up, saying, 'I'm sorry . . . thank you, thank you. I'm sorry . . .' Her voice is husky, broken yet sensual. She's edging towards the door. There she stands posed in profile. Still not looking at the young man, she's asking, 'Is it obvious?' and pulls her apron taught across her abdomen. She's four, possibly five months pregnant.

'Is what obvious?'

'The baby!'

She prods herself in the stomach.

'Yes.'

'Oh!' and she's crying once more.

The young man takes her by the hand and sits her on the bed as before. He pours another good measure of anise, but leaves it by the chessboard.

After a while Mercedes whispers, 'He almost strangled me just now,' and she sweeps back the hair that has fallen across her forehead to reveal not only the puffy bruising rapidly blackening around her left eye, but broad red welts on her neck.

'Who?'

Instantly her manner changes. 'My husband!' She raises her voice to an arrogant pitch of aggression, her lips snarl in defiance. 'The pig! He wants to kill me. It's not enough just to fucking up and go!'

'Because of the baby?'

'Yes, we already have two, no three, and we can't afford this one. We couldn't afford the last two come to that, so he's simply decided to fuck off. Bloody typical!'

'But surely . . .'

And this is that split-second eye contact of free and mutual transfer. The visibly unmistakable yet indefinable pause, in which Mercedes draws on the young man's strength. He relinquishes it without knowing how or why. It is now she who dominates.

'We give them the immortality they want,' she barks. 'Oh yes, they can't live without it they say, and what do they do . . . they run away. They just can't handle it. Men!'

And being in charge, Mercedes dictates the mood. Deftly, she adopts a mode of confidential understanding designed to elicit sympathy:

'He's a good man at heart though. He works hard: he's at work all the time when the sea's right, but we're very poor . . . and when he's not working, he gets drunk and comes to me for . . . Then he blames me, says it's my fault. So he has left me.'

'He'll be back –'

'No, he threatened to pack his bags the last time I fell pregnant. I've been sleeping here ever since; you see there's a couch in the cellar and that way I thought I could avoid his . . . I feed the kids as best I can and put them to bed. Then I slip away, a neighbour listens out for them: they're quite safe. He'll be in the *bodega* of course . . . But he found me anyway, just the once and that was enough. And so it happened. And he's gone. Oh well . . . I'm best rid of him.'

There follows a prolonged, though not uncomfortable silence, which Mercedes eventually breaks. 'I'll simply do away with myself,' she announces in a matter-of-fact way, almost as if thinking aloud, as if she has just this minute arrived at an irrevocable decision.

The young man's guts shift, the way they might when choking down a chuckle, but something in Mercedes' tone makes it impossible entirely to dismiss her words as a joke. Somewhat ill at ease and unable to gauge her true frame of mind, the young man seeks a reprieve in levity. 'Don't be silly,' he chides, suppressing an anxious giggle.

'You don't believe me!' she shrieks. 'You, you animal, you monster, you . . .' And buttons are flying, some hit his knees. Her blouse is ripped apart. The sharp cutters' scissors slung on a long cord from her belt are firmly clenched and levelled to pierce the skin beneath her sternum.

The young man would be amused by these histrionics were it not for the fact that he is ogling her, the lascivious stare undisguised, the yen to touch her all but tangible. Scissors forgotten, Mercedes is wrapping the blouse about herself. Coyly she has lowered her eyes.

'I shall do it,' she mutters. 'Perhaps not right at this minute and not like that, but I shall do it . . .'

Rain patters intensify the pause.

'You like me don't you?' Mercedes' control of the situation remains unchallenged.

'You do like me don't you?' she repeats, savouring her power. 'You can't help yourself . . . can you?'

It is the young man's turn to focus his attention on the shabby carpet.

Mercedes drops the folded guard of her arms. Little by little she moves towards him and bit by bit her blouse falls open baring her breasts.

'I'm pretty aren't I?' she taunts. 'Say I'm pretty: won't you? Why don't you look? You want to. Go on: you want to feel me, go ahead. It'll help. You could be the last man to . . . yes that's it! Wouldn't you like to be my very last man?'

The young man glances up. He crosses his legs.

'Please. Please I'm only offering what every man craves for . . . you are a man aren't you?'

Mercedes sits on the bed opposite him and lounges back on her elbows provocatively. She pouts her lips and smacks a mocking kiss.

'Come on . . . mmm? I might reconsider: and afterwards *not* kill myself. What d'you say?'

The young man shakes his head.

Pause.

'Can you write?'

The young man looks at her, puzzled and curious as before. He nods.

Mercedes has turned the chessboard on to its blank side. Chess pieces lie scattered.

'Write,' she commands.

'What?'

'God will forgive me.'

The young man frowns, then grins.

'Write, and I'll sign.' It's an order, but the young man says, 'No.'

Mercedes presses the point of the scissors into her belly. The young man lunges for them and snatches them away, scoring her chest. A reddish brown weal the colour of her nipples rises between

113

her breasts. He stands over her and cuts the scissors free of their cord. He flings them across the room.

Mercedes traces the scratch with moistened fingers.

'We have become equals,' she sniggers.

And she clings to the young man, and, squeezing him firmly by the buttocks, is burrowing and nuzzling her face into his groin. He holds her by the throat. She relaxes her grip and runs her palms round his waist. She unbuckles his money belt and loosens his fly, probing with her mouth.

On the landing outside, the basin has overflowed.

seventeen

In which, ill at ease, one Alternative Self finds itself at loggerheads with Another, much to Alexis F's bemusement; and wherein Reason, now all but resigned to failure, is still determined to have the last word.

Now I'm beginning to get really worried. Naturally I've no objection to a summary bit of fellatio (which has virtually become a literary obligation), but the potential extrapolations here give me great cause for concern. This is dangerous ground, very dangerous ground. It is at times like these that mistakes are made; irreparable damage incurred. Was it right of me to trust her? I'm convinced that she has all the right qualities, but then again she had specific instructions to steer a middle course. Shock tactics are all well and good yet need studied preparation. Issues that are forced have a habit of backfiring and I'm not altogether sure that Wayward Wendy is equipped to handle the possible repercussions; spread-eagled on the bedstead as she is, her eyes glistening, focused on some point far beyond the chandelier. Alexis F has long since joined her. He sits on the edge of the bed with his back to her, both feet on the floor, his hand resting delicately on her stomach. Above the unattended throb of the generator, their silence is becoming audible.

Thoughtfully Wendy turns her face towards Alexis. 'What d'you –' It's a false start. She tries again. 'Have you nothing to say?'

'It's time you got what you came for.'

'And what's that?'

'A need to expunge your pity.'

'But I don't pity you.'

'No, you pity yourself.'

'I abhor self-pity.'

'That's why you've come to kiss the frog, or in my case the toad.'

'And in the morning the toad will still be a toad?'

'Yes, but you'll have overcome your revulsion. You'll have plugged your fear. And you'll die happy.'

'To die will be an awfully big adventure.'

'That's a borrowed line.'

'So is that.'

'*Touché.*'

The pause is hardly worth the mention – a Wendy's breath.

'Will I die . . . ? Tomorrow?'

Taking his palm from her stomach and hoisting, folding his legs on to the bed, Alexis F turns towards her.

'No . . .' he says. 'Well at least not by my hand.'

She lifts her forefinger to touch his face expecting the scar tissue to be rough, like sandpaper, like the feel of her father's unshaven chin when, returning from the pub, he might kiss her good night. She recalls the acrid tang of beer, the hang of tobacco, and withdraws her hand.

'I won't bite,' says Alexis.

'But you have killed?'

For a while Alexis scrutinises her, unblinking, as if hoping to divine from her expression the secret that will answer some esoteric mystery of his own thinking. Eventually he says, 'Believe what you will,' and, levering himself off the bed, winds his way through the maze to a corner of the room where he squats out of sight.

After a while Wendy asks, 'What're you up to?' She doesn't expect an answer and gets none.

'Whatever it is, I wish you wouldn't do it . . .'

116

She too gets off the bed and, standing on tiptoe, peers over the walls of the labyrinth, but even so she cannot see Alexis who, with his back pressed against a wall, sits on his haunches, his arms folded across his knees, his head bowed.

'Okay, have it your own way,' says a resigned Wendy while climbing back on to the bed. Still she cannot see him, and so she begins to jump up and down. The bed springs squeal a cacophonous protest. Lifting her arm, she leaps high enough to touch the chandelier, which she sets into a tinkle of motion.

'Look, we've got our own light show!' And she gives the crystals another more determined shove.

'Come on, Alexis! Can't you see I'm not really grown up at all!' She thinks that she detects a sound, a movement from Alexis's corner, but can't really be sure in the to and fro of unfixed shadows.

'Okay, have it your own way.' Her trampolining ceases abruptly. The heavy chandelier with dull, predictable indifference eases its swing towards rest. The droning of the generator intensifies the silence.

Wanton Wendy sighs. Nimbly, on a renewed bounce, she divests herself of her sweater, then, on the next, she unbuckles her belt. With each subsequent bounce her jeans fall to her ankles and with a final act of near acrobatics, leaving her wearing only woolly socks and mismatching bra and knickers, she dives under the bedclothes. Beneath sheets pulled up to her chin, she stares at the chandelier, which continues to play with the passing minutes, ever more slowly, until all movement stops. Still the generator potters through time.

'Alexis . . . you don't have to answer . . . but . . . You're not angry with me, are you?'

'No.'

The sound of his voice startles her, not only because he replies, but because he has moved closer and she can see his head and shoulders above the stacked books.

'But you knew I'd come?' she asks, staring him straight in the face.

117

'Sooner or later.'

'You're not afraid are you?'

'No more than usual.'

'D'you mean you feel nothing?'

'On the contrary.'

'What d'you feel?'

'A need to run away.'

'But you won't?'

'Of course not.'

'It'll be all right.'

'Whatever you say.'

'Aren't you curious?'

'No.'

'You didn't ask about what?'

'That's exactly how curious I am.'

'You said it . . .' She breaks eye contact. Then, 'Does this room have a window?'

'Yes.'

'Would you open the curtains and turn out the lights?'

'You'd prefer to be in the dark . . . of course, that's understandable.'

'No it's that bloody generator! It's driving me mad! Anyway there should be a full moon.'

Wooer Wendy shuts her eyes. She is aware of Alexis manoeuvring his way around the stacks of books, though he does so without any obvious noise. She hears the sounds of brass-ringed curtains being parted. Still she keeps her eyes closed. The generator chokes on silence. A minute or so later she feels the movement of the mattress, the lift of the bedclothes and, with a slight tensing of the limbs, she anticipates the squeal of the bed springs as Alexis lays down beside her.

She opens her eyes. The room seems to be bathed in a glow of peaceful platitudes. The chandelier sparkles. 'That thing isn't going to fall down on top of us is it?' she asks, not quite seriously.

Alexis replies with a smirk, 'It hasn't done so before . . . though it might.'

He is naked. Yet, mentally replaying the immediate past sequence of events, Wendy cannot fix the moment when he actually got undressed. This bothers her. And as if to temper her worry, she briefly snuggles into the crook of his arm, only to draw herself upwards, gradually to turn her head and seek out his lips with her own.

No!

This cannot be happening. I just won't allow this to happen. It's beyond all comprehension. Wendy has completely transgressed the bounds of the brief, yet equally I feel powerless to stop her. What can we be thinking of? Seduction was never the solution, well at least not full sexual seduction. Let's face it, she is simply prostituting herself. Body, emotions. Alexis F is almost old enough to be her father. What the hell could have possessed her to do something so stupid! I honestly had far more faith in her, believed that I had instructed her better, created her to bow to my guidance – of course not blindly, but with a contained modicum of personal, sensitive discretion. I've no doubt her motives are sincere, but at the very least they are misguided. Or could it be a mere matter of intuition? Does she somehow sense that Alexis F's retreat is no more than the space he needs wherein to accept that which has to happen? Bitch!

Am I jealous? Do I think it's me she should be fucking? Yes *fucking*, that's the right word. And what of her secret boyfriend? Her lover with whom she's about to elope? Is a shrug of the shoulders and a waltz in the dark enough to dismiss him? After all I've done for her. Bitch!

I must immediately regain control. That is my role. As long as I'm in charge events will continue to unfold towards their best probable conclusion. I have the reins and they will remain in my hands until I relinquish them. This I refuse to do . . . and yet . . . do I have an option? The motions of the day have overcome me with fatigue.

These are the early hours, the tread of the midnight shift. Tempted as I am, can I truly, with an easy conscience, abandon this entire situation, and once and for all close the file and so relinquish control?

Part Two

The fly cannot sit down.

S. I. Witkiewicz
Insatiability

Part Two

eighteen

The depositions of the witnesses were presented as evidence and lodged with the investigating coroner's office. As such they are a matter of public record.

The train definitely departed on schedule.

It's a two-way country lane, not much used by traffic, but for those in the know it serves as a convenient short cut from the west to the motorway, which feeds the metropolis. Often tree-lined and throughout flanked by a fosse and hedgerows of varying height, it skirts the perimeter of an army base with secret military installations and gives a 'back door' access to the camp at one significant point. This entrance is manned 24 hours a day. The sergeant on duty recorded that he left the guardhouse at 0053 hours when he heard an approaching car draw to a halt nearby. He positioned himself at the gate and saw that the vehicle was parked just off the road some 60 metres away. 'It was one of those old sports jobs,' he said, 'with a soft top, but well maintained. I could see it quite clearly by the light of the moon.

'First the driver got out, a man, and then the passenger, a woman, closely followed by a small kid. He couldn't have been more than five or six, and scampered off towards the nearest tree, obviously in need of a pee. It was then that the man and the woman started arguing. They were shouting at each other, but I was too far away to hear what they were saying. The kid reappeared from the bushes and clung to his mother's legs. This didn't improve matters in the least and the couple continued shouting at each other. Eventually the man raised his arms in a wide sort of shrug like them foreigners do, and he stomped off in the direction that they'd just come from. The woman looked after him for a moment, then she bundled the kid into the car, got into the driver's seat and drove off. She passed me at speed, accelerating fast she was, and I watched her go until her tail-lights disappeared round the bend. I couldn't swear to it, but I seem to remember hearing the sound of a heavy vehicle, a truck or something, shifting gear as it struggled up the incline from the opposite direction.'

Not far beyond that bend, at the meet of two roads, there's a level crossing, a horizontal pole of aluminium with a built-in lantern and reflectors. This barrier swings to render either road impassable, while an official employee of the railway sits installed in a wooden hut. He represents the human element. 'My barriers were up . . .' he said, 'or down, whichever way you care to look at it. They operate automatically. And she came straight through them. Smash! Straight through 'em! Must've swerved when she saw the truck and not seen my lamps, which I might add were lit and perfectly in order. Everything was in perfect, correct working order.'

The lorry driver, who was very familiar with this stretch of road (having been born and bred in the vicinity), maintained that without fail he always slowed for this junction, even when the barrier was likely to be closed and so barred all traffic from the right. 'It's that bloody incline,' he said. 'You have to go down through all those bloody gears and then when you level off you're right on top of the bloody railway line with no real chance to get any steam up again just in case the gates are against you. Course I didn't see her till the very last second. Stupid bloody car, should've been scrapped years ago. She couldn't have had any lights on as I recall. Maybe mine blinded her, though I was definitely stopped. It's that bloody daft angle.'

*　　*　　*

'Well it couldn't have been more than a few minutes later,' said the sergeant. 'I mean I'd hardly set foot in the guardhouse when . . . boom! So I about face out again and see this ball of flames burst into the sky above those trees over there. And that's when I saw him. I mean it had to be the bloke from the car, the man who'd been driving and walked off. He was gunning it hell for leather, right across the fields towards the fire. I've never seen anyone move so fast, and I've done a few dodgy sprints myself.'

The motorcyclist, who first reached the wrecked car only moments after it had somehow disentangled itself from the locomotive, and seconds before it burst into flames, said, 'Why didn't she brake! Why didn't she brake!' Pressed for details, he said that he saw a figure, probably a man, come running as if out of nowhere straight towards the car and into the flames, which seemed to engulf him.

The ambulance driver later said, 'That one was bad; really, really bad and believe you me I've seen some bad ones. In fact it was probably that one that finally made me give up on the job. Just couldn't take it any more . . .'

The charred remains of only two people were ever found, those of a woman and a child.

The train arrived on schedule.

Part Three

... schizophrenia is merely a mistake in arithmetic.

Paul Theroux
Picture Palace

Part Three

nineteen

Involving practical ways and means of escaping Reality; and wherein contrived institutionalisation and the acquaintance of Piers Topfl provide Alexis with the makings of new directions.

They say that Alexis F is not fit. They say that his refusal to come to terms with the underlying essence of experience, no matter how brutal, has made him unfit. They say that they can make him fit; and to that end they have given him questionnaires to complete, whole pamphlets and booklets in a multitude of pastel colours, which in some cases contain upwards of a hundred questions. Some of these questions are provided with a choice of answers labelled a, b and c, but more often than not Alexis dismisses all three as being irrelevant. He fills in each form meticulously, printing in bold block capitals. But they delete his answers to substitute their own. And they decide to put Alexis F away in order to make him fit.

St Anslem's Mental Institution was built and designed during the Napoleonic Wars as a fortified gaol. In its time it has held Austrian, Russian, English, French, Prussian, Polish and even Spanish prisoners, and since then, the forbidding, castellated outlines of its buildings have changed not an iota, though the wrought iron bars on the windows have been replaced by a somewhat finer steel mesh. A high, grey stone wall separates the grounds from the main road into the centre of West Berlin. Sole access to this military-style compound is provided by the so-called Gateway to the East, a deep portal not unlike a triumphal arch, which incorporates a spacious guardroom and small armoury, now a porters'-cum-keepers' lodge. Double-decker buses stop directly outside this gate. Passengers alighting here do so either by mistake, or else they cross the dual carriageway to the international haulage depots located opposite. Save a few. Those who bring parcels, those who are friends, who are kith and kin. Those who are hospital visitors.

Trude carries only a handbag of scuffed leather. Slung from her shoulder and across her breast, it has a brass clasp over which she has curled the fingers of her mittened hand. Her face is set without expression. As she approaches the lodge, she takes no notice of the warder behind his glass partition, and unchallenged, carries on through the arch, her blank gaze fixed. Ahead. The illuminated clock at the base of the spire of a neo-Gothic chapel built on what today is a traffic island provides a focus for her attention. Afraid of being conspicuous, she walks with studied steps along the wide, asphalt drive, which is flanked by neatly tended lawns and flowerbeds, and signs that read – 'Please Keep Off the Grass'. Or – 'Men' and 'Ladies', each with the appropriate subscript of an arrow. Trude is not only concerned about possibly tripping or stumbling, but she is now also wondering about the time. Is she early? Is this the visiting hour? And bearing right, on the first path that leads away from the church, she makes for the entrance of a three-storeyed barrack room.

The sun has set and in the gloom of dusk the building presents a distinctly medieval elevation that is sombre and present. Here and there netted rectangles shine, windows lit in random patterns, but always in balanced composition. Black against white, white against black. And should a light be switched off, another will at once go on elsewhere to restore harmony to the facade. 'A testament to humanity's subliminal need for geometry,' thinks Trude, recalling

130

the design lectures she attended whilst still an architectural student; smiling a congratulatory smile to herself, but of a sudden coming to an abrupt stop. She stands watching. She remembers admiring the post-war skyscraper that housed the Faculty of Arts all aglow at night like some monstrous Mondrian monochrome, and she is confused.

Two men wearing freshly laundered, unbuttoned lab coats ignore her, keys ajangling as they pass by in animated conversation. Trude realises that she is on the wrong path, so she turns and retraces her steps as far as the church. There she takes the second exit from the roundabout and sets off for the next section of the building, which is just as austere looking and for all intents and purposes indistinguishable from its neighbour. But the sight of a telephone booth alongside the double swing-doors confirms that she is on the right track. On her last attempt to find Piers' new ward she got hopelessly lost in courtyards, in halls, and in a complexity of passages and cells. Piers had said that it was mazed like that to confuse inmates who might try an escape. And so she consoles herself with the thought that it is not simply paranoia that makes her flounder.

She descends a short flight of concrete steps and finds herself in a long corridor of unplastered brick. Punctuated by symmetrically placed, labelled and numbered doors, the walls are painted pea green to hip height and above that a sickly ochre. Between, in imitation of a dado rail, there is a thin ribbon of black. This flaky decor reminds Trude of primary school, of the nicotine-stained ceilings that abound in the city's pubs and basement jazz clubs; while the rhythmic clack of her heels on the crazed, flagged floor echoes. Cautious yet confident. About two-thirds of the way along, she pauses for a moment in front of a door that has been wedged ajar and peeps through its glazed top half hoping to catch sight of Gustav. But he's not there. Only some other man who lies with his back to her, motionless on one of the eight beds (six of these being stripped bare to the mattress, stained and unoccupied) and all arranged as in a bell-tent, spokes to a small tea table at the hub of an octagonal room over which a single 40-watt bulb burns in a chicken-wire cage.

Trude moves on. The floor slopes towards a set of twin doors, and beyond these she steps into the open again where there are cropped lawns, and murky planes, and the sun-faded silhouette of a Victorian bandstand on a dais of wood, and more oblique shadows, and rhomboid patches of light spilled from upper stories, and dim plaques that in daytime read – 'Keep Off the Grass'. Once before she had short cut this court diagonally, only to find herself in a deserted kitchen, then a laundry, then a dining area, then another kitchen, then a pantry, a closet. Now she stays close to the surrounding walls. Her pace quickens. And through another door, and through a hall, another set of swing-doors, and into another yard. Dark, bare and paved. To a fence, and alongside, and through a gap in the railings, then a full turn down a ramp of planks to the level, to the left. And more doors, in at the bottom of a stairwell, a pillar in the middle, and beneath the stairs, an entrance marked – 'Ward M (AA & DA Male)'. Trude leans her shoulder against the broad panelled timbers and a tiny wheel fitted under the outsized door on its hingeless side squeaks as it runs in its brass runner.

She enters an open-plan dormitory, a television lounge and games area at one end (including table tennis facilities), and at the other, like a jumble of transport café rejects, a missmatch of tubular steel tables and chairs. Several people (their age range indicating that they are possibly a family) are grouped round two of these tables pushed together. All at once they fall silent. And stare at Trude as if to reproach her for her unwarranted appearance. Only equally boorishly to resume their conversation, but now in somewhat subdued tones. A record is being played on a record player, which is set to play over and over – Champion Jack Dupree bemoaning the daily dose of 'ups' that 'bring him down' to the measured beat of the bounce of a ping-pong ball.

Trude takes a deep breath and starts between the tables. She is making for the central block where army surplus cots stand in serried ranks and where, amongst other inmates, Piers sits reading. As if awaiting her arrival, a man in a starched white denim jacket and blue serge trousers comes out of a small office, a cubicle behind the first of three doors on her right. 'That one with the spyhole's a padded cell,' Piers had said, with a shudder.

'Padded cell?' Trude had asked.

'For the DTs or going cold turkey,' Piers had replied.

'Cold turkey . . .' Trude had said and she too had shuddered.

The man who at first glance appears to be well into his forties but is in fact much younger, halts Trude's progress with an upturned palm and asks, 'Yes miss?'

Again Trude takes a deep breath. Her gaze rests on the single button of his jacket stretched and fastened taut across a protruding belly. 'I've come to see Piers Topf' she drawls, very, very slowly, and lifting her eyes smiles as though to congratulate herself for having managed to put the sentence together.

'I'm sorry, miss. I'm afraid that won't be possible,' replies the warder, quite affably, yet firmly.

Trude does not move. With his finger, the warder indicates for Trude to exit the way she has come. He raises his eyebrows.

'Piers!' shrieks Trude. 'PIERS!'

Everyone becomes still and all is quiet; with the exception of Champion Jack Dupree's lament and the ping-pong players who, oblivious to their surroundings, play their point to its finish. The warder takes Trude by the elbow. Gently. 'Now, miss, please . . .' he begins.

Piers has looked up from his book. He has seen Trude and the warder. He has glanced down at the page number to memorise his place. He drops the book on to his pillow and gets to his feet, uncoiling himself to his full height. In his mid twenties, he is exceptionally tall and greyhound thin. His thick auburn hair, parted in the middle, hangs in long, natural ringlets as cavalier as any regal wig of the seventeenth century, giving substance to his otherwise thanatoidal face. Slovenly and loose-limbed, he's slouching forward, shouting, 'Let it be, Rudi! Let it be!'

133

'I can't, Piers,' Rudolf snaps, 'just look at her, eh . . . Man.'

'I see her, *man*. So let her be. Ah?' Though his demeanour is pervaded by indifference, his voice carries a certain edge, perhaps as if owning up to a barely disguised plea.

'She's out of her skull, Piers . . . man, and you know it. I can't risk it . . . Man.'

'Fuckin' Nazi screw,' Trude mumbles as, with exaggerated force, she wrenches her arm free and almost loses her balance. Piers holds out his hand to steady her. He towers head and shoulders above both Rudolf and the woman, but there is no menace to his stance, no outward suggestion of any brewing violence. Nonetheless Helmut, Rudolf's shift-mate, shows his concern by coming to lean at the open door of their shared office, casually to observe and, if need be, lend support both moral and practical. Rudolf's liking for wurst washed down with jugs of beer has rendered him overweight and altogether generically round. He has a round face embedded in a double-chinned, round head, which is set on top of rounded shoulders. His tortoiseshell spectacles are round and perched on a snubbed nose. A round paunch surmounts round knees and even his highly polished shoes are round-toed. It would be hard not to assume that Rudolf is unfit, that if push came to shove he would be of little use in any physical confrontation.

'Oh come on, Rudi,' Piers continues, 'come on, *man*, let her stay, just for a few minutes, just long enough to split a straight. Okay, *man*.' And he tosses his head. His auburn curls fan up and out from side-to-side, tumble and cascade to settle as before.

'Split what?' queries Rudolf, keeping his voice down and running his fingers through his closely cropped hair. It somewhat disconcerts him to have to ask the question because he believes himself to be totally *au fait* with the latest jive and hip talk of the drug addicts and the alcoholics in his care. By keeping abreast of their slang Rudolf wants to make it plain that he is not an outsider, the enemy, but someone who can empathise with the plight of his charges, hoping thus to gain their confidence and even in part

134

to contribute to their rehabilitation. He firmly believes that they are incarcerated for their own benefit.

'Hear that, Trudi babe, the dude don't dig straight,' says Piers, adding volume as he speaks, fully aware that even the slightest display of ignorance will have Rudolf feel belittled in the eyes of the ward, all of whom are now watching the exchange with undisguised interest.

'He done flipped his groove,' Trude giggles.

'All right, all right . . . cool, man, cool it,' says Rudolf, softly, patting the air at his sides as if to calm a potentially explosive situation.

'A straight,' Piers continues loudly, 'you know *man*, a declassified narcotic.' He demonstratively sucks air in through pursed lips. And exhaling, 'A straight, man . . . a snout, a fag—'

'A tab, a gasper . . .' is Trude's butt in.

'A doofer, Rudi *man*, a common or garden *cigarette*. Man.' And Piers chuckles. He winks at Trude and playfully punches Rudolf on the shoulder. He calls, 'Hi!' at the perplexed family of faces around the two tables. They sit like an audience rented for the occasion, not knowing what is expected of them, unsure what to do next, as without further ado Piers turns and slouches off.

'See ya, Piers!' shouts Trude, and in imitation of Piers nonchalantly accepts defeat. Rudlof escorts her to the exit.

Without a backward glance Piers has lifted his arm into the air and waved a clenched fist. On his return to his cot he sits, takes papers and tobacco from his locker and begins to roll a cigarette. Helmut resumes his place at his desk, once more to leaf through a magazine. Nonetheless, he has left the office door wide open. And having seen Trude off the immediate premises and having locked the door behind her, Rudolf is now making his way towards Piers. And Piers grins, amused by the notion of Rudolf's mental processes, all those grey cells computing to memory '. . . straight equals cigarette . . . straight equals cigarette . . . straight equals . . .'

'At least the poor bugger's trying,' thinks Piers, and chortles to himself.

At the foot of the bed Rudolf waits for Piers to put a match to the strands of tobacco, which hang from the end of the crude paper cylinder. He speaks, 'Piers, I couldn't let her stay, you know that, man. It's for your own good . . . Man.'

'Sure, Rudi, my own good, *man.*'

'Come on there's no need to be like that . . .'

'Like what?'

'Less of the sarcasm, eh, man?'

'It wouldn't have hurt none to have let her stay for a minute or two.'

'More than my job's worth.'

Piers barks out a curt laugh, and, 'Right on, man! I've always wanted to hear a jobsworth say that! Brill.' Again the curt laugh.

'Yeah, yeah,' says Rudolf. 'Anyway visiting time's almost over.'

'My point exactly,' Piers replies.

Rudolf pretends not to hear and glances at his watch. 'So, what're you reading?'

Piers holds up a copy of Kesey's *One Flew Over the Cuckoo's Nest.* (Everybody on the ward has a copy whether they're reading it or not and it's always ostentatiously on display.) Rudolf has nevertheless already seen the title of the book Piers is actually reading. *The Consolation of Boethius: A Prelude to Medieval Monasticism.* The week before last it was *Cybernetics and Serendipity in Quantum Theory.*

'Okay, genius,' he says.

Gunter-the-Gimp intrudes on them, saying, 'How about a few frames, Rudi?' He has hobbled over from the pool table where he spends most of his waking hours.

'Sure. Why not . . . man,' replies Rudolf.

As a child Gunter suffered from polio and consequently wears a surgical boot on his left foot and an iron brace on his leg. He is utterly indifferent about being referred to as a spastic or even Gunter-the-Gimp (albeit not always affectionately), but is more than capable of throwing a raucous tantrum when shown understanding or sympathy or, heaven forfend, pity. He can be likewise equally riled by offers of assistance for which he has not asked. He has not lost a single game of pool for over four weeks and Konrad Pöhl, his most recent and persistent opponent, has obviously grown tired of being beaten.

'Come on, man, rack 'em up,' says Rudolf, placing his arm about Gunter's shoulders, 'and let me have a shot at breaking that winning streak of yours.'

'Fat chance,' is Gunter's boast.

Piers stares at the retreating pair. And all at once, 'Hey Rudi!' he cries, 'okay by you if I take a stroll later?'

'The f . . . !' and atypically throwing caution to the wind, 'The fuck it is!' he says with a snarl.

A hoarse laugh. Piers sucks at his roll-up. It has gone out.

And as if out of nowhere Otto Muntz materialises at Pier's side, a cigarette lighter in his outstretched hand. Forever dressed in pyjamas beneath a dressing-gown of flocked wallpaper design that could be a hand-me-down from a grandfather, and wearing an embroidered toque and Blackamoor slippers of Moroccan leather, he tends to sashay about like a benign Dickensian spectre, silently. Since he spends the best part of the each day locked in a toilet stall, he has missed Trude's arrival and departure and so, 'What's been going down?' he asks.

'Trudi came by, but Santa's Little Foglight wouldn't let her stay,' Piers explains.

'So we'll be taking a stroll later?'

'Chance would be a fine thing.'

'Bombed was she then?'

'You could say that.'

'Who wouldn't let her stay?'

'Rudi.'

'What did you call him?'

By way of answer Piers starts to hum 'Rudolf the Red-Nosed Reindeer'.

'Cool it, man, that Santa shit really, *but really* gets my goat.'
And as if for emphasis, Otto begins to grind his lower jaw laterally, slalom fashion, with the irregular monotony of a broken metronome. He is already a compulsive yawner, but this new habit is fast taking on the characteristics of a permanent affliction, somehow serving to accentuate the swarthiness of his countenance – a Mediterranean gigolo forever at war with the five o'clock shadow that rises over his sunken cheeks.

'Otto, babe, don't tell me you don't believe in Santa Claus . . .' Piers gibes. Otto's facial contortions are fast becoming as obtrusive and disconcerting as an unseemly nervous tic. As tiresome and irksome as his frequent *non sequiturs*.

'Piss off, Piers!' and yawning, '. . . it's not that, it's just so friggin' predictably American.'

'What is?'

'Well they invented it . . .'

'What? Christmas?'

'No . . . Santa.'

'What's in your bag, man?'

'I don't mean our dear old Saint Nicholas or even the Englishman's Father Christmas.' Again a yawn. 'I mean that fat, obese git with the friggin' white whiskers, the alchi's nose, in that stupid red hat, that stupid red suit with those silly friggin' black jackboots.' A token jut of the jaw and, 'It was Coca-Cola or some such that came up with that little gem . . . as a friggin' advertising gimmick would you believe!'

'So . . . ?'

'So they called it Santa Claus . . .' A yawn. He has long ago abandoned shielding his mouth behind his hand.

'And?'

'And Santa is feminine, while Claus is short for Nikolaus, which is masculine. So they created a fucking *hermaphrodite*, that's what *and* . . . ?' And yet another yawn followed by, 'I mean you can have a Santa Barbara, a Santa Ana, a Santa Maria, a Santa Lucia, a Santa Monica–'

'Cool, I dig.'

'D'you know you can drive from Montreal to Chicago without going through a single set of traffic lights . . .'

'Is that so?'

'Or you can have a San Diego, because San is masculine, a San Pedro if you like, a San Damiano, San Francisco, San Marco–'

'San José, San Juan–'

'Right on, but . . . *but* you can't have a *Santa* Claus.'

'But there ain't no Sanity Clause . . .' says Piers in English and with a smirk, the Teutonic accent of popular ridicule much exaggerated.

'Of course there ain't, what!'

'Marx Brothers . . .'

'Oh yes, neat, very neat. D'you have a copy of *Mein Kampf* that I could borrow?

'What?'

'Oh brill, that's just brill.'

'What is?'

'Sanity Clause . . .' says Otto in echoes of parody. Again a spectacular yawn. 'And don't tell me it was some sort of pre-emptive gesture towards feminism and equality and all that crap, 'cause old bollock chops there appeared at the end of the friggin' nineteenth century when universal friggin' suffrage was no more than a twinkle in the blink of an eye . . .'

'You could put it that way . . .'

'Perhaps it was *Das Kapital?*' A thoughtful pump of the jaw. Then, 'Anyway, it's just another friggin' archetypal example of American pig-ignorance and I need a dump.' Thus with a final yawn, muttering, 'Sanity Clause, that's neat, man, that's *real* neat . . .' Otto Muntz glides away towards the shower rooms, from behind looking every inch a Pasha. Perhaps this is no fanciful coincidence for his exploits and forays into the drug markets of Istanbul have long since earned him the sobriquet 'Turk', though for many the tag 'The Otto-*Mann*' tells it all.

139

With a sigh, Piers squashes the stub of his cigarette into the jar lid that serves as an ashtray. He puts his hands deep into his pockets. In the left he fingers the silver foil-wrapped pellet that Trude slipped into his palm when he reached out to steady her as she seemingly tottered on her ridiculously high platform shoes. It is not much larger than a cherry stone, but will suffice for a reasonable joint or two. He glances towards the games area where, accompanied by Konrad's impersonations of a popular sports commentator, Gunter-the-Gimp is giving Rudi a merciless thrashing at pool. It seems unlikely that Rudi and Helmut have it in mind to launch a surprise inspection tonight, a private and personal locker search, but then one can never be sure. In as much as it's far better to be safe than sorry, and using just one hand, Piers begins to peel away the silver foil with the pellet still in his pocket. Once he has it unwrapped, he swiftly pops it into his mouth and lodges it comfortably under his tongue. Hoisting his legs and lying back, his feet dangling over the end of his cot, he stretches himself out and clasps his hands behind his head. He begins to suck surreptitiously, swallowing as unobtrusively as possible. His mouth is soon awash with the familiar taste of hash, and, smiling contentedly, he gives himself over to one of his currently favourite pastimes, that of ceiling gazing.

Again she stands at the now wide open door. It's the young woman who had briefly paused and peeked in earlier, while Gustav was still out and about. Somewhat ill at ease, she shifts her weight from foot to foot. Her impractical shoes look as if they were made for anything but walking, their design being modelled on the jaded memory of a discomforted cartoon mouse. She is dressed in a much-mended leather jacket, a mauve turtle-neck sweater and flared jeans. She is slender and fragile, and seems rather tired. Her hair, once dyed to the colour of apricots, is tousled and in need of a wash. Rat-tailed slivers of a fringe drape her brow and hang into her lacklustre eyes. She watches Gustav attentively.

He on the other hand is peering at the golf-ball typewriter on the tea table at the centre of the room; his gaze like that of an entomologist examining an as yet unclassified specimen freshly pinned to a card. 'Ever seen one these, Heini?' he enquires of the vacant bed furthest from the one on which Alexis F lies curled up under a coarse woollen blanket. 'Nah, din think you 'ad. It's okay though, Heini, it dun do nobody no 'arm.'

Gustav strokes the leaden bristles on his chin. He has his head cocked to one side, not unlike a parrot; and he is listening intently lest he be asked to repeat what he has heard. Then after a while, 'Yeah, good night, Heini,' he says. 'Sleep tight an don't let the bugs bite.'

Gustav shuffles over to the next bed.

'Whato, Skipper,' he says to the bare mattress. ''Ow's the foot? Oh glad to hear it, mate, glad to hear it. Well they'll 'ave ye back on the briny afore ye can ring six bells or what 'ave you, eh?' A pause for a reply that only Gustav can hear, followed by, 'Oh, by the way, I saw yer landlady at the Kellerhoff the other night, she's mindin' yer fish an was askin' after ye. Wants to know when yer comin' 'ome. She's a real good woman that un. I told 'er you was shipshape and would be splashin' about in next to no time. Bought 'er a small beer I did . . .' Pause. 'Sure, you get some shuteye.' Then a prolonged unintelligible murmur that tails off into a muttered 'Good night,' and finally, 'I'll see to it, don't you fret none. Pleasant dreams, Skipper.'

And so on and so on; to natter at length and in rota with seven empty beds, one of which is perhaps designated as his own. An apt change of manner, an immediate change of voice and a bespoke accent customised for each new interlocutor, ever culminating with a friendly whisper, a reassuring, 'Don't fret none now!' or, 'Never fear!'

To have reached Alexis F.

'Well, Herr Bruno, my dear fellow! How are you faring this bitter autumnal night?' Gustav is addressing only those visible patches and corners of the pillow on which Alexis is resting his head and under which he has folded his forearm. 'Sorry about this inconvenience of having to double-bunk, but we've kind of got a squeeze on space as they say, what! Believe you me I'll have it properly organised in a jiffy. You watch, once I've done, the powers-that-be won't know what has hit them and they'll definitely be sitting up and begging. I'll have it well and truly fixed just as soon as is humanly possible . . . Yes, of course, somebody screwed up on the job again, that's all. Sure, you know, bureaucracy . . . same the whole world over . . . No, it certainly won't occur again, not on my watch. Now I trust you have enough room. Good, that's the show, jolly good. Incidentally . . . the lads and I are all agreed that it'll be perfectly all right for you, er, to, er, dispatch the, er, the pretender shall we say. The odd kick perhaps . . . a little shove, or a nudge. If he complains we'll jump him. A swift jab to the kidneys, what . . . that should do the trick, eh? Or maybe one or two swift ones in the ribs, that should guarantee him a transfer, wouldn't you say, eh? Do the best you can meanwhile. That's the ticket. You're a scholar and a gentleman, Herr Bruno. Yes, and thank you, Herr Bruno . . . and a very good night to you, sir.'

Thus, having done his rounds, Gustav sidles over towards Trude. Neither registering nor acknowledging her presence, he looks right through her as he shuts the door in her face. She nonetheless continues to peep through its upper glazed portion, all but pressing her cheek to the pane.

Gustav takes off his jacket. With the back of his hand he flicks and brushes non-existent lint and fluff from the threadbare sleeves, from the shiny lapels and from the misshapen shoulders. He folds the jacket exactly, lays it carefully on the floor, and turns out the light. He lies down, his jacket beneath his head. And he sleeps.

A short while later Alexis F uncoils himself from his foetal position and gets up, unsteadily, as if over sedated. He switches on the feeble light and cautiously steps over the sleeping body of an old man lying like some medieval servant across the door. Alexis pushes the door open. There is no one outside. Alexis makes his way along this indifferent corridor of green and ochre paint to the equally indifferent white-tiled washrooms. He urinates. From a dripping brass tap he splashes and pats cold water over his cheeks, but does not dry them. He returns to the octagonal room, climbs back into his bed and covers himself with a coarse woollen blanket. Prostrate, Gustav is snoring.

Just bellow the spire there's a clock in the tower of the neo-Gothic church that stands nearby. All four of its faces are illuminated. One of these shines through the uncurtained windows of the octagonal room and, despite his medication, prevents Alexis from drifting back into the cosiness of dreamless slumber.

Trude sits in a back pew of the church. She is feeling its darkness. She is feeling its stillness. Now and again, she shivers.

'Fuckin' Nazi screw!' she mouths, and wonders what's keeping Piers.

Without invitation Piers enters the room and immediately lowers himself into the chair opposite Dr Meyerstein. He sits erect, facing her across her stately desk. It is a chunky, old-fashioned piece of furniture in the solid style of a Biedermeier and its large surface, covered with files and folders of diverse colours, with notebooks, jotters and notepads, spiked memos written in a spidery script on torn scraps of paper and the insides of empty cigarette wrappers, with ball-point pens and pencils in a plastic tray, and with a sharp letter opener and a black Bakelite telephone that has not only a dial, but rows of tiny silver buttons and lights that undoubtedly flash, lies all of a clutter in apparent disorder and disarray. Dr Meyerstein has not looked up. She merely continues to study the buff-bound file that she holds in her hand. Occasionally she scribbles a note in the margin.

Piers picks up a pencil and a small schoolboys' pencil-sharpener, which he finds beside a snowstorm paperweight. Making sure that the shavings will fall into an ashtray of unused staples, he hones the lead to a meticulously fine point. It will at once break on use. He finds another pencil and begins to repeat the process.

143

When this too is sharpened to his satisfaction, he blows on the tip and, 'I hate the fuzz,' he announces, offhandedly. 'All of them, without fault or favour.'

There's a pause during which the doctor regards her patient over her half-moon reading glasses and appears to give him her full attention, though she does not put the file aside.

'When I was six years old,' Piers continues, 'the headmaster summoned me to his office. I had been reported for lifting the covers, those little round gratings,' and here Piers indicates their size with a spread of his fingers, 'those lids on top of the water hydrants that you find tucked away in some suburban gardens, usually by the front gate. And I'd been stuffing them full of leaves. It was autumn . . . this time of year in fact. I suppose I had been tidying up . . . Anyway, as I stood there on the headmaster's carpet, all scuffed boots and grazed knees, I kept asking myself – Why am I here, what have I done wrong?

'Besides the headmaster, there were two other men in that study, both of them in uniform, both of them standing, looming over me. For some time they just stared, until I thought I might pee myself. Then quite suddenly one of them pulled out his truncheon and began tapping it under my chin. "We've ways of dealing with guttersnipes snipes like you!" he snarled. His partner chuckled . . .'

Piers pauses while he selects yet another pencil.

'And before my eyes, that club, that cudgel grew, like Pinocchio's nose, till it was about two metres long. Dumb bastard! So stupid and dim-witted of him, eh? Eh . . . wouldn't you agree, Fräulein Klapsdoktor?'

Dr Meyerstein gently clears her throat. She continues to regard Piers over the gold-wire rims of her spectacles. But she makes no reply.

Instead, Piers says, 'I suffer from an inferiority complex rooted in the firm belief that I was deserted by my family . . . abandoned . . . unloved, even though we all lived 'happily' under the one roof and I was never cold, naked or hungry . . . There are many instances I could cite from my past that would confirm . . . but then again, always, always my personal interpretations have been misconstrued, have been totally wrong. Today I know what was really happening, the actual nature of the circumstances . . . and I understand . . . I accept and I can cope. And yet I've done . . . no better still . . . *do* outrageous things to attract attention to myself. Things to hurt . . .

'I have more convictions for theft and well, let's say petty civil disobedience and other misdemeanours, than your archetypal social misfit or even psychopath. Could I not be a master criminal? Definitely. Does not my IQ testify to that? Definitely. Well? Mmm? But then perhaps I *need* to be busted? You can cure me though, Doktor, can't you? What, you with your philosophies and systems of cause and effect . . . with your retrogressive therapies . . . sure you can . . . Go on, say you can . . .'

Dr Meyerstein gives Piers a broad, enchanting grin. She makes as though to shrug her shoulders. But Piers has already gone from the room.

In his place the head orderly's barrel-chested form fills the door frame. He raps on the jamb with his knuckles.

'Yes, do come in, Herr Holtzer.'

'Morning, *gnädige* Frau. Has Topf been bothering you?'

'Who Piers? No, he merely pops in every now and again with a routine reminder that I'm an incompetent failure . . . not to mention the rest of my profession.'

'I'll have Rudolf, Herr Dorfbaum that is, have a word and keep a closer eye on him.'

'There's no need, Holtzer. It is, after all, my doing that we have an open door policy and this is not a prison camp, nor a cage, and Piers is no animal. In fact he could be right . . . up to a point that is, but don't tell him I said so . . . Anyway, that's not what I want to discuss with you.'

The doctor gives the file she has been holding a final glance. Then: 'Holtzer this new patient, he's in Ward C, in with Gustav right?' Holtzer nods, saying, 'Yes, Frau Doktor,' even though Dr

Meyerstein is clearly not expecting a response. She merely carries on as if delivering a lecture, albeit ill-prepared or poorly researched, but being too enamoured of the sound of her own voice she doesn't seem to care.

'Now to briefly recap, so we all know where we are . . . he was picked up on the streets . . . yet another of the city's homeless vagrants . . . but this one had perceptibly neither slept nor eaten for a matter of days, if perhaps not weeks. He appeared to be literally dead on his feet, in a trance and all but comatose. Of course with their usual perspicacity and insight the police immediately suspected some sort of narcosis and had him dumped on the nearest Accident and Emergency unit, where it soon became obvious this was not the case . . . no drug abuse or other dependency, not even diabetes.

'So then alongside the authorities, various organisations and charities and obscure suchlike started to take an unusual interest because, believe it or not, he is, or was, some kind of minor celebrity. But all anybody really did was shunt him around until lo and behold he is landed in our lap . . . you see, basically he refuses to speak, to communicate in any way whatsoever . . .

'Nonetheless, my gut feeling is that he's shamming. He's been well watered and fed now and looked after, even pampered some might say, and he is physically robust, in far better shape than might be expected . . . given the state he was found in . . . Anyway, I contend his stupor, his probable amnesia, his loss of vocal ability to be pure and simple make-believe. He's acting. Clever . . . but acting.

'What's more, I've just been checking again through the written tests he was given and which he saw fit to complete, after a fashion; and quite frankly they tend to support my suppositions. However − there's always a however isn't there, Holtzer − in my opinion his answers are for the most part considered and contrived, the personal details he has supplied just don't tally with information that's come to light from other sources, or been gleaned from the documents found in his possession, right down to his name, or names. Oddly enough he's a DP−'

'A Displaced Person, *gnädige* Frau . . .'

'Yes, you'd think this long after the War they'd have all been relocated and settled down, those of European origin I mean . . . and politics permitting. Still, we can surmise that he's stateless, but at the same time a British resident, according to the travel document issued by their Home Office that is. Visas and immigration stamps indicate that he's a bit of a gypsy – Italy, France, Spain, Greece, not to mention the USA and Canada. Makes you wonder what brought him here . . . Anyway, he's also some sort of poet, a pioneer of abstract expressionism in verse, or so I'm told, whatever that is when it's at home. I've never seen or heard of any of his stuff, but I shall be trying to lay my hands on anything and everything that's available in print, though that's by-the-by . . .'

'Dr Pritzelwitz has proposed a typewriter be made available to him as a preliminary step towards perhaps undermining or unlocking what he likes to term "the blockade", not that he and I . . . anyway that needn't concern you. What I'd like of you, Herr Holtzer, is in a sense the standard liaison programme, lots and lots of free association, inter-personal group activity. Rudolf Dorfbaum and Helmut Kohler are very good on that score as are Grüber and what's his name . . .'

'Hans Freiden, Doktor . . .'

'Right, Gerhardt Grüber and Hans Freiden, that's the ticket, excellent, excellent . . . There's possibly a very thick layer of ice to be broken so let's see if we can't get some response, anything . . . Get Gustav on your side, he's a regular chatterbox, and tell him whatever tale you like. Get him to be friendly . . . after all, as far as we can gather our mystery man has no chums or relatives, and so on and so forth that we could turn to, so . . . Sooner or later he's going to slip up, or slip out of his shell, should I say, and I want to be there to have him when it happens . . .'

The doctor has shut the file and places it on a pile of similar buff folders.

'Well that's about it, Holtzer. Oh and Holtzer . . . there's just one other thing . . . how shall I put it . . . it's, er, his appearance . . .' and with the long, red-varnished nail of her forefinger, she taps the file several times in rapid succession.

'Yes, Dr Meyerstein, I've—'

'Oh you know. Good, that's fine then, Holtzer . . . good, good.'

It is then that she realises that Piers has misappropriated three of her pencils.

Piers makes his way to the church on the traffic island. Nobody watches him and nobody sees him enter through the west door. The church is empty, as usual. Piers steps crabwise into a rear pew constructed of crude timber, as if by an apprentice carpenter during therapy sessions. Sitting, facing a simple altar of stone adorned with no more than a plain cross of brass, he runs his fingertips along and beneath the narrow gap where the seat presumably once abutted the backrest, but has since shrunk or become warped. There he finds a small gift. It's the size of a flattened stock cube, carefully wrapped in silver foil. 'Bless you, Trude,' he mutters as he prises it from the wad of chewing-gum that holds it in its hiding place.

A cleaner, bucket and mop all a-clatter, comes into the church. Piers leaps up like some highly sprung jack-in-the-box, his hair flying in all directions. His hands spread wide, his thumbs at his temples, he's waggling his fingers and shouting, 'I'm a loon! I'm a loon! I'm a loon!'

The cleaner takes no notice. Piers skips away still keeping up his chant, 'I'm a loon! I'm a loon!' past a second cleaner who equally takes no notice. He scurries off towards the laundry where Gunter-the-Gimp will no doubt be fretting while waiting by their cart – a sort of canvas sack slung from a steel framework mounted on casters – emptied and readied for the collecting of dirty linen on their tour of assigned wards.

'Where you been?' asks Gunter.

'Comin',' Piers replies.

Gunter smiles knowingly. He hoists his trussed leg on to a cross-member of the trolley's chassis. On the other side, Piers does likewise and together they scoot along. Gunter rides more than he pushes. Piers pretends not to notice.

They drive through passages. Along corridors. In and out of wards. Clanging, clashing, smashing into walls, howling obscenities. And the ubiquitous: 'I'm a loon! I'm a loon!'

Cursing, inmates move aside.

Every day, three times a day, a woman brings Alexis his meals. Her arrival is heralded by the rattles and rumbles and squeaks of solid rubber wheels on bare crazed concrete, noises presumably made by her mobile canteen, which she leaves outside in the corridor. She brings the food in on a circular plastic tray and this she sets down on Alexis F's bedside locker. In less than half an hour she will return and clear away the used crockery to replace it with a mug of strong, already sweetened tea. She wears a blue, nylon pinafore of sorts and a paper-net cap perched high on her head. She neither speaks nor smiles. Were it not for the hump on her back it would be difficult to know for certain that it is the same woman every day. Nonetheless, it is also comforting to know that Alexis is allowed the use of ordinary cutlery.

And nothing continues to happen.

And for hours on end Alexis sees no one.

Once, a man who introduced himself as Dr Pritzlewitz came to visit. From the way wayward strands lie about his collar and shoulders, it is obvious that he is losing his hair rapidly and the length and cut of what is left gives the impression that he is unable to decide whether to ignore this premature baldness or disguise it with a comb-over. Under one arm he carried a ream of typing paper, under the other, the latest model IBM golf-ball typewriter. These he deposited on the table at the centre of the room and encouraged Alexis to help himself, adding that one never knew when 'The Muse' would strike and that being prepared is more than just the preserve of Boy Scouts. Then he spoke a little about nothing in particular, sounding knowledgeable; patted

Alexis on the knee and assured him that everything would be all right. Then he left. Left Alexis to gape through a window at a Victorian bandstand.

A week or so later, perhaps even longer, a woman who introduces herself as Dr Meyerstein comes to visit. She of the persuasive, matronly ilk whose body seems to have been cobbled together from parts belonging to at least two different people. Her upper torso is not unduly slender, nor is she unduly flat-chested, but she does have an extremely narrow waist, which without warning as it were, flares into very broad hips, fleshy buttocks and fleshy thighs. Her ankles on the other hand look dangerously thin, as does her mouth, which is painted a plush red to match her nails. Her hair, streaked with overt grey, is an unruly mop of natural tresses and twirls, like a Byzantine halo in need of restoration, all willy-nilly bunched about an angular face. Were it not for her haughtiness and that she is well into her late thirties or early forties, she might be accused of pandering to a juvenile form of inverted racism and sporting an Afro.

There are black lead and blue biro smears above the breast pocket of her white lab coat, which she wears unbuttoned and which streams and flaps behind her wherever and whenever she goes about her business, always at a pace and urgently. The abrasive edge that hallmarks her demeanour is clearly demonstrated by the tendency she has of talking at, rather than to, people. So when she visits, she lectures Alexis mercilessly, as if only a fool could construe her words to be anything but music and solace to his ears. Moreover, she is determined to make him well.

Then within two days and at all hours there came a veritable troop of visitors who turned up like a company of strolling players, each making a noteworthy entrance and each cast in many diverse roles. First there was the chief orderly, Herr Manfred Holtzer, an upright and broad-framed man. He is clean and close shaven and has large ears and a vulture-like profile, which is topped off with a wiry mane that shows frequent short-back-n-

150

sides clipping and is meticulously parted and brilliantined. He wears eau-de-Cologne. His tie, striped in imitation of some regimental design, is knotted tightly and symmetrically. His shirt collar and cuffs have been starched with deliberation. His hands are manicured and his shoes polished to a military shine. All in all he has the bearing and the manner of an NCO; one who kowtows in the presence of officers and superiors, who pays lip-service to their orders and demands, but then does precisely as he pleases, acting in accordance with his own perceptions of what is what and how things should or need to be done; which may or may not coincide with his instructions.

Those who follow Herr Holtzer appear as in a rota, recurrently and in swift succession, so that Alexis still has difficulties matching faces to names with any degree of confidence; apart from Gerhart Grüber that is, whose grace and physique remind Alexis of the studied poise of a ballet dancer or perhaps a matador. Yet whoever they are and whatever they look like, each comes with one aim in mind, and that is to befriend Alexis, to make him welcome at St Anslem's (affectionately referred to as Sami's), to become his confidante. And to that end they propose getting together, one-on-one or in groups large and small, for a variety of recreational activities – board games such as snakes and ladders, ludo, Monopoly and backgammon; though so far no mention has been made of chess. Then there's bridge and canasta, darts, ping-pong and pool. A tiddly-winks tournament had also been suggested, but was immediately pooh-poohed as ridiculously English. Somebody else put forward the idea of forming a glee club, or possibly a barbers' shop quartet. Even Gustav, though far from sociable, has ceased trying to eject Alexis from his own bed and no longer berates him when chatting to his imaginary friends.

And throughout, in impassive and preferred silence, Alexis finds it all very amusing, if somewhat irritating.

Day succeeds day.
To become another day.

And then another. The one that brings the grating squeal of misaligned, unoiled castors speeding across the courtyard towards the building, towards the octagonal Ward C that some call the Chapter House. And the two young men riding a laundry cart, hanging on either side, steering by shifting their centres of gravity, leaning this way and that as motorcycle outriders do or as yachtsmen, tacking, veering, safely to round the bandstand, heading for the swing-doors. To be out of sight when all at once a reverberating crash resounds in the halls, when the walls shake, the doors jolt and the windows shudder; and when Alexis steps into the corridor, at last curious enough to see what has happened.

The cart lies overturned. Dirty sheets and soiled blankets have spilled into a heap beside it. Snarled up in these, there's a visible forearm and the exceptionally long legs of someone flailing and flapping in a desultory attempt to disentangle himself; and kicking, uselessly lashing out as he guffaws a histrionic guffaw; while standing next to him his co-driver, a teenager wearing a leg-iron, shifts his weight from toe to heel and flutters his hands in agitation, already forestalling the would-be reactions of the warders. 'We'll get done for this, Piers, man,' he's saying, dismayed, 'no appeal, and no blood or urine tests either!'

Eventually the tall man is up. Together they right the cart, which seems to have suffered no major mishap, and having refilled it, start off in Alexis F's direction, bouncing from wall to wall as they manoeuvre it into Ward C.

'I'm a loon!' yells the lanky one as they pass.

Alexis follows them.

'Gustav's not here,' says the cripple. 'Let's nick a couple of beds.'

'No,' is the emphatic answer, and turning to Alexis, 'You in here?' He looks Alexis directly in the face and squarely in the eye.

Alexis nods.

'Which is your pit?'

Alexis points; needlessly because only two beds in the room are made up.

The boys strip the bedding and throw it into their over-stuffed buggy.

'Got a cigarette then, squire?' the tall one is asking. His tone has completely altered. Its quality and its pitch have become quite different.

Alexis offers him his pack.

'Thanks,' spoken almost as an afterthought.

He lights a cigarette, then passes the pack to the cripple, saying, 'This is Gunter . . . my name's Piers and nobody, *but nobody* calls me Lofty, right . . .' He inhales deeply, then, 'So what's your problem?' Pause. 'No don't tell me, you hear voices, right . . . You know it's amazing how many people in this place end up in the Chapter House just because they're forever gossiping with unseen chums.'

Smoke trickles from Piers' nostrils. 'D'you know why they call it the Chapter House?' he continues. 'Well it's because in the Middle Ages that was the only place in a monastery where the monks could discuss things freely, air their grievances and rabbit on to their hearts' content.'

'No. I don't hear voices,' Alexis replies softly, forming the words slowly, articulately.

'Oh you will . . . you will.'

Piers and his companion exchange grins. They mount their cart and, with a parting 'I'm a loo-oooon!' they scoot away through the open door.

Of those who in their many varied guises have invited if not his affections then his companionship, or have pandered to his passiveness and to his ambivalent lack of demands, or have encouraged, cajoled and lectured in order to precipitate some sort of response, all, unequivocally, have failed to penetrate his insouciant inertness. Nor has any one of them ever suggested taking a simple walk. Neither has it been mentioned or even hinted at that any restrictions might apply to his movements. So, strictly within the confines of the grounds, Alexis F has taken it upon himself to come and go just as he pleases.

To begin with he would stray no further than the swing-doors that seal off the corridor. Then, out. Then past the bandstand and across the yard to other sections of the complex. Then to other courtyards. Then as far as the playing fields, there sometimes to linger and watch whatever manly, therapeutic games were in progress. Until finally he would venture much further afield, over unkempt parklands, uphill through the ferns and onwards to the copse of yews and elms where once he startled, and was in return startled by a brace of pheasants. And beyond, like a rambler, on this exceptionally mild morning in late November, he is strolling along wooded trails, the very act of walking having become a backdrop shift to his solitude, an excuse for exercise spent in the ever present hope of bumping into Piers.

Theirs is a singular bond of vying polarities and as powerful in attraction as it is in repulsion. They are as inseparable opposites, oddly equal; constant and consistent, like that flood of adrenalin into the stomach, which gives rise to an affinity commensurate with the fear of rejection. And always they meet by chance and unobserved. It is not that these meetings are intentionally clandestine, they merely happen to occur when both are out and about alone. Happily to share lengthy silences. (The fact that Alexis actually spoke at their first encounter went no further, but somehow the significance of those few words did not escape Piers and the matter took on the aspect of a delicate secret never to be alluded to again.) Only to embark on urgent conversations in sudden bursts, like the breaking of a dam or the lifting of a curse. They've spoken much of themselves, though Alexis feels that one way or another he has disclosed nothing. In contrast, Piers is alarmingly frank, his addiction to heroin a permanent shadow cast over everything else.

'. . . you know, the sensation of the spike penetrating the skin, the pump of the gear into the vein . . .'

154

'That's pleasant!' Alexis is genuinely amazed.

'Yeah, sure! To be honest, squire, I think it's what I miss most. And that's odd because I have a thing about flesh. It takes a hell of a lot for me to touch anybody . . . sometimes even a woman I fancy . . .'

Alexis looks at him askance. So by way of explanation Piers offers, 'You see I fundamentally don't buy into all that Descartes crap. Thinking is the one thing that truly prevents me from being, from being myself, being in touch with myself, the "therefore I am" bit. Now H . . . heroin not only gives me a tremendous buzz and a sense of limitless well-being, but stops me from thinking. Ergo, let's all get stoned and stay that way . . . for ever . . .

'I mean, don't you ever feel like just flying away and never . . . never coming back . . . ?'

Alexis pulls what is supposed to pass as a wry face, as if seriously to consider this blatantly rhetorical question. Then, 'You mean a quick boost in the arm so you'll just think lovely thoughts and they will lift you up on the air.'

'Could be . . .'

'So why are you here?'

'Not by choice, squire. The trick-cyclist, the lawyers and my probation officers, oh happy family . . . they managed to blag the magistrate into believing that I was much too good to go back inside. So . . .' and in a voice from some jaded courtroom drama, '. . . *you shall be sent from this place to another place where you shall remain until such time as you are dried out.* That means four months, squire.'

'Four months?'

'The tax payers can't afford more.'

'Is that all it takes?'

'To come off? Maybe. But not here.'

'Why?'

'Attitude, squire, methods. Procedure . . . one, cold turkey in a padded cell . . . two, group therapy twice a week, or, I'm a junkie because . . . complete the sentence in under five words. Three, supervised parties on Thursday night. Men and women together, squire! That's double doubles. The lush, the pill-head of either sex hunting-the-thimble . . . never any chance of hiding-the-sausage of course . . . drinking orangeade. Another well thought out piece of intensified rehabilitation . . . And the rest of the time? You kick your heels, listen to the same half dozen records over and over, or are beguiled by films on TV so ancient that it's a real joy to get the actors' names right in some daft betting game usually devised as an aside to alleviate the boredom. There's ping-pong . . . there's pool . . . There's . . . There's you thinking about your last fix. How to get more junk smuggled in . . . same as outside . . . when you're not high you're hustling to score.'

'But what about the health service, isn't there some sort of a State programme, can't you get aid . . . can't you register like in the UK?'

'It's not enough. It's never enough. You know there's this chick in here who's a company director. She has regular board meetings in her room, oh yes, squire, if you're good they'll not only grant weekend passes but eventually give you a room of your own adjacent to the pleb ward. No slips mind! Though in the long run it'll make little difference. Soon as your four months are up, they'll do you. A nifty urine test and even if you're as clean and clear as the driven snow, it's goodbye Sami.'

'What? Falsify the result?'

'Shouldn't think they'd bother. No, no, they'll just file a report saying you've been a very bad boy, or girl . . . you refuse to co-operate or respond to treatment . . .'

'And then?'

'Then who knows . . . The outside is bad. The inside is bad. Though let me tell you one thing, squire, the answer definitely lies with the poor buggers in El 'n' Ef.

'El 'n' Ef?'

'The Lost and Found Ward, to you. This, squire, in case you haven't noticed, is an asylum, and certain mental disorders render persons dangerous, even violent. Such cases are stored in the El 'n' Ef. You know, if we've been very very naughty that's where

156

they put us. A few days in there to cool us off. Home sweet home, in amongst the lucky vegetables, the blessed and angry triffids . . .'

Yet insanity, notwithstanding its oft repeated allure, its undeniable pull as a potential way through a world of rational ills, in truth seriously frightens Piers. Of his friends and acquaintances on the ward, alcoholic or addict, he talks most gently, most fondly of Otto Muntz, the Otto-Mann whose brain damage is already extensive, whose speech in and about his ostentatious yawns is daily becoming ever more incoherent, illogical. A scholarship student at L'École de Beaux-Arts in Paris, he showed distinct promise as a sculptor and, despite his involvement in *l'événements* of 1968 (or perhaps because of it), was said to be heading for an illustrious career. But he would experiment with drugs, a little bit of this and a pinch of that, and now, barely five years on, he sits by the hour in self-caged exile beneath an antiquated cistern listening to the gurglings and burblings of water coursing through rusted pipes.

One December evening, the light all but gone, Piers and Alexis meet beside the bandstand. Without greeting or exchanging a word, they stroll off side by side until they find themselves on the main drive, heading towards the Gateway to the East. From his lodge the warder watches them approach, watches them pass by, and as he looks them up and down, he reaches for his telephone.

Piers and Alexis stand on the pavement outside. They stare at the traffic, the rapid sweep of headlamps, ever faster cars, lorries straining in an unbroken stream. They hear a shrill hoot from one of the international haulage depots opposite and see many, many people rush out of the building; a dense flow of humanity that divides here and there only to coalesce into different groups and reform in orderly queues; to board the waiting buses bound for the city centre inevitably all awash and well aglow with seasonal lights and decorations.

Together and as one Piers and Alexis about face. Apace, they

157

march, almost at a trot, back to the chapel where, without farewell or exchanging a word, they part.

After each excursion and on Alexis F's return to the Chapter House, Gustav would at once launch into his customary tirade. There had been a time when he had without warning exhibited an agreeable change of attitude, but this clearly affected, almost rehearsed amiability had lasted no more than several days and the biased harangues that had previously prevailed again became the norm as Gustav's habitual, if somewhat singular method of communication. He was simply an old man determined to be nasty. It would also be difficult to establish with any degree of certainty whether throughout the many weeks of their cohabitation Gustav ever spoke to Alexis directly or always via Herr Bruno (in a sense the perpetual spectre at the elbow), though whatever the address, it was without doubt meant to fire revulsion and nausea, and perhaps aimed solely towards pushing Alexis into seeking a transfer. Gustav, it must be understood, is trusted and for all the quirks and mental oddities that have led to his permanent institutionalisation, he is allowed, even encouraged, to do part-time work. And Gustav is employed in the morgue. It's one of the city's municipal morgues and is conveniently located on the premises of St Anslem's.

At university Alexis had frequently heard medical students discuss practical anatomy classes in an offhand, even callous manner, no doubt to safeguard their own inner sensibilities, but such insensitivities were indeed petty when compared to the perverse relish with which Gustav would describe the condition of, for example, traffic accident victims, or the sight and stench of bodies that had been recovered from burning buildings. As a pathologist's assistant, he was ever ready to indulge his ghoulish fancy by gleefully furnishing unsolicited yet concise accounts of his participation in each and every gory autopsy or post-mortem that had come his way. In his pocket he would carry a tape-measure, the kind favoured by tailors, and delighted in showing it to Alexis. From its old, fraying edges and despite its missing centimetres, he would note the height to which the blood had sprayed the dissecting room walls. Then he would accordingly angle the water-hose tripod (a device of his own invention and construction) and in his outsized gumboots set about jet-spraying down the tiles. It is after all Gustav's job to clean up. To steady limbs as they are being sawn from torsos. To label. To incinerate. Sometimes to weigh. To punctuate his morbid narratives by brandishing stolen and soiled scalpels under Alexis F's nose.

It's not that Alexis is squeamish or particularly faint-hearted, but he has never had any wish to learn in vivid and gruesome detail how a brain can be removed from the skull to leave no visible scars, nor marks on the scalp. That relatives who thereafter view the body would never suspect that this organ had been indiscriminately shoved into the stomach cavity along with the lungs, the offal and anything else that had been removed, sliced, diced and subjected to analysis. But he has listened patiently, both fascinated and repulsed. Now he listens no longer, but finds solace still in silent reverie away from the cadaverous smells that issue out of mouths.

Sunday visiting hours are from two in the afternoon till four-thirty. Piers lies on his bed. He has a belly ache. Lunch was grisly. He tries to concentrate on his book.

Shortly after two, Trude arrives. She and Piers sit at a table. They smoke cigarettes. Drink coffee. She is telling him about the outside. Who is on what. How hard it is getting gear. That gangrene is on the increase. And that everybody is out of veins into which they can inject. That communal works forerun amputations.

They have already said all they'll ever have to say to each other.

Piers nods. Smiles. Asks about some friends, but with little interest. He stubs out his cigarette on his makeshift ashtray. Takes the two-pound bar of chocolate that Trude has stolen for him and stands, saying, 'See yer!'

Trude goes.

On his bed again, Piers is reading. The same sentence for the umpteenth time. He gives up.

He plays a nervous game of ping-pong. Loses. He plays another. Loses.

'Gerhardt! Okay if I take a stroll, man?' he asks of the orderly on duty.

'Alone?'

'Why not . . .'

'Half an hour, max. Okay?'

'Right on, man . . .'

Piers saunters out of the ward. Then he breaks into a jog across the yard, then into a run along the corridors, eventually breathless to approach the roundabout. Then at a normal walking pace, checking to make sure he is unobserved, he enters the church where he climbs to the gallery.

Trude has heard him coming. She lights a joint. They share it in silence. Then she asks, 'The stuff I got you before was okay?'

'Yeah, thanks. You know, Trudi, you're a doll, you really are . . .'

'Sorry I couldn't get any . . .'

Piers shrugs. And Trude giggles showing her small, uneven teeth, which are becoming bad. She has shed her leather jacket and now crosses her arms beneath her breasts, grips her mauve sweater by the hem and peels it off over her head . She wears no bra. Piers grins. He watches her undress. She bears the remnants of a certain beauty, but even these are fast becoming lost in an ugly, angular thinness. A black and white film image of concentration camp victims flashes across Piers' mind. Nonetheless, he eases himself towards her.

Konrad Pöhl, Gunter-the-Gimp, Piers Topf; like the three wise monkeys of folklore, they are perched in a row on a wall. It stands over twice the height of an average man, is brick-built in Flemish bond and topped off with a rounded stone coping. A lot more substantial than its nearby complement (which has made of this city a notorious island surrounded by dry land), it forms part of the southern perimeter of the St Anslem's complex and overlooks a stretch of canal that in the east joins the Spree just north of Köpenick, skirts Tempelhof and flows southwards towards Potsdam. Dangling their legs in the air on the outside, they swing them back and forth from the knee. Konrad insists that they do it subconsciously to remind themselves of childhood, of a time when sitting in a normal chair their feet wouldn't touch the floor.

A solitary barge chugs past. Grey-blue fumes that match the colour of the day spurt hot and shimmer above the slender, flower-painted funnel. As one, the three men lift their palms to their temples and, spreading them like a donkey's ears, flap their fingers, crying in unison, 'I'm a loon! I'm a loon! I'm a loo . . . oooon!'

The barge owner disappears into his cabin. Konrad, saying nothing, nudges Gunter with his elbow to draw his friend's attention to Alexis who, dressed in a short, khaki duffle-coat minus the hood, is lazily approaching from the mound that houses the pheasants. As if by some atavistic instinct and on an invisible signal both Konrad and Gunter shuffle their behinds along the coping, marginally edging away from Piers. And leaning precariously, his arms at full stretch, Piers helps Alexis clamber up beside him. All four sit staring before them. All four are silent. With Alexis F's arrival the atmosphere undergoes a subtle change. In this unvoiced, down-turning frame of mind they are no longer in the mood to swing their legs. Instead they gaze at the murky water directly below, at the barge rounding the broad bend, at the young couple dawdling along the tow-path on the opposite bank; until eventually Konrad exclaims, 'Jeez I could do with a drink, man!' And he wipes the back of his hand across his lips as if drying off the taste of a beer.

'We ought to be getting back, don't you think, Herr Pöhl . . .' is Gunter's immediate response.

'You could be right there, Herr Gimp . . .'

'Would a swift game of pool or two be in order . . . ?'

'Well . . .'

'I've a real fancy to hustle Rudi.'

'Come off it he's not that daft.'

'No, I definitely think he's ripe for a bet.'

'No way.'

'You watch, I'll let you win a couple o'frames so he thinks my luck has changed, and then it's put your money where your mouth is.'

'What money?'

'How about a weekend pass for thee and me . . .'

'Man, he'll never go for it.'

'He's got the authority.'

'Sure but—'

'D'you not fancy a few beers then . . . ?'

'Yep! Right on, man,' as Konrad leaps, lands at the foot of the wall, and waits for Gunter who, scuffing the toes of his surgical boots, is cautiously inching his way to the ground. 'You comin' Piers?' he calls, as almost a postscript.

'Soon . . .'

'See ya then.'

'Yeah, see ya . . .'

Limping, the other trundling, they scramble towards the wooded knoll, heading towards the unseen playing fields. Gunter shouts, 'One of these days I'm going to scare those birds shitless!' his voice trailing on the breeze.

Across the canal the young boy and his girlfriend have drawn level with where the remaining two men sit. Piers at once sticks his thumbs up to his ears, waggles his fingers, takes a deep breath, only to relent and keep his mouth firmly shut. From the breast pocket of his windcheater he pulls out his tobacco pouch and his Rizla papers. Alexis offers him his pack of ready-mades.

'Thanks,' says Piers helping himself to a cigarette, adding, 'Don't mind that pair . . .' and he jerks his head at the receding forms of Gunter and Konrad.

'I don't.'

162

'It's because they can't figure out how to handle their embarrassment.'

'I know.'

'And I suppose that scares them.'

'I know.'

'They just don't know which way to look.'

'It's only natural.'

'It doesn't bother you?'

'No. Not any more.'

A calm silence ensues for a moment or two.

'This is Otto's,' Piers says quietly, holding up the cigarette lighter with which he has lit his cigarette. 'He bequeathed it to me . . .'

'What . . . ?'

'Otto's in El 'n' Ef,' he continues in the same subdued tone.

'Slipped up?'

'Yeah. Shit knows how he got hold of meth. It's his last though. He won't be out any more. Well, they won't keep him in there for ever . . . tomorrow he'll have a nice, peaceful corner where he can grind his teeth and yawn away the rest of his life to his heart's content.

'Oh fuck! Fuck! Fuck! Fuck! Only there are no ducks on this canal.'

The mortar between the coping stones flakes. Alexis tosses bits at the water. They make ripples.

'Look.'

Piers points to the young couple. The boy is tugging his girlfriend by the hand, urging her towards the hedgerows that border the tow-path, but she is resisting. Half-heartedly. They are gone; already out of sight in amongst the bushes and the undergrowth.

'Now there's a hang-up,' observes Alexis.

'It's going to be cold about the arse.' And Piers retightens the long woollen scarf he is wearing as his only concession to weather, which is still unusually mild. He too is gouging at the mortar with his fingers, lobbing loosened chips into the canal.

'Yeah . . . not to mention the shrunken goolies.'

'So what kind of father d'you suppose I'd make, squire? I mean what chances would a kid of mine have on "H" before air?'

'D'you mean Trudi's—'

'Pregnant? If she were, she probably wouldn't tell me.' He shrugs away the thought.

'Nice use of the subjunctive,' is the extent of Alexis F's counsel.

'It's all just walls within walls if you ask me.'

'Like one of those Russian dolls.'

'Or peeling an onion, layer by layer to try and find its heart.'

'Isn't the Glienicker bridge round here somewhere?'

'If I'm not mistaken it spans one of the Wannsee Lakes over there,' and with a limp-wristed flutter he indicates no particular direction whatsoever. 'Why, are you thinking of making a dash for the east?'

'Not really.'

'It would be a bit different I suppose . . .' He pauses and then, 'Now that lot over there have definitely got psychiatry down to a fine art.'

'Chemical euthanasia for the soul.'

'Oh nicely put, squire, nicely put.'

Piers flicks his cigarette butt aiming for the centre of the canal. It falls short.

'You know, squire, you keep saying you don't understand why I use. Truth be told it's quite quite simple. There's nothing else I can do. Here!' And from inside his jacket he pulls out a slim paperback volume, which he slaps against Alexis F's chest. Alexis holds it steady. He does not need to look to learn the book's title, nor the name of its author.

'It's out of the library . . . so don't forget to return it, will you, squire.'

'There's a library here?' Alexis makes no attempt at concealing his enthusiasm.

'Right on, squire, talk to the padre, sorry I forgot . . . you don't.'

'Don't? Don't what?'

'Talk. Mind you, if you were to be awfully good, they might even give you a job there, tending the tomes, what . . . ?' And he jumps from the wall, his hair splayed like the wimpled wings of the Daughters of Charity, down into the unkempt grass.

'Piers . . .' But then nothing.

Side by side they crest the rise where, with keys and key-chains that jangle at every step, three men garbed in white starched jackets and blue serge trousers worn under heavy trenchcoats appear as if out of nowhere. They arrange themselves in a semicircle, perhaps in readiness to physically confront Piers and Alexis who exhibit not the least intention of fleeing and whose paths are in any case thus blocked. All is at a standstill.

'Right, friends, game's over,' says Gerhardt Grüber.

'What?'

'You're nicked!' Hans Frieden exclaims with unrestrained delight. He is a short man and the exercise of authority gives him satisfaction.

Piers and Alexis are thoroughly searched, an orderly each to clasp tight the forearm. The total contents of their pockets are spilled willy-nilly into a polythene carrier bag and they are frog marched from the vicinity of the playing fields where a muddy game of rugby is in progress. Piers takes several tentative, long-legged goose-steps, but erupts into fits of laughter. 'Squire . . .' he splutters between spasms.

'Mmm?'

'Have a beautiful tomorrow.'

'Mmm?'

'And thanks in advance.' Piers thrusts out his hand, but the ever vigilant Helmut Kohler yanks it back before anybody's fingers have a chance to meet.

It has started to snow.

Her white lab coat is as ever unbuttoned, flares as she walks, and shows off the heavy cut of a fawn-checked tweed suit. Her shoes are sensible, brown and brogue-like. Invariably with some sort of progress chart to hand or a file to consult, her every visit evokes the thought that the very act of parading up and down by Alexis F's bed might of itself improve his condition. Her hair springs this way and that, perhaps like the ceremonial turban of some Amazonian warrior of distinction. Her half-moon glasses are folded to hang outside her breast pocket, which otherwise contains an assortment of ball-point pens and pencils. And today she has come, as it were, at the head of a delegation.

A step behind, Dr Pritzlewitz appears as though he very much needs to be somewhere else. And behind him, in a huddle, there is a representation of orderlies and warders whose names Alexis has at last come to know. From where Alexis sits upright on his bed, Manfred Holtzer presents himself tall and erect as in a full length portrait with Helmut Kohler's face and shoulders visible above Holtzer's crown, Gerhardt Grüber's forehead and eyes over Kohler's head and merely a part of Hans Frieden's cheek, nose and brow under Grüber's crooked arm. Like medical students on their daily rounds in a teaching hospital, they are all gathered in a cluster, just within the door; all that is with the exception of Rudolf Dorfbaum who in his splendid roundness takes up a stance between Dr Pritzlewitz and the pacing Dr Meyerstein. His hands clasped loosely beneath his belly, Rudolf stands like a sentry at ease, yet as immovable and unmovable as Rameses II's foot.

Of a sudden, on a turn and with the flourish of a conjuror, Dr Meyerstein produces and holds aloft the book which Piers gave Alexis, and which the orderlies confiscated.

'Had you a rewrite in mind? A sequel perhaps?' she asks dryly. 'There are definitely those sections that could be better handled . . .'

Alexis is afraid to look at her. Afraid of being mesmerised by the motion of her thickly painted lips, of the lipstick filled creases imprinted over an ever agitating, ceaseless spout of words. By now only too familiar with the nature, manner and scope of Dr

Meyerstein's deprecations, he turns his face away and catches sight of Gustav who, on peeping through the glass panel in the door and seeing his Chapter House full of undesirable, foreign bodies, hastily scuttles off. Yet Dr Meyerstein is not prone to yielding.

'Why won't you talk? We're only here to help you. You have plenty to say to Piers don't you! But that's all over . . . they're convinced you've been supplying the narcotics ward with drugs . . . have you? Oh well, it's not that important . . . you'll be discharged, and Piers too . . . soon no doubt. It would be silly to keep you two apart forcibly . . . that would be the alternative.

'Wouldn't you like to stay?'

Pause.

'Whatever it was . . . whatever happened . . . we can face it together . . . each and every one of us . . . together . . . if you'd only say something. Trust me . . . can't you?'

Dr Pritzlewitz has taken up a position beside the table at the centre of the room. For a while he seemed intent on examining the IBM typewriter as if it were an object of unfathomable perplexity and of boundless interest. Now he plays with the on/off rocker switch, clicking it back and forth, absent-mindedly marking the tempo of Dr Meyerstein's outpourings.

'Heaven only knows what possessed you to go down to the canal? I mean, were you planning some sort of escape . . . a breakout . . . you and Piers . . . and the other two? And why oh why climb the wall? It's beyond my comprehension . . . everybody's in fact, when in theory you could just walk out of the gate. And then what . . . what? Were you going to swim? D'you know how many people have already swum across the rivers and lakes hereabouts in a genuine bid for freedom? Of course not. Now they had something to escape from, a real threat . . . something dangerous and menacing to flee and were prepared to risk their lives . . . just to be able to earn an honest crust and make a decent, unoppressed life for themselves . . . but you . . . you want to run away from all that . . . you want to dig a deep hole, crawl into it

167

and cover yourself over with dry leaves, dirt and mud. Why? I'd say it's because you've just had it far too easy . . . easy-peasy, all your life I'd bet . . . and here, where everything's been done for you . . . Do I see any gratitude . . . no, of course not, why should I? Not a sausage, not a single sausage . . .'

During the pregnant pause that ensues Rudolf Dorfbaum smacks his lips, loudly.

'Silence, silence, silence . . . is that all I'll ever get?'

Throughout Alexis has been contemplating the tips of his fingers each in turn and now and then chewing on a stubborn hangnail. Occasionally he has glanced towards Dr Pritzlewitz who once or twice gave the impression of having a potentially worthwhile comment or a contribution to make, but he has thus far failed to get a word in edgeways. It has finally dawned on him that there is no socket at the centre of the room and that the typewriter is not plugged in. Apparently on the verge of taking advantage of this second deliberate pause, he clears his throat, only to be held at bay by Dr Meyerstein's calculated resumption of her fulminations.

'If you're counting on Piers, forget it. He's far too intelligent and knows which side his bread is buttered. Believe it or not, on most IQ tests he scores right off the scale. He could be a member of MENSA just like that!' A predictable snap of the fingers and, 'Only it would never cross his mind to apply. D'you know why? Because he has neither the need nor the desire to prove himself to himself, nor to anyone else for that matter. Yet for it all, probably sooner than later he's going to end up in a pine box, in a hole and it won't be the same hole you're in . . . or better still, under one of Gustav's scalpels . . . now wouldn't that be ironic . . . while you sit here and play at some sort of mute, time-share amnesia . . . well it won't wash! Not for a minute, not for a single second . . .'

Again Dr Pritzlewitz clears his throat, but his colleague is over fond of the train of her own absconding thoughts to let him have his say.

'Right, on your own head be it!' she declares with fierce finality.

'You'll know exactly what's been decided in a day or two . . . and it'll be a while before that decision's implemented. In the meantime . . .' as she brings her striding to a halt beside the table at the centre of the room, '. . . why not take advantage of this?' She flips the switch on the typewriter, and smartly about turns to leave, but not before placing the paperback book next to the unopened ream of copy paper. Her entourage follows her in single file, one by one observing some predetermined, unspoken pecking order and with bowed, averted faces, like a jury retiring to debate the foregone conclusion of its verdict.

Alexis closes his eyes. He leans against the puffed-up pillows, and with laced fingers he cradles his head in his palms.

Gustav has come back. He shuts the door and tiptoes up to Alexis F's bed in the manner of someone intent on mischief. He is carrying a parcel, about the size and shape of those cartons used by florists for transporting long-stemmed roses.

'Herr Bruno, this is the present I told you about. It's for your bedfellow.'

He lays the package beside Alexis.

'Herr Bruno? Why doesn't he unwrap his gift? Is he shy? Should I do it for him d'you think?'

Gustav snatches up the box. He's tearing away at the bindings, the Christmas wrapping. His moist eyes glisten. He raises the lid, surreptitiously; then briefly, with his fingers clamped at either end, he holds the box above Alexis. His gnarled hands tremble as he gradually rotates it to spill its contents. Instinct has Alexis jerk away and spring off the bed. He is momentarily stunned, dumbstruck; but above all confounded by an array of unexpected colour as he stares and stares at the bone, the severed tendons and the raw tissue, at the clotted blood and the fleshy flesh of a female arm rolling across his blankets and on to the floor, landing with a solid thump and settling at his feet.

'Ah come in, Herr Holtzer, come in. And how is Piers Topf today?'

169

'We've put him in F Block for now, Dr Pritzlewitz.'

'F Block, would that be in what the patients call Ward L'n'F?'

'So I believe . . .'

'Right, I see. Very well. And his state is still catatonic . . . ?'

'As far as I'm aware, Herr Doktor. At least he'll not want for company.'

'Oh? How's that?'

'That pal of his Otto Muntz . . . the one that's always yawning, he's already in there.'

'Is that so? Well. Yes, I'm expecting a report. None of it's very clear.'

'No, Herr Doktor.'

'From what I can gather it was a charwoman or some such who found him.'

'That's correct, one of the cleaning staff.'

'And how is she?'

'Under sedation . . . after all she went through a fair bit just finding him there, sitting on top of that closet like that, all naked and nibbling at that arm.'

'Quite, quite . . . poor woman. Any idea how the ruddy thing got to be in his room in the first place?'

'Well not really—'

'I mean, good Lord, man, an amputated limb!'

'It can be traced, sir.'

'Traced?'

'There's a tattoo—'

'A tattoo! That won't tell us who—'

'It wouldn't be anyone from his ward, though half the time visitors and people off the street, if you will, are coming and going as they please . . . and there are the windows. Some joker eh!'

'Or someone being helpful.'

'Beg your pardon, Herr Doktor?'

'Nothing, nothing.'

'Of course I was against his having a private room in the first place. He is too wild and too cocky for my liking, not that you'd think that to see him now . . . but then Dr Meyerstein insisted—'

'Yes, yes, I know all about it . . .'

'Excuse me, Dr Pritzlewitz . . . but how could a simple thing like an amputated arm turn someone's mind? Surely . . .'

'I can't really say. It is possible, I suppose. All the same somewhat unlikely I'd have thought. There's the shock aspect, maybe . . . but that will pass with medication and in time. No doubt a great deal would depend on circumstances, the how and the where. I mean, imagine going to the loo for example . . . lifting the lid, and the thing's already in there, pointing at you, waiting for you to sit on it . . .'

In an octagonal room furnished with eight empty beds stripped of bedding, and a tea table on which stands a typewriter, and beside which lies a slim paperback book and a freshly unsealed ream of typing paper, there sleeps an old man lying fully clothed like a medieval serf across his master's threshold. His folded jacket serves him as a pillow.

twenty

In which variations on the theory of personality projection and transference are given an airing; and wherein we learn that for Alexis, Wendy is perhaps much more than we have hitherto supposed her to be.

Poppycock! And that's putting it mildly. Poppycock and balderdash, and double balderdash! No, no, no, no, no, dearie me, no! It just won't do. Nobody, but nobody, in my opinion, loses their mind by meeting a severed limb head-on, no matter the where, when and how of the confrontation. In the loo my arse! Nice try though, Dr Pritzlewitz; but then why not hanging in the wardrobe bagged in the sleeve of one's favourite jersey, or under the pillow wrapped in one's unisex pyjamas? Because that is the stuff of Hollywood and well you know it. At boarding school, earthworms, slugs and frogs are still commonplace bedfellows, their unforeseen presence between the sheets being remedied by a good, full-throated scream. Yes shock, even acute clinical shock, I'm prepared to accept as a possibility, but nothing so severe that it can't be cured by a nice strong and very sweet cup of tea. As for catatonia, let alone catalepsy, well, in short and to be precise – bollocks and bullshit!

Now I may not be a psychiatrist or a psychologist and I'll own up to not having any kind of medical training, not even at Girl Guide level; in fact I have no qualifications whatsoever simply because through no fault of my own I had to quit school prematurely. That doesn't mean to say that I stopped learning or have since neglected my education. In fact I am far better and far wider read than today's average undergraduate. My interests are comprehensive and my knowledge is cosmopolitan. I have a special passion for European history and my grasp of this field of study, if not exactly second to none, is on a par with that of any Ph.D. student, tutor or lecturer. But this is not about my credentials. Even though I am Emotion personified, let it not be forgotten that amongst all the Wendys Alexis would have me be, I am also the Voice of Reason's ever-vigilant helpmate and oft-hailed as Wendy the Wise. Still, it takes neither genius nor a university degree to recognise that Piers Topf must be shamming; that he is in cahoots with Alexis and what's more, I would hazard a guess, that together they have devised and embarked on a scam, some sort of sublime and sophisticated confidence trick. The question is what and to what purpose? What is the nature of their game? And why in this environment, where to some extent or other, everybody needs to be faking it? And where above all, Alexis F has been pulling the wool over everyone's eyes right from the off; now to be brazenly leading the parade.

Being institutionalised is not always what it is made out to be. Often it can be more disconcerting than comforting, yet for Alexis, by his own admission, it holds an undeniable attraction. Drawing him into its web of artificial security it appears to pander to his surface needs, thereafter to accommodate his whims and fancies, and in the end serve him as a means of contrived expiation. The appeal of institutionalisation thus established, Alexis apparently resigns himself to its rigours almost as an inverted act of contrition. Were the Victorian workhouse still extant, Alexis F's name would probably feature prominently and without shame on the roll-call of permanent residents. Guilt can be funny that way. Or could it be that he is merely a devotee of Thomas Hardy's 'Age of Calculation'?

The previous place in which he was incarcerated, as he would have us believe, was run on the lines of an experimental farm using human beings as subjects, he himself featuring in the role of principal guinea pig. Yet despite his outcast status and the blatant aggressiveness displayed to him by the majority of his fellow inmates, he purported not only to find solace in the surroundings, but, contrary to his own sexual orientation, to enjoy a sense of camaraderie and companionship with the seemingly genderless Hilary. (For the record, I refuse to call homosexuals 'gay' because in my experience 'tis the last thing that most of them are. As for lesbians, well, many of them pose as the epitome of the classical virago, and that, surely, leaves nothing further to be said.) Likewise in the Berlin episode there's an element of calculated repetition. This self-ostracised Alexis is pleased to lay subtle stress on what is to be construed as his regenerative process. Though camouflaged, he is there in the first instance to charge his batteries; but by conforming to the established, cyclical course of action, he deliberately and with relish leaves himself open to the capricious vagaries of the Fates. And judging by what he has revealed of himself up till now, everything stems from a total child-like abnegation of responsibility, be it, for example, in the realms of fatherhood, or even of self-preservation.

As towards the close of the nineteenth century Auguste Comte's fellow Positivists discovered (and as more recently our latter-day hippy communards have also found out to their cost), it is a great deal more difficult being of and in the world with one's back turned to it than at first might be imagined. So, for all her abrasiveness and near unprofessional conduct, I can't help but empathise with Dr Meyerstein. She's certainly a woman after my own heart, casting aspersions and sowing doubt in the wake of her flapping coat-tails. I see her as a compassionate, composite Great Earth Mother figure with a tendency to blow hot and cold. And is it any wonder, for Piers and Alexis are definitely playing the system for all it's worth. Three square meals a day conjured up like room service, a bed and clean linen on demand, warmth and shelter on tap as it were – these are the basics that will, before one knows it, make a mockery of the outside world. Under these conditions, given the right perspective, the right frame of mind, other material considerations and ambitions along with notions of acquisition and possession rapidly fade away to a joke, to a trick of distant memory. Like any casualty of a durance one simply becomes stir crazy. It is then that the word asylum takes on its true meaning and grows to provide a source of individual tranquillity, which in turn echoes the supposedly idyllic, albeit idealised serenity of the medieval cloister. At least that's the theory. Could it be therefore that Piers and Alexis have devised for themselves a type of unspecified, esoteric order wherein they can indulge a clandestine and novel form of personalised saintliness; being forever closed off from traditional reality, not to commune with some godhead, but simply to avoid the Mab, Moloch and Mammon of everyday life? Or is that too far-fetched? Too Californian for any serious consideration?

As an interpretation it fits, but perhaps a tad too easily. To paraphrase the man – shallowness has this advantage, it's nigh on impossible to drown there. So what is Alexis actually up to, what is he trying to tell us in this labyrinthine room of stacked books where at this hour of night, in the manner of all good souls with a clear conscience, he talks plainly in his sleep. And I, lying on my side alongside him, my head at an angle, my chin cupped in my palm, my crooked elbow propped on the pillow, I, Watchful Wendy listen, and like some guardian angel, I watch. I listen and I watch to see the casual rise and fall of his chest. And I see the scars all but washed away by the moonlight that steals through the half-drawn curtains; and I hear him speak his parables, freely, softly and low.

Now there are those who maintain that sleep-talkers only mumble and utter flibberty-gibberty gibberish. This is patently not so. A short while ago I found myself in bed with Michael, a young man whom I had known since secondary school and for whom I had once carried a juvenile torch. That particular adolescent flame had long since died, but much to my amusement

I discovered that with a little riddle the embers soon became lukewarm. In short he was still quite, quite fanciable and it was a pleasure to re-meet on the occasion of his best friend's official engagement. I had been invited to make up the party at a celebratory meal because it just so happened that I was also rather well acquainted with the bride-to-be, although recently we had somewhat fallen out of touch, she understandably having new horizons and new people with which to occupy herself. Anyway, in common parlance, one thing inextricably led to another and afterwards, safely duveted like satiated satyrs, Michael and I contentedly dozed off in each other's arms.

Then I was awakened with a swift jab to the ribs to hear Michael talking to me, only to realise that though he was speaking clearly and distinctly, it was not to me. In fact he was fast asleep. The poke in the ribs had been accidental. Not only that . . . it dawned on me almost at once that he was repeating verbatim his end of the conversation that had taken place at our table earlier that very evening. Bovine-eyed and flagrantly gob-smacked I listened with fascination as he talked on, appropriately pausing to allow his companions their say, words that only he could hear, to reply to those self-same unheard questions and to entertain according to his wont with suitable witticism and anecdote. For what took an hour if not substantially more, he spoke like an actor declaiming lines long since memorised and well rehearsed, while every now and then, with a flash of recognition, I remembered things I had said, remarks I had made as once again Michael, with uncanny accuracy, furnished the same comments and supplied the same answers he had given at the time. And to the veracity of this I will swear on my mother's grave and my father's dole cheque.

Not for a moment am I suggesting that I had any immediate influence on or even contrived to bring about Michael's strange nocturnal monologue. After all, to what purpose? Neither (as it was later to be bandied about) could it have been attributed in earnest to some sort of extraordinary post-coital reaction that I,

176

Wendy Witch, had somehow magically stage managed. However, subsequent events that night, of admittedly a certain sexual bent (which I resolutely decline to detail) did teach me that I had it in me to become the mistress of some pretty weird and wonderful powers, or, as I prefer to call them, innate gifts, which I now have not only at my beck and call, but have learned to use sparingly and with respect. From the outset it had been my barefaced intention to go the whole hog with Alexis, simply because it is a well-tried and well-tested means of inducing a state of susceptible relaxation. Of course we had a kiss and cuddle, and I must confess it was an unexpected joy kissing him; something to do with the tactility and muscular sensuality of his lips no doubt, but that's by-the-by, for in truth I wasn't in the mood to do assiduous battle with his impotence. Nor did Alexis seem that bothered. His deep-rooted take it or leave it mindset makes him readily predisposed to all forms of mesmerism, and there are many.

Osculation aside, he went under, one might say, as at the springing of an opera hat, and thereafter has lain coddled in the blush of contentment, another satisfied victim of Morpheus in placid repose. A part of him believes that he is sleeping, dreaming meaningful dreams to which he alone holds the key. On the other hand, another part of him knows that I am inside those very private thoughts, flitting about and toying with those allegedly recondite symbols and mysterious images, probing and prying, skipping along the corridors of his id. He also knows that there is nothing he can do about it. So I shall let him take his ease a while longer; let him wallow in the blanks of empty thought, for tonight he will truly earn his rest. There is still much work before us. The moon begins its set and for neither of us will there be a second chance.

Frankly, I am not programmed to countenance failure. At the same time neither will I blinker myself from the possibility that I might not succeed – much to the I-told-you-so satisfaction of my detractors – those who by now stand ready to accuse me of sheer recklessness, of gross misconduct; those who will insist that I have flagrantly overstepped the mark, that I have gone way beyond my brief. So sue me. Haul me before a tribunal, parade me in front of a court martial, take me out and stand me against a wall. Or tie me to a stake, then blindfold me and shoot me. And believe me there are those who would. Yet for it all, proudly not of the professional and executive classes, neither lawyer nor clergyman, neither guru nor spy, I will persistently maintain that the path I was instructed to follow is a much-trodden cul-de-sac. Claims will of course abound that without a string of letters to my name I am not only ill-prepared and untrained, but risibly immature, though under no circumstances shall I flinch from taking full responsibility for whatever may hereafter ensue. I will not give up, not yet, not Wilful Wendy. At least I haven't closed the files and in frustration thrown in the towel, let alone an infantile tantrum based on a sneaking suspicion that it might be in my plans to fuck Alexis.

Let's be honest, this is a different game. For example, a moment's diligent research will probably show that St Anslem's, or Sami's if you will, does not exist and never has existed either as a hospital or as a prison, at least not in the neighbourhood of the Wannsee Lakes, nor within the vicinity of the Glienicke Schloss and its famed hunting grounds, nor anywhere near the Glienicke bridge, that renowned scene of many a cold, pre-dawn exchange of Soviet and American spies. Could it be that Alexis has been reading too many thrillers? Is it there, from fiction, that he selects the die of aspiration, gleans his inspiration and accordingly casts the shapes of reality? The unattainable held close to the chest, which for some might be as simple as an ivy-clad cottage with an arch of wild roses spanning the garden path, for some yachts and fast cars, fake suntans and casinos; for others it is climbing steeples and bungee jumping off bridges; for Alexis F it appears to be bedlam. That being the case, either of us could be plunged into disaster at any moment. The possibility that we have entered into a game of war with a brand new set of conventions and are just

178

starting to draw up the rules of engagement must not be ignored. But if Alexis wants war then war he shall have, though let him be warned – I make a formidable opponent.

Unless of course all the while he has been lying doggo? But I doubt it. Dr Meyerstein remarked that he was clever, good; but he's not that good. Talking of Dr Meyerstein, I wonder why she didn't make more of Alexis F's presence in Berlin. Why that city? Surely The Wall of itself is not reason enough. Why not Amsterdam or Rome? Or perhaps like Moscow in the Scottish Borders, there's a sleepy alternative Berlin tucked away somewhere in the Welsh Marches? Maybe in the long run it matters not. Alexis knows that my task is like searching for where the circle begins, relentlessly to read between the lines until intuitively I hit the right combination that will lead us, if not to capitulation, then to a generous compromise. Otherwise, as the Polish pataphysician Marek Obtułowicz would no doubt put it, the whole kit and caboodle from prologue to postscript falls into the category of yet another exercise in abject, albeit heroic futility. Hardly as tantalizing or enthralling as a company of mounted lancers launching an attack against SS panzer divisions, but at best a conundrum and at worst a bloody awful mistake, which makes me more and more convinced that we have to get ourselves back to England. It is there that it began and it is there that tonight it is playing itself out; and it is there that four-fifths of the iceberg will come to light, probably looking like some priceless porcelain cup displayed on a non-matching Woolworths' saucer.

twenty-one

In which probability might be seen to be stretched beyond the bounds of credibility; or alternatively coincidence can be accepted exactly for what it is.

On the south coast, Folkestone is as good a port as any in which to enact a melodrama, or from which to point at the sea and say:

'France is over there.'

Alexis looks in the direction indicated by the old man's finger. He sees the dip of a squawking gull and beyond, the thin grey-white band that marks the horizon. It is a colourless day, but for that, full of heightened nautical sounds and smells.

The old man drops a coin into the mechanical telescope. He bends to peep through the eyepiece. The money might have bought a bag of chips. Then, straightening up, an eyebrow twitching, he says, 'Your turn.'

Alexis puts his eye to the lens. The thin band broadens. He swings the cylinder in search of a diving seagull. And the mechanism stops whirring.

(A bottle of Coke clanked into a drawer. He stooped to scoop it out and then levered off the cap on a bracket fitted for that purpose. He gave her the first swallow.

She said, 'You seem very far away today . . . distant.'

He glanced at her swollen belly. Said nothing.

They walked along the dimly lit corridor towards the lecture theatre. She sort of waddled, her ankles now noticeably too slim for the extra weight she has to bear. After a while he asked, 'What does your father do?'

'Sorry?'

'Your father? Papa? We've been living together for nigh on three years and you've hardly once mentioned your parents.'

'My mother organises charities.'

'And your father?'

'I haven't the slightest idea where he is.'

She handed him the bottle, empty. He lobbed it at a waste paper bucket and almost tripped over the steps down to the lecture theatre.)

'Are you all right?' the old man has asked, taking Alexis by the elbow to steady him.

'Yes.'

'It sometimes happens . . . that dizziness . . . when you get up too quickly.' He relaxes his grip, 'Of course these things are designed for midgets.'

'Children?'

The old man chuckles. As he does so, a little cluster of silver-tipped hairs just below his lower lip separates out and lifts independently from the rest of his goatee beard. Alexis turns back to face the sea. He rests his forearms on the railings, relishing the feel of the wind, the tang of salt water. Beside him the old man suddenly seems to straighten up, to fill out and grow taller, as if with studied poise to become more of an elderly, dignified gentleman and one familiar with assuming authority.

'You're not a holiday-maker of course.'

'Of course.'

('Of course we shall expand this idea at our next session,' said the professor. 'Meanwhile I'd like you all to read . . .'

181

Going through the door, she gave him her notebooks to carry. Apart from the odd date, the pages were all blank. It wasn't as though she had lost interest. She clasped his hand. Lightly. To ask, 'Will he know his father?' twice patting the bulge of her stomach. She sought no reply, instead forced a giggle and added, 'I never saw mine . . . or rather, I don't remember seeing him. I was probably eighteen months old when he left.'

'Left?'

'Ran off with my uncle's wife.'

Pause.

'He got *her* pregnant. And scarpered. Quite a scandal.'

'You've had no contact with him?'

'None . . . and the entire family are obliged to keep their mouths shut, not a word. We're one hundred per cent orthodox on that score. I could ask my grandmother . . . but she's always so ill. I simply don't think about him.'

Beaming at the sight of pending motherhood, the porter made a show of holding open the heavy door for her. The second-hand sunlight pooled in the dusty hall under the neo-Gothic arches of their nineteenth-century redbrick Alma Mater. It wasn't warm.)

'I hope I'm not being unduly forward . . .'

Alexis looks at the elderly gentleman and smiles feebly.

'I'm not homosexual, and anyway you're too old and too wise to succumb to a casual pick-up.'

Alexis looks away.

'No that's part of it. Normally I wouldn't dream of addressing a total stranger. But there's something in your expression. Something about your eyes.'

'The way you just can't help your gaze from always straying towards a cripple or a moron perhaps . . . specially if you're closeted in the same waiting-room or seated in the same railway carriage?'

For a moment the gentleman is silent.

'Bitterness doesn't become you.' A considered statement,

followed by, 'I'd like very much to buy you a drink because . . .'

He adjusts his tie. Then he peers down at the beach, possibly at the same pebble that has attracted Alexis's attention.

'Because—' But Alexis cuts him short:

'It doesn't matter. I'll gladly have a drink with you.'

'In that case I shall tell you all about it.'

Yet before he can say any more, Alexis links his arm through the elderly gentleman's and, having spotted a pub sign not far off, steers him along the sea front. His companion has begun again, 'I'm a gambler. A successful one at that . . .'

In mid-stride he twists aside. Their arms uncouple. As intended, the movement allows Alexis to take note of the gambler's clothes. His bespoke suit is of a fine grey herring bone. The jacket is waisted and fashionable – not exaggerated, but tailored to compliment age. The white shirt he wears has a stiff collar, cuffs that are starched and spotless, and would no doubt have been as precise were they of Regency lace. The tie, military. He wears no hat and his hair, with its ashen wings swept over his ears, looks as if it might be daily trimmed and singed.

'I'm a gambler,' he repeats.

Pause.

'A lucrative profession as you can see, though it has cost me a wife and countless lovers, indirectly of course.'

'Of course.' Again Alexis surveys his companion. There is an aura of a bygone era about him and Alexis is struck by the thought that he might be dealing with a leprechaun in disguise. For a moment he wonders why it is that people never really see one another, not even when the opportunity readily presents itself, such as at bus-stops and in cinema queues; but the gambler is talking once more:

'I have a daughter you know. She must be well . . . close to your age I should say.'

Pause. Alexis expects him to produce a photograph. But they walk on. In silence. Then:

'My credit's good all over Brighton, that's where I live. And believe me some of the very best gaming clubs are to be found there. Oh I've tried the established houses such as those in Monte Carlo, Nice, even Las Vegas, but somehow they're wrong. They're artificial. Too much glitter and razz. They're geared to making or losing fortunes. To chance. In all that grandeur they lack finesse, they lack subtlety. Nothing there smacks of the profession or the career, and gambling's a job like any other. Don't get me wrong, those places are full of professionals like myself but I always say an accountant will work better if his office windows don't overlook a fun fair . . .

'Oh I know what you're thinking, big fish in a small pond, and in some ways that's true. But in exercising his capabilities a man must also acknowledge his limitations. In the end it boils down to the society he's prepared to keep . . . or tolerate. After all, we're free to choose exactly how much evil we take on board. Here we are . . .'

The pub? It's a pub. Small, but pretentious and designed to cater above all to the ambivalent tastes of a passing trade. Originally Edwardian, it has full-turned the chrome and plastic revolution to become an unskilled reproduction of its former self. Nevertheless it is a pub and the curt thud of darts hitting a board makes Alexis feel at home.

('Must you go and play tonight?'
'Why not?'
'It could be any time now!'
'Nonsense. Don't be so hysterical. You've weeks and weeks to go.'
She might have pleaded. Like a beached whale, she might have cried. But they both knew that he would be gone before the month was out.)

The gambler says, 'A beer I'll wager.'
'Please.'
'Yes, there's a lot of the scholar about you.'

184

'What d'you mean?'

'How do I mean what? That you put across the air of somebody well educated or how do I know that scholars are beer men? It's simple. If university does one thing it teaches you to live on next to nothing and to drink ale. Also to enjoy it. What's more you look at the sea the way a man looks at a chessboard . . .'

'Two pints of bitter please.'

They carry their overfilled glasses to one of the four vacant tables in the middle of the lounge. There are two other customers there and they sit at opposite ends of the bar. In a mouthful, the old man drains half his mug, then, plucking a neatly pressed handkerchief from his waistcoat pocket, he dabs at his whiskers. And, 'Of course you're wondering . . .'

Alexis is on the verge of answering, but the old man's upheld palm stops him from speaking.

'Even if you're not, let me say that you're about to leave the country, that you came to Folkestone in order to catch the ferry, but it's off season and there's only one boat a day, which you've missed. So you've decided to get a bus to Dover and then sail on the midnight crossing to Boulogne. Now the purpose of our drinking together is to wish you bon voyage.'

'But—'

'But nothing. You're curious. Curious as to how I know these things. Well perhaps I don't. On the other hand everybody has a "tell", a little something that gives them and the game away, and it's a gambler's solemn duty to spot these little signs at the drop of a hat. Then again perhaps none of it's true . . . but since people demand reasons I've given you one. Cheers.'

The bitter curbs Alexis's hunger, yet he can't understand why it was that he made no effort to eat earlier. He lights a cigarette and watches his companion sip another long draught of ale. He fiddles with his matches. The gambler has forgone tending his beard, but is asking, 'Would you care for a snack, a sandwich? I think they have an excellent buffet here.'

'No. Really no thank you.'

The old man finishes his pint and moves to get up.

'No let me . . .'

At the bar Alexis is kept waiting while the barman finishes telling a new customer the latest joke.

'That's very kind of you,' says the old man as Alexis sets a brimming glass before him. A bank note lies folded under his beer mat, ready for the next round. And the next.

'You see,' he begins slowly, 'it's Saturday and I can't work on Saturdays. Not any more. That's the why of inviting you for a drink. At least that's part of it.'

Other than to furrow his brow, Alexis makes no reply.

'I used to say to myself, I don't gamble on Saturdays because the banks are closed and I don't hold with playing unless I've considerable cash to hand . . .'

He glances at the bank note as if to say I've got enough for both of us tonight.

'But that's not true. There was a time when I earned most of my money on a Saturday.'

'The sabbath?' Alexis quips.

The gambler laughs heartily, his head bobbing.

'Yes, that's nice, very good, the sabbath. But no . . . not so long ago . . . well a few years now, I was playing at a small club in Brighton. Incidentally, I'm here in Folkestone to resist temptation . . . anyway I was a regular at this place. In fact for many it was my only known address. And early that evening, that Saturday, I received the telegram. A tragedy, it said. My daughter . . .

'I stacked my chips, and without a word strolled off, alone . . .'

And silence.

Alexis smokes.

The bartender is crushing ice-cubes.

They drink.

A street lamp flickers through an unwashed window.

The old man slides the note towards Alexis.

'Would you get them?' he asks.

186

'Sure. Oh and you were right, I am catching that ferry from Dover, only it goes to Dunkirk.'

And now settled again with a fresh mug, the gambler resumes his narrative. 'I never learned the exact details. You see to be quite frank she was virtually no more than a name to me. And *they* wouldn't tell me anything . . . her mother and . . . not that I'd ask. Nothing. You know prior to her death I'd heard rumours that she was pregnant, even that she'd given birth to a baby boy. A grandson would you imagine? But would anybody tell me? Write to me? No. No, no, no.

'That night, the night of the telegram, I walked. And walked . . . Lord knows where. By dawn, it was spring by-the-by, I found myself on the street where I lodged. Ordinary rows of ordinary Victorian houses divided into apartments, one to a floor, with a common staircase. Well I expect I was in a daze, probably a little tight. Just stumbling along when I registered footsteps in front of me. I looked up to see this young girl and at a glance I could tell she was a tramp. No that's not true. It was partly the resentment – how dare she be alive, by what absurd right when my daughter . . . I've no doubt she was a perfectly moral woman. A pretty little thing. Yet somehow, she gave me the impression of a third-rate stripper who had spent the night 'hostessing' in some dive. That shouldn't upset a gambler you might think. Still it didn't seem to matter, nor did I take any further notice, but trundled on. Possibly she slowed to let me pass her. Anyway, eventually I climbed my porch steps, and it wasn't till I had entered the lobby that I realised I was inside the wrong building. So out I came again, just as she drew level with the door. She quickly skipped into the next house, the one in which I lived. I went in after her.'

A pause. To lift his glass, to drink. And, 'My flat was on the top floor. Isolated. I knew none of the other tenants, and they didn't know me – working unsociable hours you see, but that's not the point. As I turned the first-floor landing I almost collided with the girl. She stood there, calmly to ask, Why do you follow me? I replied, I'm not, equally calmly. And she moved, giving

187

me room to go on by, but . . . but to this day I can't tell you what it was, something, her mere presence, I don't know, something forced me to grab at her throat. She did nothing. And I was squeezing. Coldly she stared me in the eyes . . . no screams, my grip was tightening. She didn't cough and she didn't choke, or splutter, as if she wanted to help me kill her. All at once her eyes rolled back horribly. I thought she was about to die and became fully aware of what I was doing, but before I loosened my grip, she began to kick and scream. We fell fighting to the floor. I could not take my hands from her neck. She hurt me, but at the time I felt no pain. Then I heard the sound of a door opening. She was beneath me. Somebody was yelling something. I released her. And tailed off. From the ground floor I looked up and saw a man peering down the stairwell. Though it could not have been more than a fleeting glimpse, we stared at each other intently and for what seemed to be a long time.'

The old man pauses again. He sighs, pulls out his handkerchief. Alexis reaches for his empty glass. The old man rests his hand on Alexis's and says:

'I'm drinking with you because . . . because you bear an uncanny resemblance to that man.'

twenty-two

Wherein, providing scope for more than one interpretation of events and ever compliant with the mysterious ways of Emotion, Wendy wealds her magic.

Well ... we're getting on ... we're getting on ... (as a certain playwright would have it). At least Alexis condescended to have himself persuaded back to England, be it only briefly and at no doubt the start of what promises to be another venture, or more accurately, another escape to foreign parts. I can't help but wonder why he summarily chooses to do so much gadding about and what is it that he is actually fleeing; especially since his performance is taking on a most unsatisfactory aspect and his actions are becoming more and more contrived. Could it be that the true extent of his limitations is coming to the fore of its own accord and he has resorted to the double-bluff of blatant repetition in the misguided belief that even if I do notice I shan't consider it significant? Then think again, Alexis, think again. You're not dealing with one of your dunderheaded dairymaids or gullible goose-girls now. Leave the simpletons be to the pages of your fairy-tales. I'm not one to be tumbled willy-nilly in the hay during harvest only to be forgotten by thanksgiving. Better scholars than you have tried.

Yes, I freely admit I have a bee in my bonnet about my lack of formal schooling, about having been denied access to higher

189

education. It's illogical, I suppose; though strictly speaking I have no capacity for logic, neither formal nor symbolic, and it plays no part in my machinations. But then what does? After all there's more at stake here than just a scroll of paper embossed in Latin or a photograph posed in graduation cap and gown, neither of which would I ever have dreamed of having framed, let alone displayed thereafter on a piano or on a mantelpiece or, heaven forfend, hung on a wall. Not in a million years. Never. But somehow the mere knowledge of having a diploma or a degree would have curtailed the resentment and sufficed in satisfying every sporadic need of pandering to the norm, or worse still, every errant wish of keeping up appearances. Though I'm somewhat at a loss to grasp why it should be reduced to a matter of keeping up appearances, and if so, what appearances? Or should that be whose and for whom? For those who still deem it right and proper that women be treated as inferior citizens and privileged to be confined to kinder, küche and kirche. That ubiquitous, immovable and two-faced, not so silent majority, on whose behalf governments pass all sorts of laws and issue all sorts of acts; but legislation notwithstanding, in their heart of hearts, they and their ilk will never cease calling a bird a chick, a nigger a spade, a yid a kike, and a honky a honky, all the while gravely paying lip-service to the principles of equality espoused in feminism and in the tenets of anti-racism.

And so in my insignificant little village, my insignificant little certificate would have been proof enough where it was needed of my capabilities and potentialities. It would have served to snub those good, rustic neighbours, experts in husbandry and furtive match-making, who have long since marked me down as a fully paid up member of the barefoot and pregnant brigade, fit only for mediocre breeding. Why else – their argument must go – would I have a clandestine lover? And why in this permissive society, in this day and age of liberal sexuality and contraception on tap, why on earth would I be running away to get married of all things . . . and in secret at that? Well the answer is simple. Were I to announce my intended departure, to openly declare that I was going to keep house for that sot of a father no more, then in the interim before actually leaving, the tension and the anguish would become insufferable. At first I would probably cope quite well with the calculated despondency, the helpless-without-you posturing, but eventually, and to my cost, my siblings would melt my resolve with their persistent lost-boy looks – Curly kneading and tugging at the crocheted hem of his unironed surplice, Toots furiously bending discords in augmented sevenths from an open-tuned guitar, and the twins peering out from behind yet another unfathomable reality – individually and as one they would have me shot down, emotionally blackmailed me into mothering them to the grave. Theirs and mine. But especially mine, a thin slab of plain marble inscribed with an epitaph anachronistic in its foresight and reading: Wysiwyg Wendy – The Silly Girl Who Was Too Forthright.

Okay, having got that off my chest, I'm now going to step into I-told-you-so mode. From the moment I took over and began working off my own bat, Alexis started to disclose things about himself that up until then (while under the care and in the illustrious hands of others) he had been at trenchant pains to mask. Admittedly it was almost by accident, a sort of impromptu giving up of no more than a scant nibble here and there, but enough to indicate that with a measured construct a pattern might eventually be made to emerge. The Folkestone punter, who in my opinion shares particular traits and physical characteristics in common with the head orderly at Sami's, provides further affirmation of that which was already becoming apparent during the entire Berlin episode. Alexis F's desultory demeanour, the underlying aimlessness ascribed to all his miscellaneous, self-centred adventures undergoes a change. He recognises that his being does have a bearing on other people, that he can act in the interest of others, and accordingly he does something selfless, something useful, at least useful in his own estimation of what is required. The seaside gambler, albeit, he aids unwittingly, at a second-hand distance as it were.

191

Within these strictures, the recurrent theme of fathers and fatherhood, even be it absentee fatherhood, takes on a significance of note. Since a propagation of the species by procreation is the only unarguable justification for the existence of humanity (anything else by way of meaning and purpose being just so much icing on the cake), Alexis F had come to equate his failure as a parent with failure as a human being *per se*. In consequence, he had plunged into living all manner of parables born in the wake of death and out of discredited yet reanimated notions of guilt and retribution. A self-made isolationist, he had no role in society and had resolutely shunned cogent intercourse with his fellows. Until now. And if I didn't know better, I might once have accused him of solipsism.

But enough of this speculative tomfoolery. Given the current state of worldly affairs, the question may indeed lie in to father or not to father, but that's no excuse to sound off like an intellectual black hole. All the same, though it presently puts itself forward as being of keystone importance, this train of thought may yet prove to furnish an altogether far too facile explanation. Native cunning and homespun wit has yet to be dispensed with, especially since Alexis has in his inimitable repose just avowed that I constitute no danger to him. So I shall not be in the least surprised if any minute now it takes but a little push, a gentle loving nudge for the last of his defences to be breached, even though in a last-ditch stand he erect a motte-and-bailey castle, secrete himself in its keep and surround the stockade with a deep, deep moat.

But softly, softly . . . Let's not get ahead of ourselves. Cleverness, commendable as it may be, needs perhaps be tempered with a reminder of the words of Marshal Pierre Bosquet who, on witnessing the charge of the Light Brigade at Balaclava remarked, '*C'est magnifique, mais ce n'est pas la guerre.*'

twenty-three

In which Alexis recognizes that there is no easy way out and that even a latter-day anchorite must sooner or later succumb to flow of the tide.

A mile or so off the cliff-indented coast of an Aegean island, there stands a rock. In shape it roughly resembles a wedge of cheese on its side and covers an area of perhaps three, possibly four acres, its thin end tapering leeward, pointing north-east and out to the open sea. The island and the rock are connected by a deeply submerged ridge of irregularly spaced stones and rounded boulders lying like the scattered remains of a monstrous vertebra, their whereabouts known only to a handful of local fishermen. The singular peculiarity of the tides and the attendant currents render this underwater thoroughfare more or less passable on foot shortly before dawn and again after dusk, but only once a month. On the island, well south of the spit, which thus abruptly plunges to form this hidden causeway, there's the village of Virrisydes replete with church and belfry, walled cemetery and a partially excavated Roman villa. Nearby, several recently erected luxurious holiday bungalows dot the hillside. Seen from there the rock presents a sheer face, both alien and hostile. However, beyond this seemingly inaccessible bluff, the scarp slopes, levels to a field of moorland scrub and gorse, then gently falls to a breeze-blown beach; a secluded and sheltered

193

cove where, out of sight from the village shore, a flat-roofed adobe has been built.

On the lime-washed wall in the entrance porch Alexis has drawn a large square and meticulously divided it into a chequered pattern of 27 rows and 27 columns. Each of these smaller squares represents one day and all but nine are marked with a cross as an indication and a reminder of the time he has spent on the rock. Alone. He has allotted himself two years of silent, eremitical isolation and in retreat remains unvisited, save every other week when a retired, crippled fisherman calls bringing bottled water, fresh meat, fruit, eggs and milk, and sometimes writing paper and kerosene for the lamps, all in accordance with Alexis F's instructions. These, sealed in an oilskin pouch, are written in symbols and left in a crate attached to a mooring pole on the beach's jetty along with the wherewithal to pay for the next fortnight's supplies and generously to recompense the old man for his troubles. Like the earliest primitive Corsican traders, neither Alexis nor the fisherman have spoken to or seen each other since the day these arrangements were made, not even at a distance.

Before moving into the cottage, Alexis stocked the cellar with a liberal quantity of various wines, liqueurs and spirits as well as a vast array of tinned foodstuffs, and these are still far from exhausted. Though the soil round about is thin and hardly fertile, he has stubbornly managed to cultivate some vegetables and, as a result, has developed a peripheral interest in the indigenous flora. A study of those sturdy plants that grow wild in the surrounding fissures and crevices has now added to the general relaxation he otherwise derives from his books and from solving chess problems. Ever critical, he has been content to play and replay the games of his favourite masters, by and large as a leisurely diversion from his principal task, a definitive analysis of the provincial language, its dialects in particular and its evolution as demonstrated by its somewhat sparse writings. Alexis F's thesis is nearing completion.

This morning Alexis has clambered up to the highest point of the rock. To sit and to watch. Listening to the sea, his back warmed by the newly risen sun.

All at once his attention is caught by an unexpected movement below him and to his right. Alexis gets to his feet, the better to see a small boy scrambling out of the sea and on to a narrow strip of smooth pebbles at the base of the cliff. There the boy hops from foot to foot as he peels off his wet espadrilles and wriggles his toes. He becomes aware of Alexis F's presence. Peering up, he squints, and though standing in shadow, shields his eyes with his fingers as if from the glare of the sun. Then he waves. Alexis waves back. Espadrilles forgotten, the boy tentatively picks his way on tender soles towards the uneven steps here and there crudely hewn into the rock face. Steadying himself with his hands, he begins to climb; at first moving cautiously, in places on all fours like a young animal on new-born legs, then more confidently becoming as sure-footed as a mountain goat and as graceful as a gazelle or a young deer mindlessly reliant on instinct. Every now and again he pauses to glance up, to check that Alexis is still there, perched on the top step. Waiting.

And now in front of Alexis, their faces are on a level. For a second their eyes meet, then the boy's flit to some spot under Alexis F's lip and finally away altogether. Rapidly. His thumb and forefinger twirl the stem of the flower that he picked from a crack in the stones on his way up. And with all his might he concentrates on the spin of its yellow petals.

Alexis says, 'Hello . . .'

No reply.

The boy stares past the flower and at the ground. His bleached hair catches the sun as he tosses his head from side to side. Without warning. Without taking his eyes from between his feet, he stills the flower and urgently offers it to Alexis, saying, 'It's for you.'

'Thank you.' It is so long since Alexis last spoke English that he is aware of mouthing, of forming his words self-consciously, deliberately, lest he betray any trace of an accent as he asks, 'Shall we put it in some water?'

The boy sifts dirt with his toes. Silence. Alexis begins again, 'Shall we put–' But the boy has raised his hand. He is reaching out, and gingerly touches Alexis F's cheek, at once jerking back his hand. To touch again. To look at Alexis and say, 'If we don't give it some water it will die.'

Alexis stands. He feels the boy's fingers probing for his palm. And hand in hand, side by side, without a word, they walk down the rugged incline towards the cottage.

The boy has opted for the only comfortably upholstered chair. Seated well back, his spindly legs stick out horizontally while his elbows are splayed at such a stretch that only their knobbly tips are in contact with the padded armrests. He asks, 'Can I play with that?'

'Yes, but there's a special way of playing . . . It's called chess, shall I show you?'

The boy nods. Alexis explains where each piece goes. How it moves. How it kills. The boy is sharp on the uptake and eager to learn. He is captivated by the knights, delighted by their dog-leg leaps, their devious mode of entrapment. And as if warming-up, giggling, clapping, he jumps them about the board without once making a mistake.

Their first game is over in a matter of minutes.

'Well, sir, you beat me at chess! Congratulations. Now may I suggest a small libation, a little refreshment, what d'you say? A drop of port perhaps?'

The boy nods. He wrinkles his brow, narrows his eyes and compresses his lips into his very own version of a serious expression.

'A cigarette?'

Alexis picks up a wooden box. There are no cigarettes in it. Alexis doesn't smoke, yet there are times when he feels certain that he did. Was it a pipe . . . or perhaps he rolled his own?

The child pretends not to notice the adult's momentary yet

196

obvious confusion, the pregnant pause before Alexis abruptly turns and leaves the room. Hurriedly the boy gets down from the chair, and glancing all about as if to miss nothing, scurries off after his host. He draws level with an open door beyond which a much cluttered desk is clearly visible. 'Papa has one of those!' he cries with delight, indicating the portable typewriter. 'It makes letters.'

'Yes, would you like to write something? Your name, maybe?'

The boy doesn't answer. He waits for Alexis to make the move. Alexis walks into the kitchen. The boy follows.

'What *is* your name?'

The boy remains silent.

'How old are you?'

'Six and a quarter . . . and a bit.'

'And where did your mummy and daddy go?'

'Nowhere.'

'Nowhere? Didn't you come with them in a boat?'

He shakes his head.

'Where are they?'

He hooks his thumb over his shoulder, presumably in the direction of the island.

'In the village?'

He nods.

'Do they know you're here?

He looks down at the floor.

'How did you get here?'

'I walked.'

'You walked! You walked across through the water?'

He nods. Quickly and a number of times.

'Weren't you afraid?

He shakes his head. Once.

'No. It only came to here,' poking at a spot just below his knees, 'and I could see the bottom, no sharks, no crocodiles, but I would have heard one coming.'

'But it couldn't have been light then?'

'Just a little. I crept out when I woke up. And I went to the beach, and I walked, and I saw the road under the sea, and −'

'But they'll be worried about you. Your mama and your papa.'

He shakes his head.

'No they don't care about me. They just sleep on the sand all day, and all night in bed. They were asleep when I ran away.'

'How am I to get you back?'

'I don't want to go back! I want to stay here . . . with you. We can play more chest.'

Alexis shrugs. He busies himself with crushing oranges. After a while he looks down at the boy, winks, and pours him a full tumbler of juice. The boy offers to share it. Then they eat breakfast.

The day is the boy's. To begin with he asks to be shown Alexis F's living arrangements and they embark on a tour of inspection as conscientiously as any admiral and his entourage would when reviewing the crews and ships of a new command. Not that there is much to see. In keeping with its purpose, the adobe provides for a thoroughly Spartan lifestyle. Nonetheless, the large and ancient brass bedstead holds some interest. The boy tests the firmness of the mattress with his tiny fists and finds it yielding, his grimace suggesting that it's possibly somewhat too soft. He sits on its edge, bounces up and down, gingerly at first, but then with more confidence, gradually manoeuvring himself towards the middle. The bed starts to judder and rock on its castors, bedsprings clang and clatter. And in one swift flowing movement the boy is on his feet, bouncing for all his worth as on a trampoline. The squeaking and squawking protests of the bed are outmatched by the boy's howls of laughter and shrieks of joy. It is perhaps something that elsewhere he has been forbidden to do. Alexis smiles what he hopes is a smile of approbation and encouragement, but as he does so the boy jolts to an abrupt halt, his attention caught by an old sea-chest.

'Treasure!' he exclaims, leaping from the bed and towards the metal-hooped trunk that stands beneath the uncurtained window. He struggles with its lid and, having managed to unclasp and lift it, his disappointment is all but palpable as he discovers the chest to be full of nothing more than bedding, towels and linen.

'But where's the gold? The pirates' gold!' he cries, his small-framed frustration mounting. 'I know . . .' he mutters shortly and with an air of reflection as one wholly undaunted. 'I know . . . it's still buried and . . . and we have to find the map . . . with a black cross on it . . . and it's hidden . . . and it's hidden . . .' Pause to scan the room as in a game of I-spy. 'I bet it's in . . . one of these!' as he skips over to the headboard where he fiddles and fumbles with the bed-knobs, one by one trying to unscrew them, but without success. Finally, determined not to be outdone and in an obviously modified phrase and a tone of voice borrowed from an exasperated, albeit resigned adult, he decides, 'Well, once we're finished here, we'll just have to search the island from top to bottom.' Then, as they are about to leave the bedroom, he catches sight of an icon of St Sebastian painted on glass, and spends a while staring at the garish Byzantine figure in contemplative silence.

The kitchen holds no secrets as such, though the pump-handle (which Alexis delights in yanking three or four times whenever he passes), does take some patient explaining. It is mounted on a shelf beside the stoneware sink, which in turn is fed by a single, dripping, chrome-plated tap. Without entering into the mysteries of plumbing theory Alexis tries to convey the notion of spring water being sucked into an underground storage space, then filtered, later and as required to be manually pumped into a tank on the roof. The boy listens attentively, nodding his apparent understanding, and being plainly relieved on learning that this water is not really for drinking or cooking, but rather for washing. Short of running his finger round the rims of stacked pots and pans, across plates and dishes, and of asking what every jar in the cupboard contains, he continues to display an insatiable interest in everything he sees, all the while commenting on the overall sparseness of furnishings, on the bare walls and the considerable mess to be found in Alexis F's study.

Outside, he points out that the rain-barrel leaks. Alexis F's indifferent acceptance of this seemingly vital information gives the boy a brow-furrowing moment's cause for concern, but this is soon forgotten on the discovery of an arcaded external staircase that leads to a small turret-like structure on the roof. It is here that the cistern is housed, and it is also here that Alexis stashes his camp-bed and a few ex-army blankets for sleeping alfresco. In wide-eyed astonishment, the boy admits to never having slept under the stars and, after taking in the flat-calm vista of a wine-dark sea, but above all after being reassured that this is where they shall be spending the night if he so wishes, they set out on an exploratory trek across the rock. As one discovers and the other rediscovers its pink sandstone contours, its weatherworn ledges, its fissures, nooks and crannies – any one of which could be an Aladdin's cave of diamonds and jewels, of golden goblets and silver broaches, of precious rings, combs and clasps and silks from the Orient, all purloined by Barbary buccaneers long days since – so the boy remains indefatigably talkative and tirelessly curious. His appetite for questions knows no limits, and Alexis gets the feeling that he considers each and every answer he is given before fixing on committing it to memory, tidily and exactly. He has to know what each flower, each plant and shrub is called. The insects that grub around them. The name of every bird that skims above their heads. And as and when it happens to be apt, he implicitly expects Alexis to own up to ignorance; even demanding during a subsequent game of hide and seek that, despite much mutual pantomime cajoling and bantering, they both freely confess to cheating, to peeking through their fingers. At last to agree on a long swim to round off the morning.

How do limpets cling?

Why do waves go white on top?

The boy doggy-paddles with great proficiency and shows no fear of water whatsoever. Nevertheless Alexis is very mindful of not getting too far out of the boy's depth, as also of the possibility of being caught unawares in one of the freak currents that occasionally pervade these shores.

If you've got an old sock we can fill it with sand and make a football . . .

They lunch on thickly buttered crusty rolls, smoked tuna and a salad of sun-dried tomatoes, cos lettuce, horse radishes, red onions, black olives and goats' cheese, all liberally soused in a dressing of olive oil, mustard and crushed garlic. Having lent a hand in its preparation, everything is very much to the boy's liking. He samples the wine, taking a tiny sip. And again. But with a wrinkling of his nose and a puckering of his lips rejects it in favour of the orange juice. There are figs for dessert. Then sated, they decide to leave the washing-up for later. Alexis suggests a siesta, but no, not even a short nap. And it's back to the beach for more guessing and spying games, for more football and questions, questions and questions.

Where does the salt in the sea come from?

Why don't clouds make a noise when they bump into one another?

At last too wearied to do otherwise, Alexis lies back in the shade of a small, tufted dune and rests in peace. With plastic bucket and improvised spade, the child digs contentedly. He is building sandcastles while simultaneously treasure hunting. Soon he is certain to unearth the ill-gotten gains of Captain Hook or Long John Silver, or better still Barbarossa, all of whom, arguing amongst themselves in a cacophonous range of comic strip voices, give him a multiple choice of conflicting instructions on how best to conduct his search. Every so often, he takes a break and shouts to attract Alexis F's attention, to secure his approval or to seek advice. Later he wanders off on his own to collect shells. And towards evening Alexis spots a pair of dolphins, scarcely visible dots far out to sea. Time ceases to have meaning as man and boy watch the creatures at play, revelling in their acrobatic antics till at last they leap over the horizon. Enjoying a satisfaction akin to that achieved at the end of a hard day's work, Alexis proposes that they retire for another drink.

'I'm tired,' the boy sighs. And lifts his arms to be carried. Alexis hoists him off the ground. The boy hooks his arms around the man's neck. Then, 'What happened to your . . . ?' but he falters and turns his face away, saying, 'I'm not tired any more, put me down, I'll walk.'

Alexis sets him down.

A glass of milk, a sandwich. The boy lounges in his armchair. They're about to have yet another game of chess. At the cost of a bishop and a pawn, the boy has commandeered all four knights for his side. But he can barely keep his eyes open. They close, he smiles. He flutters his eyes open and mutters, 'My name's Jay.'

'Jay? Is that . . .'

He's asleep.

Alexis waits until the boy's breathing becomes slow, deep and regular. He drapes a blanket around Jay's shoulders, wrapping it closely about the small body as he scoops it into his arms. In spite of the fast fading light, he carries the sleeping form with ease, tenderly hugging it to his breast. And with a sure-footedness that comes from familiarity he swiftly descends the cliff face. The waters over the causeway will soon be at their lowest and it is imperative that Alexis make it back on to the rock before the tide turns.

By way of unlit alleys and dark, narrow streets, he scurries through the village, which in age-honoured fashion already gathers itself together for sleep and betrays no signs of the furore that beset it earlier during the day.

News of the foreign boy's disappearance had spread with the forked-tongue speed of practised gossip. While the frantic child's parents drove into town to report the disappearance, certain widowed mouths heaped scorn upon them for their unnatural, barbaric ways. It was put about that only a thoroughly godless and selfish mother would consider farming out her child to the care of strangers, let alone leave it to its own devices wholly unsupervised. Others spoke in undertones of perverts and kidnappers, of tinkers and gypsies. Jews from the mainland were mentioned in passing and an uncommon sense of urgency, apprehension and disquietude began to prevail. In the minds of the most vociferous, with each embellished rendering, the child's gruesome fate became more firmly sealed. Yet all agreed that it was ultimately a matter for the authorities. They after all had the resources, the manpower and the proper equipment. Even so a few young goatherds who tended flocks on the nearby hills formed themselves into an unofficial search party and scoured the local grazing grounds looking into potholes, caves and disused quarries. Some searched the olive groves. But all to no avail.

Now in the far distance a dog barks. It is answered from afar by another dog and they begin to howl in concert. Propane lanterns still burn in the bar and shadowed rectangular pools of light spill from the unshuttered windows. The sounds of men at leisure punctuate the cicadas in their incessant nightly chorusing. And unseen, Alexis creeps into a porch and through the side door of the church. He finds himself in a small vestibule. To the right lies the sacristy. There, as he lays his burden on a large sofa that is shedding horsehair, Jay wakes, smiles, slips his thumb into his mouth and falls asleep once more. Alexis adjusts the blanket. He brushes the boy's fine blonde hair out of his eyes, leans forward and kisses him on the forehead.

Ghost-like, Alexis F returns the way he came.

Sun-doped women in horizontal, bikini-clad acts of sun-worship lie coddled by the tremors of a layered but peeling heat shimmering on a secluded stretch of white sand. The beach at Virrisydes is situated well off the beaten track and boasts an air of exclusivity. Here there is no chance of overcrowding, for its whereabouts have yet to be discovered by the run of the mill holiday-makers – operators and participants alike.

It is late afternoon.

A man ambles up to the prostrate, motionless form of his wife.

He stands at her feet throwing a long cooling shadow across her sun-soaked body.

'Swim, darling?' he suggests.

And behind Polaroid sunglasses her eyelids flicker him into focus.

'No . . . No, Adrian, I don't think so,' she replies, her tongue a little thick from the drugs she has been taking.

A smile, and the man turns and runs down the beach as if chasing the outgoing sea.

The woman lifts herself on to her elbows to watch her husband, to see tanned and sinewy back muscles roll to the rhythm of pumping arms. Her fingers curl, she scratches at the sand. Picking, sifting. Picking and sifting.

Yesterday she could have strangled him without a second thought, without a qualm. In fact she almost did. But then she should never have been asked to live through a day like yesterday. It simply wasn't fair. Nobody but nobody should ever be subjected to such horror. Not the sleeping-in and waking up alone in bed and coming to the realisation that there is no one else in the bungalow, that wasn't at all bad. If the truth be told, it felt rather good and made a welcome change. The finding of a note on the kitchen table from Adrian saying that he'd gone off for a ramble, and assuming that he had taken Jay with him was to be accepted as nothing out of the ordinary. But somewhat later to learn that her son had gone missing, and after uselessly and fruitlessly searching, to fully grasp that her son, her only son, had actually gone missing, with all that implied, was the beginning of an unspeakable nightmare. The combination of fraying nerves and an overripe sensibility brought about an inexorable cascade of visions as if to mock the interminable snail's pace drive to the nearest town along roads of melting asphalt already fit only for dog-carts, donkeys and the tread of vagabonds in this godforsaken, bug-ridden backwater of a country. Vivid pictures of Jay lying in a bleached ravine with broken bones poking through his skin and surrounded by lunging vultures pecking at his eyes. Jay fathoms deep in muddy waters, tangled in seaweed, his fantailed hair swaying, gently, his eyes staring, staring. Or being molested, tortured by a paedophile cloaked in a grotesqueness of Dickensian proportions, Jay's eyes a dead terror, blanked out in abject fear. While policemen fill out forms and ask inane questions over and over, in bad, badly pronounced, broken English, saying they can do nothing until help arrives from the mainland, maybe a helicopter, maybe tomorrow. Her state of panic now at hysterical breaking point. Adrian insisting she wait outside and leave it to him, but not being Jay's biological father he could well afford to be complacent. And with just a trace of menace Adrian begging her to stay calm. At which moment, unable to take any more, she physically launched herself at her husband's throat. They struggled. The police intervened. She had to be restrained until a doctor appeared with a syringe, with a bedside manner acquired during an internship at a London teaching hospital, but above all with a handy supply of sedatives. And the effects of these, one three times a day, she can feel coursing through her veins, making a sluggish thing of her body, and of her mind, a lethargic haze.

She scans the beach. Her son is safe, found last night in the sacristy by one of the faithful, a washerwoman bringing freshly laundered and ironed vestments for the following day's service. And this morning the doctor pronounced Jay physically whole and sound, without even a scratch, untouched and unharmed. Nevertheless he reports that the boy tells a wild and fanciful tale, the result of too many cartoons on television no doubt; though an over-eager psychiatrist might care to make something out of an arrow-pierced minotaur with not a bull's but a dragon's head, and of a magic lever that hurls geysers so high into the sky that they fall in multi-hued showers of rubies, amber and gold, of emeralds and sapphires, topaz and quartz, all spewed from the clandestine depths of a pirate's underground hoard.

'Thank God, thank God . . . But Jay, my love, my sweet, won't you tell mummy where you've been?'

'I just went for a walk on the water.'

And indeed there is Jay at the water's edge, securely watched, safely squatting on the shore, poking holes in the wet sand with a stick, his gaze forever straying to the rock that stands a mile or two further along the coast. And while Adrian tries to amuse him with shallow-floating imitations of a walrus, or possibly a crocodile, a dinghy with an outboard motor lurches away from a nearby jetty. It carries two men, one of whom wears a uniform. The woman lowers her head to her towel and once more closes her eyes.

The old fisherman and the police officer make their way up the beach. The police officer raps at the adobe door with his knuckles. It is opened almost at once. With a discreet wave of his other hand, he indicates that the fisherman should remain on the porch. He then mumbles a sort of apology-cum-greeting and asks to see Alexis F's papers. Alexis invites him in and goes to fetch his documents from a drawer in his desk. The police officer glances at the faded cover and, from behind very dark glasses, frowns. His bushy eyebrows meet above his nose. He flicks through the embossed pages, each imprinted with a visa and overlaid with a mass of smudged entry and exit stamps. Here and there he inspects one more thoroughly. He looks at the photograph, then at Alexis. At the photograph again. He gives a shrug, a barely perceptible lifting of his arms and he confiscates the documents, 'I'm sorry, you'll have to come with me.'

'What's wrong?'

'Your visa hasn't been renewed. Almost two years see!' An alternate raising of each eyebrow.

'What will happen?'

'You'll have to go!' A sarcastic grin. 'Perhaps be escorted to the frontier, or even officially deported.'

'Deported! To where?'

'That's none of my concern. Let them do what they like with you, why should I worry? I'm just a cop not immigration . . .

Anyway, as for that other little matter . . . there'll be no charges, but we don't have to tolerate your type here do we? What did you do with his sandals?'

'Sandals? Oh they're probably still at the foot of the cliff.'

'Well let's go and get them.'

From the dinghy, Alexis could see his reception committee on the jetty. Drab, charcoal-grey silhouettes lumped together, screaming and yelling long before the boat was moored. Much of what they shouted escaped him. Lost in the general noise, the hubbub. Strange phrases, the esoteric obscenities of old women with ploughed faces and black shawls draped over white heads. They form a writhing corridor through which the police officer and Alexis must pass. An ancient and withered hag trundles forward, her long skirts bowing about frail legs. She spits at Alexis. The crowd jeers. The witch shrieks, 'Gallows-bird! Gallows-bird!'

The mob takes up the cry. More people are gathering. Villagers, bewildered sunbathers. A stone strikes Alexis in the back. Another and another is thrown. The officer has doubled his pace. He drags Alexis by the arm.

And from somewhere in the background somebody shouts, 'Here! Quick, give me the camera!'

twenty-four

Devoted to a reckoning of accounts; and in which Alexis at last discovers that, freed of feeling, the past exists only as a matter of record. Consequently some ghosts are laid to rest.

And they say the camera doesn't lie!

Tosh and piffle!

Now that may be me repeating myself in a rather un-ladylike manner and sounding neither particularly sophisticated nor even urbane; but then why should I claim to be either, especially when obsessive political correctness (or paranoid crap as I prefer to call it) is still very much a thing of the future?

Photography is the art of illumination, of ethereal sculpting, and just as there are as many realities as there are witnesses to any event, so it all depends on how one sheds light on one's subject. It is all inordinately simple. As at the flick of a switch and in a mere moment's consideration, everything becomes crystal clear. Moonshine and disfigured tissue may well take on the aspect of horny, reptilian scales, yet therein lies the rub. From the outset Alexis has been predictably manipulative with the truth, but to put it mildly, he has now committed a cardinal sin. Far worse than splitting infinitives and mixing metaphors, he has fallen foul of treason, he has Judased himself. Betrayed by bed-bouncing. By not paying due care and attention, he has slipped up and forgotten that it is me (or 'I' if you must) who is predisposed to playing at trampolines, and not some symbolically neglected merchild on a mythical Aegean rock where Alexis purports to be a self-ostracized Jonah practising for perpetual bachelordom and the loneliness of a solitary old age. I think not.

And so there it is. A tiny slip perhaps, but with its pinpoint isolation, like a bolt from the blue it makes for squaring the circle. In other words there is no vintage sports car travelling at speed along country lanes towards the metropolis. And there never has been. It is therefore not being driven by a man with a small moustache who has a predilection for foreign gestures. There is no woman and no child in the passenger and dicky seats. Nor will their corpses be burned to a frazzle, nor will the pervading sweet stench of smouldering flesh be held at bay with handkerchiefs sprinkled in cheap eau-de-Cologne. And if the converse of all that is untrue what of the rest? If there was no Eden, no Adam and Eve and therefore no original sin, what need does humanity have of redemption? If the child is the father of the man then Alexis has fathered no child. But in social compliance, in his eagerness to role-play and in his fear of rejection, he has opted to enslave himself in his own fiction. Just as Polish uhlans with wooden lances and sabres drawn charged Nazi tanks solely in the imaginations of screenwriters and film directors simply to further patriotic conceits, so Alexis has chosen to indulge in a fantasy, an intangible cage of his own making. There he daily wanders the echoing rooms of a leaking, draughty mansion built by a man mad enough to believe himself to be Lear (be that Shakespeare's deranged king or Edward, the Victorian poet of literary nonsense fame). Boarded up in mind and soul, a spectre in his own lifetime, he is ever abroad seeking a faithless wife to blame and unconceived generations to save from corruption. And until such time as Alexis decides to move on, and move on he will, no amount of research, cajoling or analysis, psychology or psychiatry will make the slightest bit of difference. Buried bones always rest more soundly undisturbed.

Shit, I'm in danger of slipping into purple prose again, but what the hell! At least it hasn't come to doubting my own existence. Yet. And so lying on my side alongside Alexis F, my head at an angle, my chin cupped in my palm, my crooked elbow propped on the pillow, I, ever the Wiser Wendy, no longer listen. I am a guardian angel no more. But still I watch the casual rise and fall of his chest as finally he sleeps in the rhythms of his own natural sleep without my traipsing through his grey cells or surreptitiously bending his ear. And I see, awash in mercury, one by one, the scars fading with the waning of the moon, while those that remain he already wears well and with grace.

Soon it will be dawn and time to grow up. I shall dress and softly kiss him on the brow, gently so as not to disturb his adventure-filled slumbers. With a stifled sigh and the merest hint of regret (for he wouldn't have been the first man to have benefited from having some sense fucked into him), I shall leave him to a life lived at the back of the mind, in a labyrinth with no centre and no horn-headed monsters stalking the tunnels intent on the kill. And even if he were in need of a silver thread, why should I be the one to give it to him? Reason will never conquer feelings nor will it allow itself to be subjugated by emotion. So, since it is best for all concerned that I fly, I shall steal away just as I came, on tiptoe, wellies in hand, until I reach the gravelled courtyard and the sweeping drive that leads to the river. There shod once more I shall turn my back on this tired mansion that Alexis has adopted as his ancestral home. And in the name of long journeys I shall stealthily make my way to the arms of a man with whom I shall be married in secret, and far, far away.

And all the while Alexis will be dogging my every step, right up to the colonnaded portico and to the edge of the unkempt lawns once landscaped and laid out like a miniature Versailles, where naked, he will come to a halt to wave his arms in some ritualistic, esoteric semaphore in a final bid to attract my attention. This I will ignore. And he will retreat into the shadows and, pressing switches and pulling levers, he will turn on the fountains and set off the fireworks. The last of night will explode into a myriad points of varicoloured light revealing star clusters and constellations ridden by goblin, djinn and banshee. And the coruscating heavens will cast primeval rainbows across the play of fountains in an entertainment of regal splendour, which though some 20 years premature, is worthy of any millennium fête not to mention the world's end. But there will be none. None to applaud, none to oooooh and none to aaaaah, not even Wayfaring Wendy wending her weary way home towards the rising sun, forever the usurper, but a figment of whose fey imagination?

twenty-five

Wherein Alexis concludes that every new end is but a half-remembered beginning, that Cycles must remain Cycles, and that Reason and Emotion will forever make strange bedfellows.

And before yet another gradual incline, with no apparent rhyme or reason, the train will slow to a crawl.

One of Alexis F's fellow passengers will nod to his companion and ask, 'What's happening?'

'Perhaps it's a station . . . ?' the other will suggest.

'But this is back of beyond?'

'Yes . . . and it's very beautiful, I must say, the mountains, the forests and that . . . but for always, I mean to live here day in, day out, well no . . . not for me. I bet they haven't even got street lighting.'

'Nor to mention decent sewage . . . eh?'

Alexis will take his baggage, a single ex-army knapsack from the rack above their heads. By way of farewell he will smile at them as he unlatches the compartment door and leaps on to the low boardwalk platform. A few faltering steps to trot alongside the still moving train until once more sure of his balance; the notion of being alone responsible for this delay to some eight coaches, and the sight of their gaping occupants, it all amuses him beyond measure, but no doubt any thought would have evoked the same knavish grin. For Alexis has come home.

The Walrus (so obviously nicknamed because of his long, drooping moustaches) will be sitting in the shade of the tiny shed that serves not only as a waiting-room, but also as the left luggage, lost property and ticket office. His railway official's cap will be set askew, tilted over his eyes. He will be sleeping and probably won't notice Alexis F's unorthodox arrival. Alexis will be tempted to creep up on him, to kick the stool out from under his fat arse, a crime of which he had once been wrongly accused, long, long ago, and for which he had been punished. But he will merely shrug and start off on the mile or so of meandering dirt-track that links the station with the village snugly tucked away in the upper valley.

He intends first to visit the priest. He wants to thank him, for what? He doesn't know. Marching, whistling no recognisable tune, rather a series of haphazard notes, he will be content. The earliest spring crocuses will be in blossom.

At the manse gate he will meet a gardener. He will be disappointed, for he will not recognise him. He will be further upset by the gardener's words, 'Old Father K? No, he's not here. People are dying you know.'

And of a sudden Alexis F's plans for the entire day will seem to be in severe jeopardy, if not altogether doomed.

'Thanks,' he will grunt. He will shoulder his knapsack and walk on towards the church, then turn on to a path heading for the south transept. From a distance he will see a woman dressed in widow's black kneeling beside the grave next to his mother's. She will be weeding, tending, watering the flowers that will soon bloom there. And nearing her, he will see that her clothes are tattered and in sore need of repair; that there are buttons missing from her blouse and the wrinkled globe of one sagging, purple-veined and brown-nippled breast is visible in sharp profile.

She will hear Alexis approach. She will glance up. And startled, she will jump.

'Lucy!'

And she will be old. She will stare at Alexis who will be about to draw closer. But she will shoo him away, her hands flapping. Alexis will not move, he will simply gawk after the retreating form of Lucy tottering, yet somehow so sure-footed as she flees along the hillside.

Mother's grave will be well kept. Freshly turned soil will show on its surface. Father lies buried in the adjacent plot where, like the march of cut-out soldiers, a bas-relief procession of saints has been carved into the headstone. Alexis will laugh. And laugh.

'Zufa's' is the cracked and faded sign hand-painted on slats of timber hung over the tavern door. Nobody remembers who Zufa had been and nobody can trace his name in the village records, nor connect it with the various family ties of any past landlord. During Alexis F's childhood Zufa presented the most common topic of speculation, especially for the then innkeeper – Bartek's father – a portly, blue-jawed man who was never more regularly cursed, never more frequently blessed than in Alexis F's cottage. (Was it not Bartek who had toppled the Walrus from his chair and let Alexis take the blame? Was it not Bartek who, almost a year his senior, had taught Alexis to stalk lovers in the woods and, safely hidden in treetops, to pelt them with fir-cones at the most crucial of moments?)

Inside it will be dim and musty. The four men who will be sitting at a circular table and playing cards will pause in mid-hand. In silence and bluntly they will scrutinize Alexis, only shortly thereafter to resume their game with renewed vigour. There will be a man standing behind the bar. Bartek by name, he will be of solid build and wanting for a shave. Alexis will book a room. Bartek will speak cordially as befits a host. Alexis will pay for a week in advance. Bartek will call Alexis 'Sir' with deference, but without any suggestion of recognition or of kowtowing. Alexis will order a brandy addressing the man by name, but the latter will recoil from such familiarity. He will gaze at Alexis who will be smiling. Eager to chat, to be accepted, Alexis will asks questions pertinent to this type of community. Bartek will respond, limiting his answers to a 'Yes' or a 'No' where it will suffice, ever cordially but coldly, as one satisfying the wants of a passing stranger, a customer (maybe an unwelcome one at that?), a stray traveller being cautiously treated to the minimum maxims of hospitality.

Alexis F's enthusiasm dampened, he will lean against the counter and study the card players. As through a mist he will see the adult expressions of boys whom he may have known for a while years ago. He will try recalling names, placing them in lists. And in time, he will find labels that bear no correlation to these faces before him who will feature in no part of him. Anywhere.

And everywhere he will go it will be the same reaction, the same ever present suspicious glance; when the women's chatter will become a swallowed whisper and when men will make noteworthy, but unshared discoveries at the bottom of their half-filled tumblers or on the ground beneath their feet.

An afternoon will be spent by himself locked in his room. There, ceiling gazing with daylight fast fading to the tap of the ivy stems that encircle the window frame, like the mosses and lichens that cling to the walls of a neglected, desolate house where Alexis was born, and where the barn gate will still creak on its hinges.

A supper to be eaten alone. He will drink alone. He will get drunk alone. His father's endemic defence of every riotous hour squandered away in this bar will tonight pervade his unfettered recollections over and over again. Enthralling tales of music, dancing and winter sleigh bells. A fight; and the entertainment deemed incomplete unless somebody gets chivvied or at the very least sliced open with a blade. The gift of fly-buttons bought on impulse for Bartek in memory of a boyhood jest will needs-must stay unpacked and forever remain upstairs carefully wrapped in this evening of gloom.

Alexis will get lost, unexpectedly. He will have been walking for several hours and in the general direction of the disused sawmill, either strolling at a brisk pace, or else resting and smoking. In reflection, each thought at once forgotten, as he will have ambled through groves, through acres of dense forest, perhaps in deliberate circles over hillock and by coppice; until finally coming upon a clearing where, away from the ferns and the grasses, amongst tall pines, a woodcutter's shack has been erected utilizing the steep contours of the land to form a natural, rear wall. On its insignificant porch an old man will be found bobbing in a rocking chair. He will have been watching Alexis.

'Come for a haircut?' he will call from afar.

'A haircut . . . ?' Alexis will tentatively finger his collar-length hair. 'No I don't want a haircut,' he will reply.

But the old man will have entered his hut and, by the time Alexis will have reached the porch, the old man will have come out again, combs and scissors in his hands.

'Sit down please.' He will indicate a bench of roughly hewn wood.

'No, I really haven't come for a haircut,' Alexis will insist.

'Haven't you time? Surely you can tell the time can't you?'

Impossible as it is for Alexis to comprehend, this man is undoubtedly the old peddler, a lost familiar from childhood who was already ancient when Alexis was a baby. And today he appears as one unchanged.

'Yes,' Alexis will manage to stammer. 'Yes . . . I can tell the time. The grandfather clock only has one hand because instead of five divisions between each of the digits from one to twelve, there are four, and each of those represents a full fifteen minutes, so the time can be accurately estimated to the nearest quarter of an hour.'

The peddler will smile. He will pointedly look down to the bench; while confused and duped by the eeriness of this encounter, Alexis will sit, as if on command. The peddler will begin to clip at his hair. Starting on the left, he will work towards the back and eventually move on to the right.

Silence, but for the steady snip-snipping of scissors.

Then, 'So you're home?'

'You wouldn't think so.'

'Oh . . . why?'

'Nobody knows me.'

216

'Nobody?'

'Well you, you're the only one.'

'Are you sure of that?'

'Yes . . . Yes I'm sure.'

'No they don't have it in the village. Why try to steal it?'

'Is that a riddle?'

'Riddle me a riddle . . . no . . .'

And back to the snick-snicking of the scissors.

A thin, scraggy cat will have pounced on to the rocking chair. After kneading the unyielding and mindless of failure, it will curl itself up for sleep. The peddler will sigh, and, 'I've been waiting for you. I was told you would come.'

'But it's pure chance that I'm here! Anyway who told you? Lucy?'

'It doesn't matter. Have you come to stay?'

'Does that matter?'

'Yes.'

'Why?'

'Because they're afraid of you.'

'Afraid? Is it—'

'No your face doesn't bother us, it might not fit but it doesn't bother us . . . though I don't see why something couldn't be done. There are people, specialists . . .'

'How often can the same machine have a re-bore?'

'Oh sit still, please.'

'Why then?'

'Why what?'

'Why are they afraid?'

'Well not of you, not the person, the individual, but just afraid. D'you understand?'

'No.'

And Alexis will be up and running. Running and running. And the old man will be yelling after him, 'You're not finished! Come back! Where are you going? You look like a cretin! I've only done one side!'

*   *   *

217

In the abandoned stores of the sawmill Alexis finds a two-man tent, mildewed and stashed to rot with much other unusable junk purloined from the liberating armies during the War. A relic of someone's chimeral past, he carries it across his shoulders; a change of warm clothes folded inside. The border is not far off.

The customs officer ignores Alexis F's burden. He can't make up his mind. Should he or should he not officially brand Alexis with an exit stamp? Slowly he rocks the little-used rubber seal over its ink pad, and then, as if on impulse, slams it down on to a page already littered with crude overlapping imprints smeared willy-nilly all over the place. Handing the travel documents to Alexis, he pauses, once more to take note of the photograph. He is about to speak, but apparently thinks better of it and motions Alexis away with a limp gesture, as though condescending to throw a lost ball back to children at play below his windows.

There's no traffic. Alexis ducks under the barrier.

It is dawning.

The feeble lights of another customs post shine dimly but a short distance away, and altogether in a different country. Alexis veers off the road. He hurries along over the sods of still frozen earth, parallel to the wire fences that separate nations.

Both customs posts being well out of sight, he sheds his load and edges his way to the barbed wire. Turning, he walks towards its counterpart, counting every step. There, at the second fence, he about faces and returns half that number. Leaving a large flat stone to locate the spot, he fetches his tent and pitches it squarely in the middle of no man's land.

The purr and rumble of engines disturbs his sleep. (In dreams a puppy came to sniff at the canvas? To mark the guy ropes?) Alexis F clambers out of the tent. He sees two soft-topped jeeps. Four uniformed men ride in one, being dangerously thrown from side to side. There are also four men in the other, but these wear different uniforms. They're racing across the hardened clods and from opposite directions. They drive very fast, bouncing. It is difficult to gauge which group will reach Alexis first.

218